The NO-PRESSURE Pact

MARIA RIGOU

AUTHOR'S NOTE

The word that we use in Argentina for nosy is *chusma*. Some other Spanish-speaking countries will say *chismosa*. And it's true, that's what I am. I am nosy. So nosy, in fact, that I eavesdropped in on someone's conversation on a train in Switzerland, and this book was born. This story, is, in fact, inspired by real life events. However...

I did not actually attend their luxury vacation. I wasn't invited, shockingly. But in my head? I did what any self-respecting romance author would do: I turned those people's private conversation into *a wonderful love story*. You're welcome.

So if you ever see me on public transportation, whisper softly, because you never know if you're about to become the main character of my next book.

———

The No-Pressure Pact is an open door romance novel. This means that it has on-page sexual content between two consenting adults. Additionally, there are mentions of panic attacks and other mental health topics on page, though the events take place off page. There is use of profanity and explicit language throughout the story. Mature readers only. **Please read with care.**

To the ones rebuilding themselves, piece by piece, and wondering if they'll ever feel whole again—you will.

I hope this story reminds you that you don't have to be whole to be loved.

PROLOGUE
MANUELA

Two years ago

THE ROOFTOP SMELLS like money and grilled peaches.

Not in a gauche, new-rich way, but in that curated way where the peaches are probably organic and the prosciutto draped over them was special ordered from an artisan producer in the mountains of Italy. It's all very *New York*, I've come to learn.

Elle's engagement party hums around me, the string lights overhead trying to look casual. Linen and glassware, heels tapping on the slate tile, the occasional pop of a champagne cork.

The city sprawls behind it all, golden in the late summer dusk.

I'm posted near an olive tree taller than me, doing my best impression of someone who belongs here. I've been in

New York for over a year now, long enough that the skyline almost doesn't make my breath hitch anymore. Almost.

"Manu!" Elle appears through a knot of guests, a flash of white linen dress and bare feet, carrying a drink in each hand like she's out clubbing instead of at a very fancy party in her honor. There's a flush high on her cheeks, either from the summer heat or the cocktails, and a strand of blonde hair has escaped the sleek bun at her nape.

Her eyes catch on my wrist. "Oh my god, that bangle is spectacular."

I glance down, twisting it so the metal glints under the string lights. "Thrift shop on the Lower East Side. Isn't it cute? Ten bucks and a little elbow grease."

I moved to New York City from Buenos Aires over a year ago, and Elle and I took a quick liking to each other. She's the one who helped me get set up in the city—navigating the real estate situation, subway transfers, and avoiding looking like a tourist in my own neighborhood. We knew each other from before I moved since we worked on adjacent teams before I moved to this one, and now we report to the same arrogant asshole. But in the time since I've been here, we've been getting closer. I would definitely consider her my closest friend.

"Stop," she says with a delighted gasp. "Don't show Nicole. She would actually die. She loves thrifting, especially for unique jewelry and art."

I laugh, already picturing Nicole with an entire curated

collection she'd claim was just stumbled upon. "Okay, I'll be careful," I say with a smile that she returns in earnest.

"I've been looking for you." She hands me one of the glasses, a low container with a suspiciously orange fizzy drink. "Come, there's someone I want you to meet."

Before I can protest, she's steering me away from the safety of the olive tree. My low heels catch slightly on the slate, the tag in my thrifted dress itching between my shoulder blades in exactly the place I can't reach.

We stop near the railing, where a man is standing with a drink on one hand, the other tucked into the pocket of his slate-gray trousers. He's not holding court like some of the others in attendance, more like watching from a comfortable distance. But when Elle stops beside him, his attention shifts immediately.

"Hey, Connie," Elle says, beaming at him, then turns to me. "This is my friend Manuela. Manu, this is Jack's cousin."

I take him in quickly—brown hair that's just a little too long to be neat, a couple of strands falling toward his forehead; deep brown eyes that seem to take in more than they give away; warm skin, like he actually spends time outdoors. And the faintest shadow along his jaw, as if he didn't bother shaving for this. There's a steadiness about him that makes the rest of the crowd seem louder, more performative by comparison.

He straightens, offering his hand. His grip is warm and firm but not rushed. A subtle squeeze before he lets go, and I feel the world slow down around me.

"Hi," he says, voice low and even. "Connor."

"Hi."

Elle's name gets called from somewhere behind us—a singsongy "Elle!" followed by a wave of laughter. She glances over her shoulder.

"Back in a sec," she says, already heading to the other side of the rooftop terrace. "You two talk."

And then it's just... us.

The quiet lasts a beat too long. He takes a slow sip from his glass, thumb brushing along the rim as he lowers it, gaze flicking toward the skyline before coming back to me.

"That's a good spot you had over there," he says finally, nodding toward the olive tree. "Best angle of the city from up here."

I tilt my head. "Is that your polite way of saying that you know I was hiding?"

One corner of his mouth curves, not quite a full smile, but it changes his whole face, softens it. My stomach twists a little, in a good way. "Just observing. Big difference."

"And which were you doing before Elle dragged me over here?"

That gets me a real smile, quick but genuine. The kind that reaches his eyes and makes the corners crinkle. His fingers tap lightly against the side of his glass. "Probably both."

He studies me for a moment longer, like he's waiting to see if I'll fill the silence.

"You're not from here?" he asks. And it's an odd question because to me, it's a little obvious that I'm not. The thick accent alone speaks volumes.

"What gave it away?" I shake my head with a soft smile on my lips. "Argentina. Small town in the mountains called Tres Fuegos. Moved here almost a year and a half ago. I work with Elle."

He nods once, jaw ticking like he's tucking the information away. "What do you think so far?"

"About New York?" Or about Elle? Or about this whole glittery Manhattan thing I still don't feel part of? Sometimes it feels like I've walked onto the wrong set entirely, I want to say.

He tilts his head in confirmation.

"It's... a lot. Loud. Fast. Expensive." I make a face, and he smiles and nods. "But there's always something to look at."

That earns me yet another smile, slower this time, and I catch the faint dimple in his left cheek.

Someone calls to him from across the terrace. He glances over, then back at me, the smile still lingering.

"I'll remember to stand where you stand next time," he says, and there's a flicker of something playful in his eyes before he excuses himself.

I should probably leave now. Instead, I drift through the house, past strangers in tailored clothes and women who look like they belong on TV. I stop by the grazing table and try a little bit of each of the cheeses on display and take way too long to decide which of the seventeen different kinds of olives I'm going to eat. By the time I make it to the kitchen, chasing water and quiet, I find him again.

Not on purpose—just the natural end point of my escape route before I sneak out of this party and head home to my quiet and dull apartment.

He's leaning against the counter, scrolling through his phone with one hand, a half-finished beer resting on the marble beside him. The overhead lights are softer in here, the hum of the party muted through the closed glass doors.

Connor looks up when I walk in, thumb pausing on his phone screen.

"Hydration break?" he asks, nodding toward the bucket of fancy glass water bottles sitting on ice.

"Strategic retreat," I say, grabbing one and twisting off the cap.

"Are you going to pull an Irish goodbye?"

"A what?" I reply, head tilted in confusion. It's not a term I've heard yet, but this doesn't really surprise me. "I don't think I know that expression."

He smiles, soft and a little crooked, like he's amused I don't know. "Leaving without saying goodbye. That's an Irish goodbye."

"Oh." I huff a laugh. "Caught in the act, I guess."

His eyes glint as he sets his phone down, finally giving me his full attention. "But then you ended up here instead."

"Yes, well." I wave a hand vaguely toward the ceiling. "The rooftop was getting loud."

I shift against the counter, water bottle cool in my hand,

suddenly aware of how quiet it is here compared to every-where else.

"Yeah," he says, mouth tugging up just slightly. "The kitchen's better. No small talk."

I lean against the opposite counter, mirroring his posture. "Isn't this technically small talk?"

"Maybe. But I like this version better."

The way he says it, steady, no rush, eyes holding mine, makes my stomach do something inconvenient again.

"Is that your thing?" I ask. "Standing on the sidelines and letting everyone else do the talking?"

His gaze dips briefly to my mouth before he answers. "Sometimes."

The glass doors slide open again, laughter spilling in and footsteps moving closer, then fading as someone closes them behind them. The air between us feels charged in a way it didn't out on the terrace. Maybe it's the close quarters, maybe not.

"That's my cue," I say, turning around to leave in the opposite direction I came in. "See you around."

He doesn't hesitate. "I hope so."

I don't let myself smile until I'm two blocks away.

1

———

MANUELA
MONDAY

THE ELEVATOR JOLTS just enough to make me wonder if today's the day it finally gives up on me. A fitting metaphor for this dreary Monday, honestly.

By the time I reach the seventh floor, my canvas tote bag is digging into my shoulder, my hair is frizzing from the late summer humidity, and I've mentally drafted three different versions of my resignation letter—all of which I won't—can't—actually send, because this job is the reason my permanent residency is still in progress. Toxic boss and all.

I swipe into the floor's modern turnstiles, past the wall of glass awards our creative agency likes to brag about, and head straight for my desk. April from strategy gives me an exhausted smile, and I nod in return. She used to be friendly with me, even inviting me to brunch with her friends on the weekends and the occasional post-work happy hour, before I got moved onto the Horizon account and jumped from the strategy team into managing accounts. Now she simply winces sympathetically when I'm in her vicinity, like someone watching a car wreck happen in slow motion right before their eyes.

"I swear to god, this week is testing me," Elle Winslowe, my friend and coworker, says. She's been repeating the same combination of words once a week since she got engaged a little over two years ago. She sets her large designer purse on the desk next to mine and takes a sip of whatever drink she's enjoying on this balmy fall morning, ice shaking as she moves around the space.

"What happened?" I say, just as my phone pings consecutively at least eight times. I place my bag under my desk in the only small space my tiny cubicle can accommodate. Elle's desk is sandwiched between mine and a large window overlooking the Hudson River and, if you squint and do some Olympic-style gymnastics, the Statue of Liberty.

"The wedding is in three weeks," she says with an exhale, hooking up her laptop to the monitors in front of her and clicking her mouse an exorbitant amount of times. I open my mouth to say something, but she interrupts, continuing with her venting session that is so common at this hour, no matter the day. "Mind you, I'm leaving Wednesday," she emphasizes, her eyes widening for dramatic effect. "Wednesday."

"Is there something I can do to help with wedding stuff?"

"Oh, no thanks, babe," she says while she glances at her

buzzing phone on her desk. "I already added them to the list."

I laugh, shaking my iced coffee to get the last few sips out from the bottom. New York City in the late summer is muggy and overwhelming. And although Buenos Aires was very similar, the pace in this city and the sheer number of tourists add an additional layer of anxiety that has me on edge the majority of the time.

"How was your weekend?" I ask, moving in a similar way to what she's doing. This has been our routine for the past year or so since I got promoted into a new role and our boss, James Jameson, decided it would be better suited if Elle and I sat right outside his office. Sometimes, when we are at work way past closing time, Elle and I like to theorize about why he's such an anal-retentive prick. Other times, we go inside his office and move his sticky notes a fraction of an inch towards the edge of the desk.

It's highly unprofessional but also a very good way to unwind and destress, even though our jobs are anything but. We work at a creative agency that caters to non-profits specifically, so the work is low stakes and low urgency but highly rewarding.

"I got my nails done," she says, wiggling her fingers in my direction, "and touched up the tox on my forehead and crow's feet, you know, just in case." She does something weird with her face, trying to show me the unnatural ways the muscles of her face don't move at all.

"That's nice," I say, although I can't really relate. I don't think I've ever gotten my nails done since I moved here, choosing instead for a more do-it-yourself approach since everything is so expensive in this city. And Botox? Yeah, that's just a pipe dream at this point and something I should be saving for, just like I should be saving for a down payment for a house. "Are you all packed?"

"Yeah, Jack's parents flew out yesterday, so they took a suitcase with them," she says absently, moving her mouse and opening her email app. The new messages load fast, hundreds and hundreds of them populating the screen in front of her. "My dress is being delivered tonight to the house, and the shoes should be, fingers crossed, in by Wednesday at the latest."

I smile and nod, just like I do most of the time Elle talks about things I can't, quite frankly, understand. The way some of these people talk about their lives and their money just astounds me at times, and it's nothing like what I'm used to. I come from a small town in the mountains in Argentina, where the majority of the people are middle or working class. I'm a first-generation college graduate and worked very hard to get where I am, and it's a shock to hear these things sometimes.

"Are you excited for the trip?" Elle asks without looking at me. She's scrolling through emails, half-distracted. "I think it's going to be so good for you."

"Yes," I say quickly.

But the truth is I'm feeling a little anxious about it. Two whole weeks before Elle's wedding, stuck inside a house with the same group of people that makes me feel slightly out of place on a regular basis? Not my idea of fun.

"I mean, I *love* the idea of ninth-wheeling this romantic vacation in the Alps."

"You jest," she says with a lopsided smile and a slight glance in my direction. Her long blonde hair is tied in a low bun like usual, a sharp, crisp line down the middle of her head and her strands pulled back with such tightness I'm surprised she can even think. "But honestly, babe, who even cares about that? The house is amazing, and you'll be able to relax and not think about work for two whole weeks."

I nod, even though she's not looking. I've already made peace with the fact that I'll be a background player in this group—the kind of person who's in all the photos but gets cropped out when they make it to someone's feed.

"Oh! I forgot to tell you—"

"Manuela, get in here, please," I hear James call from his office. Except it sounds more like *Man-you-elle-ah* than how you would actually say my name.

"Hi, James, good morning," I say with a smile as I enter his office. It's the corner office on our lower floor, but he treats it as if it were the one-hundredth floor in the most prestigious building in Manhattan.

"Yes, good morning," he says dismissively, reclining in his overpriced chair with his feet crossed on the desk. If this isn't a power move specifically to intimidate me, then I don't know what is. "Did you see this?"

He points at an article pulled up on his computer about an upcoming cold front.

"I did," I say. "But the forecast doesn't call for rain, so the installation shouldn't be affected. And honestly, I still don't fully understand Fahrenheit, but I don't think it'll be that bad."

James drops his feet to the floor, eyes widening like I just confessed to embezzlement. I swear I can see him foaming at the mouth with anger. If I've learned anything in the months since he's been my supervisor, it's that he's volatile and things with him change a lot. It's always better to be prepared.

"Manuela," he spits, "you live in America now. You have to get used to the way we do things here. For fuck's sake."

I blink up at him, trying to really understand why this is important. The app on my phone can easily convert the temperature, so why is he berating me this way for accepting I'm having difficulty with something that is so easy to correct? But I flush nonetheless, the heat curling up my chest, to my neck, and finally rising to the tips of my ears, where it sits and burns.

But with everything with James, it's easier to smile and nod. It's not the first time he's made somewhat derogatory comments about me and my style, as he likes to refer to some of my more... Latin-American nuances. I overheard him once talking to our HR rep that my accent was too thick and he didn't understand when I pronounced the word "strategy." Another time I mentioned how it's summer in Argentina over the holidays and I was excited for my first-ever white

Christmas, and he muttered, "Classic third world country," under his breath.

"Understood," I say simply as I tap my foot on the carpet, waiting for the final instruction before I vent to Elle.

"Fix it." He adjusts the bottom of his sticky notes so that they are perfectly parallel to the edge of his desk. "No one is going to emotionally engage with the exhibit's storytelling if their hands are cold."

It's fruitless to argue with him for many reasons. The biggest one being that I cannot control the weather.

"You got it." I smile despite the heaviness that lands on my chest. I don't think I've had one civil conversation with him since I started in this new role. And it infuriates me because it seems like all his common sense goes out the window when he's talking to me. There's nothing we can do about the weather, even if we had all the money in the world, and the campaign with the immigration justice organization we work with is going to be amazing regardless.

He dismisses me with a wave of his hand while the other one moves his computer mouse impatiently, clicking until the log-in window for his email flashes in his eyes. I turn on my heel, walking back, Elle looking at me with eyes wide and a subtle shake of her head. She wants to strangle him for me, I know that.

And I agree, but I also really enjoy my job, and I've worked my ass off to get to where I am. So I shake my head and walk back to my cubicle and sink into my chair without a word.

The hum of the office fills the silence—keyboards clacking, phones ringing, James's muffled voice bleeding through his door. I stare at my screen, not really seeing the blinking cursor, and Elle just sips her drink like nothing happened.

It's our unspoken pact: she won't push me to talk, and I won't crumble in front of him. Not here. Not yet.

2

MANUELA

"HE'S SUCH A FUCKING DICK!" Elle screams at the top of her lungs the moment we step through the building's doors. There's a regular stream of people walking out with us and another significant amount in and out of the subway entrance at the corner of the street. All of them turn to watch what's going on, but Elle continues cursing, her indignation entirely on my behalf.

This is normal New York City behavior, I remind myself —crying on the street or the subway is practically a rite of passage. I haven't done it yet, but I've come close. Maybe today will be the day.

"Why do you let him treat you like that?" Elle says, pushing her purse up her shoulder forcefully. "I just—"

"Elle," I say with a sigh. I'm resigned, really, at this point. There's nothing I can do to change him. If he's a racist asshole, then let him, but there's too much riding on this job for me to do something about it. "It's fine."

"It's not fine." She turns again and takes her phone out of her slacks pocket, her thumbs moving wildly on the screen. It's almost like I can see her thoughts whirring in that brilliant brain of hers. "I'm going to text my dad, and he—"

"Absolutely not," I cut through her spiraling thoughts, and her thumbs slow down slightly. She looks up at me expectantly, like I should give her a definitive reason to abort whatever she is doing right now. Her dad is a big-name attorney and was able to hook me up with a firm that took care of my Green Card process, and luckily, it's been smooth sailing. "It's just a few more months, I swear."

"Girl," she replies, sighing dramatically and draping one arm around my shoulder, tugging me towards her. "You are fucking amazing. I hope you know that."

"Sure," I say, shrugging it off even though a small part of me wants to lean into it.

We walk in silence for a beat, the city buzzing around us, and we let her optimism carry us down the block, even if mine is running a little thin.

After a few blocks of chitchat, we each go our separate ways, and I wander through the city streets in the direction of my apartment.

By the time I get home, it's close to eight, and the grime of the city has clung to me like a second skin. My blouse smells faintly of coffee and printer ink, and my feet ache from a day pacing between my desk and James's office. The air in the apartment is heavy, muggy in that way it always is since the A/C died last fall and our landlord keeps promising he'll "send someone."

I kick off my shoes by the door and undo the hair tie from my half-hearted bun, my curls falling limp over my shoulders. There's noise coming from the living room—music, maybe, or just a few too many voices talking over each other. Camila must still have people over. I vaguely remember her mentioning something about her graduate school friends stopping by after happy hour, but I didn't think they'd still be here. Not that it's unusual. She entertains more than I do, which isn't saying much.

"*Hola*," I call softly, not expecting anyone to hear me.

My roommate appears at the end of the hallway, barefoot, holding an almost empty glass of wine. Her dark hair is in a messy braid, and she's wearing one of those matching lounge sets that makes her look impossibly chic even though she's clearly been drinking for hours. She smiles when she sees me—not cold, just a little too bright to be completely genuine. "Come meet everyone."

She's also from Argentina, and we ended up as roommates after she graduated with an MBA at Duke and moved to the city for her job in finance. My cousin's husband is somehow related to her, and they connected us a little over two years ago once she knew she was moving here. It happened that my lease was up at the time, and I wanted a little more space and a building with an elevator, so I decided to live with a roommate.

It's been a drastic change in my life—starting with the fact that it somehow feels like I'm regressing. When I lived in Buenos Aires, I didn't have a roommate, so it just makes me feel like despite having landed the job of my dreams and living in an amazing city, I'm not quite there yet.

I hesitate. "It's late, and I haven't had dinner yet."

"We have food. And they're nice," she insists with a grin, leaning against the wall like she has all the time in the world. Which, to be fair, she does. She was laid off a few weeks ago and has been struggling with finding a job. She mentioned something about having a sixty-day grace period before her visa expires or else she'll have to go back to Argentina. "*Dale.*"

Before I can make an excuse, someone in the living room calls out in Spanish, the words tumbling with the kind of ease that makes my chest ache. *Qué boluda,* followed by laughter that sounds like home.

"And then the *señora* tells me she's never been south of San Clemente, and I say *ah bueno,* now everything makes sense." Laughter erupts. Not the polite, overly loud kind people give when they don't actually find something funny.

Curiosity wins. I step into the living room, barefoot, smoothing my curls down with one hand. The lights are low, and the playlist is some *cumbia villera* remix I barely recognize. Two women are cross-legged on the floor, one half-asleep on the couch.

"Someone said something about San Clemente?"

"Why?" one of the women responds. She has dark long

hair down to her waist and a breezy sundress that is draped over her legs. She looks at me with inquisitive eyes, almost like I'm intruding in on her life.

"I'm from Tres Fuegos, just up the mountain."

"No fucking way!" she screams, and she shoots up from her perch on the floor in complete surprise.

"What did you just say?" the blonde woman says. Her hand is resting on a small baby bump, but she's looking up at me like I just told her I'm the queen of England. "Tres Fuegos?"

"Yes." I laugh, slightly skeptical. "It's in Córdoba."

"My ex-boyfriend is from there. Santiago Williams."

"Shut the fuck up," I say, and suddenly, I'm invested. This has never happened to me in the three plus years since I moved here. Occasionally people have asked me if I know someone or other, but it's a big enough country that the chances are minimal.

"*Que chiquito es el mundo.*"

"Wait a minute," Camila says, looking from one friend to the other, blue eyes wide. "How is this even possible?"

"I don't even know because you have to zoom in real close to even see my town on the map."

"Oh, by the way, everyone, this is Manuela." Camila gestures loosely and shakes her head, like she can't quite wrap her thoughts around what is happening. I move to sit on the floor in between the girl who mentioned San Clemente and my roommate.

"This is Sol, and Clara with the baby on the way, and the

one asleep on the couch is Mica. She's also in finance and had a terrible week." I smile, and Sol sits next to me.

"I can't believe it," she mutters to herself, taking out her phone and quickly texting someone. "How come we've never met? I mean, we would have crossed paths eventually. With all that nothing to do in the summers and all."

I laugh again because I'm still shocked. "I don't know. Do you know the Williams siblings? I'm the same age as the youngest."

"Ah, that must be it. I'm much older," Sol says, tucking her legs back in a way that makes her look so effortless. She has tiny tattoos all along her arms, almost in random spots on her skin. There's a set of stars, some sort of bird, and a lot of different flowers sprinkled throughout.

Camila is nodding along with the conversation and smiling, almost like this is giving her an enormous amount of joy. There's something deeply comforting about the shorthand of shared geography, and I can't believe there's so much overlap in our lives, and this whole time it was just a matter of listening a little bit closer to what Camila and her friends were talking about.

"Anyway," Sol continues, like this little diversion is just a normal thing that happens to them and not potentially something life-altering to me. "Finally, the lady gave me the empanadas and let me go, but that made me, like, forty-five minutes late to my wedding. It was clear my marriage was doomed from the start."

Clara snort-laughs and chokes on her water, and Camila

moves slightly to tap her on the back as she coughs. "We're celebrating Sol's divorce," she whispers in my ear, and I nod as if I understand any of it.

"I miss empanadas," Sol says, with a smile on her face and a shine in her eyes.

"Oh my god," I say. "I haven't had a decent one since I moved here."

Sol nods solemnly. "My mom put some frozen ones in her suitcase one year and got detained at customs at JFK. I cried for, like, three hours. Not for her but for the empanadas."

They all laugh again, and this time I laugh too—not the awkward kind I usually default to at Elle's parties, but the easy kind that feels like letting your shoulders drop. When I finally stand to leave, Camila lifts her glass with a knowing smile.

3

CONNOR
THURSDAY

"Bro," I hear from behind me just as the footsteps slow down. I'm sitting at my desk, two monitors plus my laptop in full view and my headset halfway off, still cradling over one ear. And for fuck's sake, if I hear that word one more time… If I had a dollar for every time someone called me "bro" in this office, I wouldn't need a trust fund.

"What's up?" I say, removing my headset and placing it on the desk. My finger is moving of its own accord and tap, tap, tapping on the tabletop. It's the fifth time Cash has interrupted me in the past fifteen minutes, and I'm starting to think that he must be either very good or really bad at his job because he's never doing anything. He's grinning like we're best friends.

"You're the only one who isn't participating in the fantasy football league, bro."

I sigh and turn to face him. He's wearing slacks and a

white shirt, sleeves rolled up to his elbows and an obnoxiously expensive watch on display. His Patagonia vest has seen better days, but the company's logo shines brightly on his chest, like a beacon of supreme pride. Almost like the ultimate flex. A finance bro through and through.

"Right," I reply, glancing at the time on my watch even though I know I have another thirty minutes before the next calendar block. "Haven't had a chance to look."

"Oh, no worries, dude," he says with a chuckle. It's almost like a combination of confusion and annoyance that I haven't, in fact, had a chance to leisurely sign up for a fantasy football league I have no interest in. "But if you could at least sign up before leaving for the trip, that would be awesome."

I nod slowly. "Sure," I say as I unplug my laptop from the dock. I stand, not aggressively, just fully, and Cash takes a small step back. I'm taller than him by a few inches, and it shows, especially when I'm this close. "I'll see if I get to it after work."

"That's fire," he says, a half step behind me now as I turn away.

Fire? Jesus Christ.

I don't say anything. Just keep walking.

The office is still buzzing behind me—calls, pings, the low drone of overachievers who think working themselves to the bone for a deal is a noble pursuit. I used to be like that. Used to want to be the best at this. Until I started asking myself what *this* even was.

By the time I'm on the street, it's dark. That in-between

time when the city shifts—less finance, more Thursday bar crowd. A strange quiet hums under the usual noise, like New York itself is catching its breath. Summer nights usually mean packed sidewalks and rooftop laughter, but tonight the air's unseasonably crisp. A rare break from the humidity. The kind of night that should feel like a gift.

It doesn't.

I loosen the top button of my shirt and start walking. I could call a car, but I'd rather take the long way home and move my body. Pretend I'm grounded and all that shit.

My phone buzzes in my pocket, and I don't even have to look to know it's my father calling. I almost let it go to voicemail, but I don't. Because not answering somehow feels worse.

"Connor," he says in that clipped, efficient tone he uses for his quarterly earnings calls. "Did you confirm with Joe about dinner tomorrow?"

I pause at the crosswalk. "I told you, I can't commit to that yet."

"It's just dinner," he replies, like that makes it harmless. "He's a partner at Vista. They're looking to expand their team. It could be a good move for you."

There it is. A good move. A step on the path. The words land with the weight of decades of him trying to mold me into something solid and comprehensible, someone he could point to at dinner parties or charity events and say *that's my son.*

The path has always been their world, not mine.

Grades, internships, Ivy League, analyst, associate, VP. Each rung on the ladder its own box I'm expected to check, not because I want to climb it but because climbing is the only acceptable motion. The only proof I'm not falling behind.

And for years, I did it. I ran until my lungs burned and called it ambition.

But lately, all I can feel is how narrow it's gotten. How the *path* feels less like a staircase and more like a windowless tunnel. Not even a light at the end.

"I'll... see what my schedule looks like," I say because it's easier than no. I will deal with the aftermath later—a problem for future me.

"Good," he says, already satisfied. "And bring Athena if she's back from the Hamptons."

The light changes. I start walking again. "Sure, Dad."

"Proud of you," he says and hangs up before I can answer.

I slide the phone into my pocket and keep walking, letting the city swallow me block by block until the gold-lit awning of my building finally comes into view.

"Evening, Mr. Paul," Alfred says as I push into the lobby of my building. His tone is warm and familiar. He's always been polite but never fake, which is exactly why I like him so much. He's wearing the most doorman outfit there ever existed, but it suits him and his role just perfectly. The building where I live is as subtle as a slap in the face. Gold leaf trim, floor-to-ceiling mirrors, velvet benches no one ever sits on, and a chandelier so large it looks like it was brought in directly from Versailles in its own private jet. The ceiling is domed and hand-painted by an artist I should remember but don't.

The residents love it. Take real pride in it. I once saw an older man with sparkling New Balance shoes give a ten-minute speech to a real estate agent about the *original plaster work.*

I've lived here long enough to stop noticing the extravagance. But sometimes, when I come home late and the lobby is quiet like this, the opulence screams at me and makes me feel lonely.

"Hey, Alfred." I give a tired half smile. "Cold tonight."

"For summer? Absolutely," he says, tapping something on his tablet. "The city doesn't know what it wants lately."

I chuckle lowly. "Tell me about it."

"You're later than usual today."

I nod. "Meetings."

He gives me a knowing look. "Long meetings make for short lives, you know."

"I'll quote you on that."

The elevator dings before he can answer, and I step inside. The metal doors close, and I stare at my reflection for the brief ride up—crumpled collar, under-eye circles, a man who looks like he needs eighteen hours of uninterrupted sleep and possibly a new identity.

My apartment is quiet and dark.

Athena's absence hums through it, not like an echo but a

gap. A missing note. Her presence lives in the empty side of the bed, the untouched custom-made coffee mugs, the closet that's now perfectly organized because she's not around to wreak havoc with all her clothes strewn about.

She moved out seven months ago, and I still haven't told anyone. It's final this time—not like the other handful of times we've been apart for a few months and end up getting back together, that comfort in the familiarity of knowing someone.

Every time my mother calls, she asks if Athena's coming to brunch next Sunday, and I stall. Say she's busy or at the Hamptons' house with her parents, which is much easier than saying that I ended it, explaining why, and then having to listen to my mother go on and on about the expectations they have from me, how *eyes will be on you two soon, and maybe you can have Grammy's ring whenever you're ready to propose.*

Her voice always drips with expectation, like she's waiting for me to catch up to the life script she's already written in her head. Husband. Father. Managing Director. In that exact order.

It's not that Athena was awful. She wasn't at all. She was ambitious. Polished. Of a good family. Everything I was raised to want and definitely fit into those expectations my parents—particularly my mother—droned on and on about.

But every time we talked about the future, I felt like I was standing on a ledge. And when I finally jumped—when I said *I can't do this anymore*—I thought I'd feel free. Instead, I landed in silence. In questions I couldn't answer. In a body that stopped sleeping and a chest that wouldn't loosen no matter what I did.

The night I went to the emergency department, I thought I was dying. Full-on chest tightness, blurred vision, hands going numb. I left the office at ten and collapsed on the sidewalk, not dramatically like in the movies—just slowly, knees buckling, breath clawing at my lungs. For a second, I swore this was it. That my body had decided it couldn't keep running at the speed everyone else demanded of it.

I told the nurse I had no prior history and that I worked in investment banking, and she just nodded like that explained everything.

And maybe it did, and I was more of a stereotype than I wanted to admit, and the only thing missing from being a walking finance bro was actually using the word "bro" in conversation.

I open the fridge and grab a beer, then let the cold bottle rest against my forehead for a second before twisting the cap off. The invitation to Switzerland is still stuck to the fridge, printed on thick cream cardstock like it's a royal event. Jack and Elle's names are in bold script at the top—my cousin, the golden boy, marrying into money like expected and somehow still likable and down to earth. He invited me a year ago, back when I was technically with Athena. We were supposed to go together, and I think she expected I would propose during the trip because the hints started early on and kept coming. That part didn't stick.

The pre-wedding trip is two weeks in a chalet somewhere near Lucerne. Hiking, boat rides, scenic trains. Jack's friends are all investment bankers and start-up founders who grew up together. I'll be the odd one out, which says something, considering I grew up adjacent to them.

The apartment smells faintly of cleaning products, which somehow makes it worse.

On the counter, my abandoned experiments sit like quiet accusations: the dead sourdough starter I forgot to feed, its surface collapsed in on itself; a stack of clean, unused recipe books from the month I thought cooking might fix me; the guitar propped in the counter with sheet music still clipped open to lesson two.

I keep thinking the right thing will spark something. *Anything*.

Shake me out of this gray fog.

But every time, I start with this surge of determination and end up here again—restless, flat, circling the same empty rooms.

Jack keeps saying the trip will be good for me, that I'll have fun. "It's a chance to unplug," he told me last time we talked. "Just show up, man. We'll take care of everything."

Unplug. That's what everyone keeps calling it, like I'm a device overheating. Maybe I am.

I should one hundred percent skip it. But I won't. Because it's also expected of me to show up at this family affair, where everyone who is anyone will be seen, and I cannot disappoint my parents, it seems.

Athena would've loved this trip. She thrived in these circles, fluent in the language of clinking glasses and polite laughter. I would've played the part at her side, and my mother would've been satisfied. But now it's just me, and I can already hear the questions waiting when I get back.

I take another sip of the beer, then let it go warm in my mouth. Two weeks. That's all. I'll fly in, smile at the right people, eat some fondue, and keep my head down. Be normal. Be *fine*.

And maybe if I fake it hard enough, it'll stick.

4

———

MANUELA
MONDAY

THE CUSTOMS OFFICER barely glances at my passport before waving me through. Outside the security area, the airport hums with early morning activity—roller bags rattling, carts stacked with suitcases, children half-asleep on strollers, parents sitting down and taking a moment to breathe. The floor shines too much, like it was polished just for this party. I chuckle at myself because I wouldn't put it past Elle.

I blink at the brightness. Everything feels louder, greener, lighter.

The flight wasn't bad, exactly. But it was long, and my neck is sore from the awkward angle I held it for most of the red-eye. I don't sleep well on planes—I'm used to the long distances, but the amount of bodies around me makes me jittery. Last night, the man next to me had sharp elbows and a tendency to sniff every few minutes, which in turn made me incredibly paranoid because I really can't get sick.

I didn't say a single word to him, simply tried not to breathe in too deep.

At baggage claim, the carousel is already moving. I stand behind a family wearing matching sweatshirts that say something about *#FamilyTrip* on the back, with the year in ginormous glitter font under the tagline featuring their last name and what I assume is supposed to be a funny play on words. They're arguing loudly in English about whose turn it is to check their connecting flight information. I hug my coat tighter around me and keep scanning for my suitcase, half afraid it didn't make it.

My carry-on duffel is slung awkwardly over my shoulder, the strap already digging into the spot where I hit my shoulder with the door on the way to the airport yesterday afternoon, and I wince without meaning to.

I finally spot my suitcase on the belt. The light blue-and-white ribbon my mother tied to the handle is the only thing that distinguishes it from the sea of black around it. I pull it off the belt and set it on the ground and start heading towards the exit.

I pause for a second near the arrivals area. Elle sent a whole itinerary for getting to Lucerne. A train to the city center, transfer at the main station, then about an hour to the final place where someone will be waiting for us. It's not hard. Just... a lot.

And I'm more tired than I want to admit.

I got here a few hours later than the rest of the group, which should be at the house Elle and Jack rented by now. The cheaper flight was worth it, though it means walking in by myself, which only sharpens that familiar sense of being a step behind everyone else.

I sit on a bench near the sliding glass doors. A breeze sneaks in every time they open, soft and cool and smelling faintly of coffee and diesel. I close my eyes for a moment; I should get moving, but it feels good to stop.

There's always this strange beat the moment right after I land in a new country, where I feel like I'm exactly where I'm supposed to be. Not because I belong here in any real way but because I belong in motion. It's been this way since I finished college and decided to stay in Buenos Aires, where life moved faster than in Tres Fuegos, and the quiet independence of growing my own career and owning my life gave me the momentum to keep going. It makes me feel capable.

Like I've built something of a life, even if most of the time I'm still trying to prove it to myself. And even as the last three years have been a constant reminder that sometimes things take longer than planned.

I pull out the train directions Elle sent a few weeks ago and double-check my route. One step at a time.

"Fancy seeing you here."

I glance up. Connor's standing a few feet away, leaning slightly on the handle of a suitcase that looks like it's already lost a fight. There's a small rip on one corner, and the zipper is holding on with what looks like sheer willpower. He's got sleep lines on his cheek and his hair is doing something chaotic, like he ran his hands through it too many times and gave up halfway on each of those attempts.

"Oh—hey, Connor." I blink up at him, caught off guard. I didn't even know he was coming, and now he's suddenly in front of me, tall and very real in this crowded section of the terminal. For a second I'm not sure if I should stand, wave, or just stare. Of course Elle never mentioned he'd be here. Why would she? He's part of her world, not mine. And besides, nobody knows that when I first met him, I had the slightest crush on him.

"I ended up on a different flight," he says, dropping his bag with a sigh. "Had some miles to redeem, so I took what I could get. Figured I'd catch up with everyone here."

"Ah." It's all I manage because I'm still wrapping my head around the fact that he's actually standing here, talking to me.

"And then my flight got delayed out of JFK, and I spent six hours next to a guy who kept trying to explain the difference between sparkling water and club soda like it was an advanced chemistry lesson."

I laugh. "There's a difference?"

"Apparently," he replies, lifting one shoulder casually. "Something to do with added minerals that give one of them a salty taste? I can't even recall the details, to be honest."

He drops the duffel draped around his shoulder with a

soft thud and sits next to me. Not too close, just enough that I can feel the warmth of him in the cool morning air.

"Are you heading straight to Lucerne?" he asks. His brown eyes appear lighter today, even in the clinical light of the airport.

I nod. "Trying to remember which train I'm supposed to get on first. It's all very organized in Elle's spreadsheet, which is great, but also slightly overwhelming after an eight-hour flight."

"I've got some notes," he says, fishing his phone out of a pocket on his oversized coat and immediately scrolling through it. "Although I thought I'd just follow someone smarter looking than me and hope for the best."

I raise an eyebrow. "And you landed on me?"

"Obviously." He shrugs again, and the movement, combined with the way he's saying it, makes my stomach flutter. "You give off capable energy."

"Thank you," I say, and then after a beat, "I think?"

We stand and start walking together toward the signs for the trains. His suitcase clunks every few steps, even on the smooth tile of the arrivals area, and I try not to let the scene make me laugh.

"You know," he says, glancing over at me, "I didn't expect to see anyone I knew this early. Figured we'd all just magically appear at the house looking suspiciously well-rested."

"Well," I say, "you're halfway there."

He raises a brow. "Yeah?"

"You showed up."

Connor lets out a soft laugh. "And the other half?"

I shrug, grabbing on to my suitcase's handle with a little more force than intended. "Debatable."

"Ouch," he says, pressing a hand to his chest. "That's brutal."

"Just calling it like I see it."

He smiles, easy and unbothered. "Guess I'll have to win you over on the train."

The train platform isn't too crowded yet. We scan the board and find the right platform number, then walk toward it in companionable silence. The train arrives within a few minutes, sleek and quiet, and we get on without issue, heading towards the suitcase racks. I lift mine on, and Connor follows with a low grunt, almost like he's laughing under his breath at himself— but the sound comes out rougher, heavier, and it catches me off guard. It's nothing, really, just a noise, but it lands too close to the base of my spine, sharp enough to make me suddenly, annoyingly, aware of him. And when I glance up, he's already watching me, like he's just as surprised to notice me back.

We find seats near the window facing each other, and within a few minutes, the train starts moving. The view is already beautiful—green hills, small houses with flower boxes, glimpses of water just beyond the trees.

He stretches his legs out and leans back with a sigh. "So," he says, eyes closed as if he's intending to sleep the whole way to the first station where we need to change trains. "Any pre-trip regrets yet?"

"Not yet. You?"

He tilts his head to either side, stretching his neck. "Hmmm, ask me again in two days."

I watch the countryside pass. It's quiet in the train car. Peaceful, in that in-between way where no one expects anything from anyone yet. Where all you have to do is be exactly where you are, going in the exact direction you are heading in.

"You're quiet," he says after a while. Not in an accusing tone in the slightest, simply making an observation.

"I'm always quiet," I say. I want to add that I'm not usually the quiet one in a group, but it's unnecessary. We're friend-adjacent, and he doesn't need to know every detail of my life and my feelings.

"That's true," he says. "But I think it's on purpose."

I glance at him, the words catching me off guard. His features are so relaxed, unlike anything I've seen recently. Normally, he's buttoned-up and stiff, eyes always on his phone or thumbs typing furiously, even with his girlfriend next to him, talking loudly and gesticulating wildly with every story she tells. A lot of the men in the friend group are the same. *Finance*, was what everyone told me. Like their chosen professions just keep them on edge constantly.

Connor doesn't elaborate. He watches me for a beat before looking back out the window.

I lean my head against the glass, unsure what to say to that. It's not a bad observation. It feels like more than I expected from someone who's mostly existed in my periphery until now.

"You don't talk much either," I say.

"I talk enough."

"Is this a competition?"

"Only if I'm ahead, obviously."

That earns him a smile.

The train speeds up, gliding past a patch of farmland and a field of yellow wildflowers like the ones we have back in my hometown, except these look more distinguished—definitely European because it's like they're classy. I could take a picture, send it to my best friend from back home, Martina, so that she can get her husband, Jacinto, to grow these for her, but it feels better to just look. To keep this moment to myself.

"Can I ask you som—" he says.

"How's work?" I blurt at the same time.

We both pause, then laugh, the sound spilling out too loud for the quiet of the train car.

"You first," I say quickly, waving a hand for him to go on. It's a basic question, definitely making small talk, but something I've seen so many people do in these types of situations before. It's polite, I think, and breaks up the silence of the whole scene.

He leans back against the seat, considering. "It's... fine. Busy."

The words come out steady, but there's weight behind them. For a second, I don't know what to say because it's the most standard answer anyone can give. Almost like being busy is something you should be proud of. It's also, I notice, the most words we've ever exchanged in the three years since I've been in New York, and I don't hate it one bit. Even if it sounds rehearsed, scripted.

The train slows a little as we pass a cluster of green hills dotted with chalets, and a local train station is a blur outside the window. He turns slightly towards it, his knee brushing mine. It's casual. Probably accidental. But I feel it all the way in my bones.

"I'm glad for the time off," he adds after a second. Connor's eyes move from my eyes to my neck and linger on the crescent moon pendant I'm wearing, partially visible among my hair. "And we're actually required to take a two-week break every year because of..." He trails off and gestures with his hand. "Boring regulation stuff. So no one will be contacting me." A faint smile. "Which is my favorite part."

There's a beat where I'm not sure what to say, so I match his smile. The train hums beneath us.

"Me too," I say, soft but steady. "Glad for the time off, I mean."

Connor leans back again, clearing his throat. "Alright. Your turn."

"For what?"

"To ask something inappropriate."

"Connor," I say with a smile on my face. I'm starting, finally, to feel tired and drowsy, the adrenaline of the flight over and the mixture of everything slowly fading. I imagine my expression is sleepy and somewhat unhinged. "I already asked a question. And it was not inappropriate, thank you very much. Extremely polite."

He laughs, a hearty laugh that makes his body shake. He crosses one leg over his knee in that classic man pose and looks at me, a crinkle in both his eyes.

"I don't have any inappropriate questions."

"Liar."

I think for a moment, hum to myself. I desperately want to ask about his girlfriend—the one who's usually glued to his side at every social function we've ever overlapped at—but that feels completely out of bounds. We're friends. Or close acquaintances in the same orbit. Either way, it's not my place.

"She's not coming," he finally says, eyes fixed on the window, tracking the blur of trees and fields and rolling hills just outside. "In case you were wondering."

"Oh." It's all I can manage, taken aback. I noticed her absence from the social events where we'd see each other this year, sure, but assumed it was a fluke, with the summer keeping a lot of us busy. I didn't expect him to name it.

He glances at me, then away. "Yep."

There's the noncommittal shrug again. The one shoulder lift that's so easy to miss. Except it's not. It's the kind of shrug that hides something sharp underneath, like the full story is heavier than he wants to carry out loud.

I don't blame him. We *are*, after all, just friends. Or maybe friend-adjacent.

We both look out the window after that. Nothing pressing or heavy. There's something nice about the shared silence—it's filling the space between us in a cozy, enveloping way, even if what just happened was charged with tension and hums with something new and unexpected.

Something I can't name. Not while I'm tired and the train is still moving.

5

MANUELA

We don't talk much for the rest of the ride. Not because it's awkward but because it's comfortable in a way I haven't felt in years. Every once in a while, Connor points out something out the window—the edge of the lake through the trees (there's more than one throughout the journey), a church spire in the distance—and I nod, smiling, letting the silence stretch.

Changing trains in the Zurich central station is less chaotic than I imagined. The station is massive but organized, with high ceilings, warm lighting, and the kind of tile floors that make our suitcase wheels echo a little too loud, even with the hundreds of people moving about at the same time as us. We walk side by side without saying much, following the signs. Connor buys us both lattes from a kiosk without asking what I want—he guesses correctly, which is either impressive or terrifying or maybe says a lot about how predictable and bland I am.

Our connection train is smaller, slower, with wide windows and wooden accents that look almost movie-like. Nothing like the sleek European trains I saw all over the internet during my research. This feels more local, like a best-kept secret. By the time we are winding around the lake, the conversation picks back up, low and meandering and really nothing of substance. Music, the worst jobs we've ever had (mine: helping out at my small town's library in the summers—dusty shelves and no A/C; his: a landscaping job up in the Hamptons where the owner of the house made him trim the grass with kitchen shears).

When we arrive at the tiny dock town Elle flagged in the itinerary, it's clear this is the part where things get ridiculous and so very much like my friend.

"I thought the house was in the mountains," I say as we step off the train. The air is crisp and cool, and it smells like winter is coming. There's a faint smell of damp grass and bread, like there's a bakery somewhere just out of sight. We are the only two people standing on the platform, the other bodies having retreated to their final destinations in hurried steps as the train pulled away from the station minutes ago.

"It is," Connor says, pointing. "Up there, I think."

He's right. Perched high on a hill across the lake, tucked between green ridges, is what look like multiple converted chalets with massive windows and wraparound terraces. In the center, there's a large building that looks similar to the houses—most likely the hotel part of the resort where we're staying. There's a long staircase leading down to the water and a little boat gliding towards us, the Swiss flag moving against the wind.

"*Me estás jodiendo,*" I murmur. "We're taking that?"

"I believe the itinerary called it a *boat transfer,*" he says, reading off his phone. "Very casual, very normal."

The boat looks like a cross between a water taxi and a Bond villain's preferred method of transportation. We wait a few moments, and a chipper man with a large gap between his teeth and a striped shirt gets off. He smiles and nods, muttering, "Yes, yes" as he grabs our suitcases. I look at Connor, expecting some sort of confusion, but he's helping the man load our luggage into the boat, like this is, in fact, the method of transportation we should be taking.

The lake is impossibly blue. Not turquoise like the Caribbean, not murky like back home—just deep and cold-looking and still. My shoulders stay tight as the boat pulls away from the dock, the water slapping against the sides louder than it should be. I grip the edge of the seat and try to keep my expression neutral, even as every tilt makes my stomach tense.

I keep my gaze fixed toward the shoreline, where the trees are beginning to change color—patches of gold and orange breaking through the green, mirrored perfectly on the surface of the water. It looks like something out of a postcard, the kind of view that should make me relax. But I stay sitting too straight, palms flat on the seat, as if letting go would tempt the lake to swallow me whole.

The ride takes maybe fifteen minutes, long enough for the breeze to lift the edge of my hair and for Connor to tilt his head toward the sun and say, "Okay, fine. This part is kind of nice."

At the far end of the arrival dock, a small stone platform leads to the base of a funicular track that looks like it was built into the hillside. Waiting for us is a teenage staff member in a crisp white polo, checking our names off a list on a tablet that is partially strapped to his chest.

"You're with the Paul-Winslowe party?" he asks, already turning to unlock a gate that is built into the terrain. If I weren't paying attention, I would never guess it was there.

"Apparently," I say.

The funicular rattles up the hill slowly, like it's trying not to disturb the trees. The incline is so steep that every few feet, my instinct is to grab on to the handrail inside the cab. The view, on the other hand, is spectacular. The peaks of the tallest mountains are lightly dusted with snow, and all the trees seem to be a different color, from deep yellows to golden oranges and faint reds. It reminds me so much of fall in Tres Fuegos, of those crisp mornings when I used to walk to the café and the whole valley smelled like woodsmoke and fresh bread.

But this isn't home.

And the ache sneaks up on me in a way I'm not prepared for.

I haven't seen my family in over a year. Between the complications of immigration paperwork, the difficulty of traveling during the early stages of the Green Card process, and the constant shuffle of everyone's schedules, two years have come and gone. My older sister sends me voice notes every day about random things that happen to her or to fill me in on the town's latest gossip, and my parents try to video chat at least a few times a week, but it's not the same. I miss them.

It's not that New York isn't exciting or full of potential. It's just that sometimes the pace of it all feels like a blur I forgot to consent to. And now that I'm this close—so close—to permanent residency, it feels like I'm suspended in place. Waiting for something to change without being able to move.

And somehow, riding up a hill in a silent glass box in a foreign country makes all of that sharper. I've never felt farther from home. Or more like I'm supposed to pretend I'm fine.

Connor hasn't said anything in a while. He's watching the view, too, arms crossed over his chest, face unreadable. I let the silence stretch between us, too full of my own thoughts to try and fill it with niceties or small talk.

We pass a narrow clearing, and suddenly, the resort comes into view. That helps. It gives me something else to focus on.

Something unreal.

At the top, there's one final surprise: a gold-plated golf

cart with cream leather seats and a tiny screen that flashes our names in block letters.

"You've got to be kidding me," Connor mutters.

The driver, wearing a short-sleeve button-down and aviators, doesn't bat an eye. "Welcome," he says in a thick accent. It sounds more Italian than German to me, but what do I know? "We'll be at the house in three minutes."

Connor shoots me a look. "This feels extremely on brand for your friend."

I laugh. "Right? I was expecting fancy, but this is a full-blown lifestyle catalog."

We bump along a narrow winding road, through a grove of evergreen trees, past what I'm pretty sure is a yoga pavilion. And then we round a curve—and there it is.

The house.

More modern than expected, with floor-to-ceiling windows, sprawling decks, and stone steps that curve into the mountainside. It's definitely equal parts Bond villain lair and luxury spa retreat in the Alps. I think my jaw actually drops.

Connor whistles low, hands tucked into the pockets of his pants as he turns three-sixty and looks around us. "Okay, so... how do we act like we belong here?"

I snort and catch myself, but he's already smiling in my direction. "You do belong here."

He doesn't smile back right away. "Meh," he says with one of those shrugs, the sound deliberately disinterested. There's a flicker of something else beneath it, a small shift in his posture, the way his shoulders go a little rigid, like the comment landed in a place he didn't expect.

Like maybe he thinks I meant *that kind* of belonging. The old-money, trust-fund-boy kind.

The kind that is in such opposition to me, a working-class immigrant who doesn't belong with this type of crowd.

I almost clarify—almost say *I meant it as a joke*—but then he looks over at me again, expression soft as he decides not to take it personally.

"Anyway," he says, a touch lighter, a polite smile on his lips. "Lead the way."

6

———

MANUELA

WHEN I WAKE up from my nap, the light in the room is golden and low, casting long, dark shadows across the floor. For a moment, I have no idea where I am, because it's an expansive, white, and blinding room, *almost* surgical and very different to my bedroom in New York.

Then I remember—the flight, the trains, the boat across the lake, and the absurd golf cart with heated seats. The house.

Everything was quiet when we entered, and I assumed the group was either out doing something or resting in their rooms. Either way, I was drowsy with sleep and headed up to the top floor where my room was waiting—a small note from Elle on the bed welcoming me to the trip of her dreams letting me know they were down by the lake if I wanted to join.

I stretch without moving much, blinking slowly at the

wooden beams that crisscross the tall ceiling. The room is beautiful in a way that feels effortless. Clean lines, a linen duvet in the softest cream, a single vase of flowers on the sill. The window's cracked open just enough for a cool breeze to sneak in. Beyond, the lake shines wildly, the sun setting behind the peaks like in a movie. I think I see a pair of swans swimming by the shore, but I can't confirm they're there. It's nothing like home, that's for sure.

I didn't mean to sleep so long. Just meant to rest my eyes, maybe check a few messages and go through the itinerary so that I can be up and ready to go whenever the group is moving. My phone is still face-down on the nightstand, and for once, I don't reach for it. Outside, the world is quiet except for the faintest clatter of plates, the low murmur of voices drifting in from somewhere below.

Dinner, it seems.

I sit up slowly, the sheets soft against my skin, and try not to think about how long it's been since I felt this still. Not just tired, but static in that rare way, like your body's here but your mind hasn't caught up yet. It happened a lot in Buenos Aires, when I would go back to Tres Fuegos to visit, and the small-town living consumed me in ways I didn't expect to love so much after living away from it for a decade.

I should message my mom, let her know I made it safely. But the thought of explaining where I am, of describing this place over voice notes and a series of photos and videos, feels overwhelming right now.

I run my fingers through my hair, twist it up into a messy

knot, and pad barefoot to the window. The terrace is visible from here, two stories below and set back on a platform that juts into the trees. There are string lights overhead, soft and warm, and a long wooden table being set with mismatched dinnerware and bowls that look like they belong in a food magazine. Someone uncorks a bottle of wine. Someone *oohs* and *ahhs* at the movement. I can't see who it is, but I recognize the cadence of the sounds from years of listening to the same chants.

It looks like a scene from a movie I'm not quite in yet. But I'm close.

I slip into the ensuite bathroom, splash cold water on my face, and change into a loose sundress I stuffed into my suitcase last minute. I don't think it's warm enough for me to be wearing too few clothes, but from where I stood by the window, it looked like the outdoor heaters were doing their thing and keeping everyone toasty even in the crisp fall evening. The air smells like rosemary and soap when I open the door and tiptoe out into the hall.

I don't run into anyone on my way downstairs, but I do snoop around the house. All the bedrooms look identical, except for one on the second floor that seems to be Elle's— it's almost the entire length of the house and potentially bigger than my whole apartment back home. There's no sign of the bride, so I continue making my way down the stairs in search of her and food. By the time I reach the back terrace, people are already gathering around the table in loose clusters.

Connor is leaning against the railing, his hair slightly mussed from sleep, a bottle of sparkling water (club soda?) in hand. He looks over as I step outside, and the corner of his mouth lifts, lazy and amused. "Good nap?"

I nod. "Didn't mean to crash that hard."

He raises the green bottle like a toast. "You and half the house, it seems. I think everyone's in recovery mode, getting ready for the week."

A breeze moves through the trees on either side of the house and rustles the string lights overhead. A server is setting down a plate of olives at the table. Someone else is popping open another bottle of wine, this time followed by loud laughter. The conversation around us builds like a soft tide.

Connor nudges his chin toward the seats. "You hungry?"

"Starving."

"Come on," he says, tipping his head towards the table.

Elle is standing at the head, naturally, laughing with Hannah, one of her bridesmaids, and her boyfriend, Sterling, who also happens to work with Jack in whatever finance bro thing everyone on this trip does. They're part of the tight inner circle, the kind of people I've seen at every dinner and weekend gathering since I joined this friend group, though I still mostly hover at the edges.

Right next to her, Jack is deep in conversation with Banks, another one of their college friends, something about rare watches and who still buys them.

"And then the dealer told him it was a 1997 prototype

that only went to royal family members, so of course he bought it," Banks says, not realizing how ridiculous it sounds.

"It was actually a good deal," Cash, another of the bros, adds. "You can't find those under six figures anymore."

Connor snorts into his drink and walks to the other side of the terrace. I head towards my friend, and before I can even utter a word, she's squealing and trampling me like she hasn't seen me in a thousand lives. Never mind that she saw me just a few days ago at work.

"Oh my god, you're here," she says, squeezing my bicep and admiring me, head to toe. Almost like I'm a vision and she can't quite believe I'm here. "I told Jackie you'd pull out at the last minute," Elle says, still holding on to my arm. "With your immigration stuff and all." She says it low, close to my ear, like it's a secret, or maybe if she says it too loud, the gods will get angered and revoke my *almost* permanent resident status.

"I told you I was going to be here," I say, with a smile on my face. I would never bail on her wedding, and it never even occurred to me to simply show up for the wedding and then go back to New York. She's been talking about this trip for a year at least, and I want to celebrate with her. "It's beautiful. All of this."

She follows my gaze across the lake, then down the length of the table, like she's seeing it all for the first time. "Jack's parents wanted it to be... I don't know. Special, I guess. A big send-off for both of us."

"It's definitely that," I say.

She leans closer now, wrapping one arm around my neck, and lowers her voice. "Just wait until you see the boat party next week. Don't pack anything you're emotionally attached to. You will get wet."

"Noted," I say with a laugh, but there's a hollow edge to it. I know she means well, but it's easy for Elle to say things like that when a lot of her problems can be solved by money. Not saying that she throws money at them, but... I digress.

My friend flits away a moment later, called over by another girl from the group, Amelia, waving a bottle of wine, and I'm left standing alone, watching everyone settle into their seats. Laughter rises and falls like waves. People are already starting to shift into vacation mode—looser posture, louder voices, the kind of easy camaraderie that happens when no one is worrying about alarm clocks or deadlines.

Connor takes a seat at the other end of the table, deep in conversation with Banks, still going on about the watches, while his girlfriend Nicole scrolls on her phone. Connor's listening, half-focused, holding a glass of something pale in his hand. When he looks up and catches my eye, he lifts his brows slightly, like we're sharing an inside joke neither of us said out loud.

I look away before I smile too wide and find myself sitting next to him, drifting into his orbit like I've been doing all day. It's almost like the universe is conspiring and has decided we are now buddies for this trip, given the coupled status of everyone around.

"You survived the bro corner," I say under my breath.

"Can you actually believe that people hold entire conversations about watches?"

"I believe it. I mean, I once bought a sandwich that was forty dollars, and I still talk about it to this day."

Connor laughs loudly, tipping his head back. His whole body shakes, and his eyes are shut so tight in amusement that the only thing I can do is stare in awe at this man who suddenly looks so different here, on vacation, than when we are back in New York.

Not that it should surprise me. I've watched him for years from a careful distance—at parties, group dinners, birthdays—always composed. Like there was an invisible line he never let himself cross.

But here... he's loose. Untethered even on the first day of our group vacation. And I can't stop looking.

"In my defense," I add, and a chuckle escapes me, "it had really good pickles. Like, insanely good."

His smile is crooked, and I stare at him some more, sipping from a drink that magically appeared in front of me while this whole thing was happening. The night is soft around us as the lake reflects the last light of dusk, and the hum of conversation rises again. Hannah toasts to the couple, and we all clink glasses together.

"For what it's worth," Connor says as he leans in slightly, his shoulder brushing mine—not enough to make a scene, just enough to remind me he's still here, "I'm glad you came."

I glance over, watching the profile of his face lit by string lights and ambient lighting, and for a second, I don't know what to say.

The night settles into a rhythm—courses arriving one after the other, more stories, more references I don't fully follow. I keep my head down, my smile polite and practiced. Part of me wants to fade into the background completely like I usually do.

7

―――――

CONNOR

THERE'S an expensive hush to the air. The floor-to-ceiling windows reflect the lake, and the mountains are barely visible in the moonlight. Dinner dragged for hours until the bravest of them all finally called it and got up to go to bed. The itinerary the next few days is insane—very much fitting Elle and Jack's personalities.

Boat rides and hikes and day trips to waterfalls and ice caves and potentially a (mandatory?) whitewater rafting excursion... a little bit overwhelming, but I'm hoping it'll help me escape, relax, forget about the dumpster fire that is my life back in New York.

The job that eats every waking hour and still feels hollow. The apartment that's too quiet without Athena but was suffocating me with her in it. The inbox that refills the second I clear it, like scooping out water from a sinking boat. The friends I barely see anymore because I keep canceling plans at the last second. The recurring feeling of having a life I don't want at all, but also not knowing what the fuck I want out of my life either.

I pad barefoot down the stairs and through the hall, the polished wood cool against my skin, aiming for the kitchen and hoping for any warm beverage that could help me sleep. Tea. Or water. Or something to settle the low buzz behind my eyes that has me seeing slightly double.

Everything's been wiped down. Marble counters gleam, the citrusy-cleaner smell still faint in the air. The built-in fridge—somewhere on the far wall of the kitchen—hums softly. For a house this big, this scene feels surprisingly still.

I reach for the cabinet and nearly jump when I see her.

"Sorry," I mutter because I really should have seen her. But she's curled on a stool by the island, half-hidden in shadow, barefoot and wearing a pair of soft pajama pants and a T-shirt that keeps sliding down her shoulder. Manuela's blonde hair is loose, a little messy, and she looks exactly how you hope to look when you don't expect anyone to see you— comfortable, cozy, and somehow still a little magnetic.

Maybe it's the alcohol speaking, but I really can't stop looking.

She smiles like she's been caught but doesn't mind. She lifts one of the mugs already set on the counter. "I was about to make tea."

"Same." I nod toward the kettle, already filled.

We move without talking, finding spoons, picking out bags from a wooden box filled with blends I've never seen before. Basil and hibiscus flower with cardamom notes. I'm not a huge tea connoisseur, but that really doesn't sound very appealing.

There's a rhythm to it that I wasn't expecting, unspoken and easy. She slides a mug toward me as the water starts to boil, and I hand her a teaspoon before she even asks.

It's domestic, almost. Foreign, in this strange house.

When the tea's steeping, she turns on the stool and leans back against the counter, facing the lake. "This place doesn't feel real yet."

I get it. The glass, the magnificence, the view. The way everything looks designed up to the tiniest detail. Manufactured in a way that can make you feel cozy. "Feels like at any point, we're going to realize it's really the set of a movie."

She grins. "Right? I keep expecting someone to yell 'action' at any given point."

That makes me laugh, and I let the sound fill the space. Being with someone who doesn't pretend this is normal. That's what makes it different. I grew up around this—outlandish vacations, spectacular homes, scenes pulled straight from Nancy Meyers movies. It was always there, expected. But it never felt real to me. Not common. Not mine.

Maybe because I knew the price tags that came with them, not just the dollar amounts but the pressure—the constant push to prove we belonged, to keep up, to want more, more, more. My parents certainly thrived on it, but I never did. I never learned how to look around a room like this and feel at home in it.

We take our tea into the sitting room off the kitchen. Couches built for sinking into and potentially falling asleep, windows wide enough to make the lake feel like it's part of the room as it glitters in the moonlight... There's a floor lamp in the corner casting warm light across the room, making everything feel cozy.

We sit, mugs in hand, a little apart. Not distant. Just... careful.

After a while of staring out, she says, "I think we're the only ones not sharing a room tonight."

I tilt my head toward her. "You sound surprised."

She shrugs. "Not surprised. Just... watched? I don't even know that's a fair conclusion of what's happening. Sometimes..."

She drifts off mid-sentence with a deep sigh. I want to probe, to know more, but I leave it, letting her look out onto the lake and the slow darkening of the mountainside as the houses around us start shutting off for the night.

"You could've brought someone."

"I don't really know anyone that well," she says, sipping her tea. "At least, not enough to share a bed for a couple of weeks."

"Fair."

A beat of silence passes. Then, from upstairs—barely audible—a faint sound. A breathy gasp. A moan.

We freeze.

Her eyes meet mine, wide. And then, like the tension breaks all at once, we both burst into dramatic, over the top laughter.

"Oh my god," she whispers, laughing so hard she has to stop and wipe under her eyes. "This house has no sound-proofing."

"Apparently not."

She takes another sip of tea, then sets the mug down. "God," she says with a sigh. "I miss sex."

It's so sudden, so honest, that it stuns us both. Her face goes red in an instant, and even in the dim light, I can see how it reaches the tips of her ears. "*Dios*. I didn't mean to say that out loud."

But I'm still laughing. Not at her—but at the realness of it. "You kind of did."

"I really didn't." There's a tiny squeak at the end of her sentence, and then she buries her face into her hands, lightly chuckling into them. I don't know if she's also buzzed like I am, but she's definitely relaxed, guard down. "I didn't. I swear."

"Well." I pause, contemplate my next few words. We are the only single people in this group, and we will, most likely, be partnered up for all activities that require a buddy on this trip. "Same."

She turns toward me, blinking. "Yeah?"

I nod. "It's been a few months." Seven, to be exact. But who's counting, really?

There's a pause. She doesn't make it awkward at all, but

she studies my face, looking for whatever answer she's been after since this morning.

In this moment, I don't even think it's about sex—not really. At least, not for me. It's not about getting off or scratching an itch. It's about what it could mean. The chance to be close to someone, to let myself be seen for once instead of performing.

I don't know if she feels any of that. Maybe it's just attraction for her. Maybe it's nothing more.

The silence sits between us, just like it has all day. Heavy and rough around the edges, yet comforting and stable.

Then Manuela says, "Can I ask you something?"

I nod.

Her gaze skims the table, like she's debating whether to risk it.

"What's... going on with you and Athena?" The words come out carefully, almost like she's afraid they'll break something.

For a second, my chest tightens. I keep my eyes on the tea swirling in my mug, willing my face to stay neutral. "We broke up seven months ago."

She doesn't jump in, but it looks like she wants to say something along the lines of *duh, it's obvious since you haven't been with her and she was always dragging you around.* But she doesn't. Manuela waits patiently for me to be ready to say something.

"She wanted more structure. A plan and timelines. I get it; she deserved to know where it was all going after so many years together. And I couldn't give her that." I shake my head, trying to find the words I haven't uttered to a single soul because it makes me uncomfortable to divulge so much of myself and to lose control of the narrative that threads my life.

For as long as I can remember, I've lived like everything depends on what people see when they look at me. If I stayed on script, people nodded with approval. If I strayed, even for a second, it felt like the floor tilted under me.

Telling the truth about Athena means opening the door to everyone else's version of the story—my parents' disappointment, my friends' pity, the quiet *what's wrong with him* whispers I've heard my whole life about other people. And once those versions exist, mine would stop mattering.

"I built my whole life on plans," I admit, almost to myself. "Every move mapped out five steps ahead. I used to have a five-year plan." A hollow laugh slips out before I can stop it. "Now even the next five weeks feel blurry."

Her brows draw in.

"I thought I knew what I wanted. A lot of what I wanted had to do with familial expectations—a career, a stable relationship, marriage, and kids. And then I got half of that and... I don't know." I shrug. "It felt like someone else's life. *Feels* like someone else's life."

Manuela is quiet, but her presence is grounding. She moves her body in my direction, switching her angle enough so that now I'm the center of her attention. She's nodding along like she totally gets it. And maybe she does, and I want to prod, but how do I even ask? What do I even ask?

"There's this itch I can't shake," I say. "Like I should be doing something else, but I have no clue what. I keep waiting for a sign or a moment or something, and all I get is noise."

"You sound like someone who needs a vacation," she says softly.

"Or a personality transplant." Or maybe a new group of friends.

She smiles again, tucking a leg beneath her. "For what it's worth... I think you're doing okay."

It's a simple thing to say. But something about the way she says it makes my chest ache.

We sit there a while longer, letting the tea cool. The laughter and flirtation from earlier lingers, but quieter now. Like we're both aware that something shifted.

She glances towards the stairs. "I should probably sleep before someone else starts up."

"Let me know if you need earplugs," I say, keeping my voice light.

"Only if you snore," she throws back, already walking away. "Don't we share a wall?"

I watch her go, her steps soft against the floor.

Then I lean back on the couch and take a long sip of lukewarm tea.

I don't know what this is becoming. But for the first time in a long time, it doesn't feel like nothing.

8

MANUELA
TUESDAY

THERE'S a knock on the door. Before I can stretch or even utter a single word out of my mouth—a customary "I'm coming" or even a "just a second"—it swings open.

Elle stands in the doorway, framed in her sheer white robe, sunlight behind her haloing her figure. She tips her head forward dramatically and groans, like she's in a classic nineties rom-com, waking late for a wedding brunch.

"*Buenos días*," she says in her most theatrical voice yet. She has consistently practiced Spanish with me at work for the past year or so, ever since we started sitting next to each other. She says it's because she needs to be able to talk to her housekeeper turned dog sitter turned master of her home, but I think she does it so that I feel closer to home. "You look alive."

"Good morning," I return, squinting at her and stretching diagonally across the bed. The other side feels cool and welcome in the heat of the room. I swing my legs out of bed. "You slept well?"

"Tried," she replies, pulling open the blinds. Outside, the terraced landscape glows—the maples turning gold, the alders faint red, the sky a sharp blue behind the mountain peaks. "Gorgeous morning."

The light is soft and golden—not harsh but just enough to make waking feel like an invitation were it not for the abrupt presence of Elle. There's the lake again, smooth as glass, and a hint of mist pooling over the surface that wasn't there yesterday.

Last night felt oddly important, even though nothing major happened. I don't feel self-conscious, remembering what I said about missing sex. Mostly, I feel surprised Connor agreed, casually. And how honest it felt. There's something quietly comforting about that.

The floor is cool on my feet but not cold. The house feels quiet even though I'm almost sure everyone is up and moving and getting ready for the planned excursion.

"You good?" Elle asks casually, sitting on the mattress next to me.

I nod. "This mattress is amazing. And I'm excited for today." I stand and take a slow sip of water from the glass I left on the nightstand. "A waterfall hike feels like a perfect plan to start the vacation."

"Duh," Elle says, eyes flitting around. "We're headed to these caves with, like, interior waterfalls?" she says like it's a question. "It's, like, a twenty-minute bus ride from Interlaken, but we have to get going because that is two hours away by train. And we have lunch reservations, and it's, like, a three-kilometer hike to get to the restaurant. Totally peaceful."

I grin. "Sounds like a postcard."

"Exactly the point." She smiles. "Alright, get dressed and meet us downstairs for breakfast. We roll out in half an hour." Then she glances over with that familiar Elle grin that I've gotten to know so well in the past three years. "Coffee first."

I watch her close the door, and for a moment, I breathe. Outside, I hear chairs shifting on the terrace below —people stirring. Soft laughter, someone shaking an iced coffee.

I pull on leggings and a cozy sweater—one of those light but warm basics that travels well and is aesthetic enough for this crowd. My hair's thrown into a loose knot. I let the glow settle around me as I slip into socks and quietly leave the room.

Downstairs, the open concept kitchen is already awake and moving. Steam curls from a huge French press on the island, and there's yogurt and fruit, bowls of granola and honey, fresh bread, a plate of sliced cheese and cold cuts. Someone from the house staff is quietly placing fresh croissants in a basket.

Connor is already there, leaning against the counter and studying the options before him. A classic continental breakfast that makes everything look so good.

He gives me a small nod and pushes an empty mug in my direction.

"Morning," he says softly. The undercurrent is still there—unspoken and warm.

"Hi," I reply, reaching for the French press and pouring some into the rustic ceramic cup in my hand. "Looks good."

He doesn't say anything else, but he meets my eyes over his mug as he drinks, eyebrows lifted slightly. I smile behind my own cup, a blush threatening to form on my cheeks for no reason at all.

Elle claps her hands, cutting through the easy chatter in the room. "Train leaves in thirty. Everyone fed?"

Banks peers at the half-empty plate in front of him. "I think I just ate six croissants. Is that too many?"

His girlfriend, Nicole, audibly gasps, turning her body towards him. "Oh my god, babe, what?"

Banks shrugs. "Vacation rules, babe."

They are one of the couples staying with us during the week. Nicole, Hannah, and Amelia all grew up with Elle and are in the bridal party. Their partners—Banks, Sterling, and Cash, respectively—are acquainted with Jack somehow and all, coincidentally, work in finance too.

Connor chuckles quietly next to me, and it vibrates in my chest. I don't know when I started noticing that about him. The way even his smallest reactions seem to ripple outward, making me want to lean a little closer. Maybe it was last night, in the intimacy of the dim lights and the words that sounded like a secret just for us two.

Jack stands, stretching. "Alright, crew. Let's move before we get too comfortable and the sun starts hitting the deck just right."

A few minutes later, we're walking downhill towards the small town adjacent to the house, leaves crunching underfoot. The train station for this town sits at the center, and it's the exact opposite of the way we arrived—but nestled into the most charming town I've ever seen.

The morning air is crisp but refreshing, and everything has a dewy look to it. It smells like pine needles and earth, and the breeze has a bite that finally wakes me. Elle hooks her arm through mine, squeezing it lightly.

"I'm glad you're here," she says quietly. "I know this can be... a lot."

I laugh softly. "You know I wouldn't miss it for the world."

She squeezes again. "Yeah."

Our transportation arrives at the platform within a few minutes of us reaching it. A clean, tidy three-car train painted bright red with shiny windows. We settle into seats near the windows, and the view slides past slowly as we pull away from the station. The mountains rise sharply, the lake stretching wide and deep blue beside us, mist still clinging to its surface.

Connor sits directly across from me, his arm draped lazily over the back of his seat, eyes fixed out the window. Every so often, his gaze flickers toward me, just for a beat, then away. I'm surprised by how easy it feels. And not at all like I'm being watched—which is the exact feeling I've had for the past three years. Instead, it's inquisitive, alive. As if he's trying to figure me out a few seconds and glances at a time.

It's disarming. Knowing he and Athena aren't together shifts something—almost like the rules of the room quietly rearranged themselves when I wasn't looking. There's a lightness in him I don't remember from the past two years, a looseness in the way he sits, like he's finally breathing air that belongs to him.

It reminds me of the Connor I first met at the engagement party, a little bit more... uninhibited.

Jack kneels in his seat, glancing between the group. "So, what are we thinking? Swim at the waterfall?"

Sterling groans dramatically, followed by a loud "bro" from Cash, one of the other finance bros in the group. "Are you trying to kill us?"

"Adventure builds character," he replies with a big smile on his face that is aimed at his soon-to-be bride.

"Yeah, when you're in your twenties," Elle points out. "We are way past that, babe."

I catch Connor's eye, smiling. "Says the woman who made us climb into an open-door helicopter ride over Manhattan and called it a 'scenic ride.'"

Elle doesn't even blink. "It *was* scenic."

"You had your eyes closed the whole time," someone says —maybe Cash, maybe Sterling—but the entire group erupts in laughter.

"Worth it," Elle declares, flipping her perfectly styled blonde hair over her shoulder.

I hide a smile behind my hand, watching her work the group like a pro. I've seen her lead agency meetings with this effortless charm and a natural gift for orchestrating chaos with the flick of the wrist.

Connor catches my eye again. "What about you? Feeling brave?"

"Define brave," I say, although I straighten my spine and square my shoulders to appear as such.

He lifts a shoulder. "Hiking up a cold mountain trail to willingly throw yourself into glacial runoff."

The train rounds a bend, the lake glittering far below, sunlight flashing off the surface like it's been freshly polished. Behind it, the mountains climb higher and steeper, dotted with trees that have started to lose their leaves, the deep burgundies and reds of the leaves barely holding on to the branches.

Connor shifts slightly, his knee bumping mine for a second before he draws it back without comment. I don't move either, but I feel the space between us buzz a little more.

"Okay, but seriously," Banks says, pushing his sunglasses up his nose. His watch is obscenely shiny, and I wonder if it's one of those special editions that is worth more than my yearly salary that they were talking about last night. "Is there, like, a snack hut at the top? I need to mentally prepare."

"Oh my god, babe," Nicole whines. "You *just* had breakfast."

"We have lunch reservations," Elle says. "And we packed snacks. Relax."

Banks leans back with a content sigh. "That's all I needed to hear."

The banter keeps going, light and quick, and people get on and off the train at different stations. For a while, I stop thinking about Green Cards and a manager that is sucking the soul out of me and how long it's been since I've seen my family. For the first time in weeks, I feel like I'm not catching up to my own life—I'm actually in it.

The train slows as we approach the station, the voice over the speaker announcing our arrival. Everyone starts gathering their things—backpacks, sunglasses, water bottles—and Elle gives us a small briefing.

"Okay, it's a short walk to the trail entrance, and then we'll start the hike. It's not hard, but if you're dramatic or out of shape," she says with a pointed expression at Banks, "now's the time to stretch."

9

———————

CONNOR

"THE AIR SMELLS COLD." It's the first thing that crosses my mind the second we step into the trailhead. It's wide and steep, with a very well-kept gravel path that leads into the mountain. I don't mean to say it out loud, but I hear a few mumbled agreements from the group behind me.

Everything is crisp and a little damp, like the sun hasn't had a chance to stop by and dry everything up from the morning mist. I'm not usually a nature guy, but even I can admit this place is stupidly beautiful. The trees are large and towering, and the paths are winding with no end in sight. Just a trail up the mountain to what I think could be something at the top or maybe towards the side.

We've barely made it fifty feet, and already Banks is complaining. "This incline is disrespectful," he mutters, taking exaggerated steps up the path.

"You've walked twenty feet," Elle says, not even looking

back. She looks spry and athletic in her earth-toned athleisure. Athena used to wear those matching sets all the time on the weekends, even if she wasn't going to work out. I never understood why she did it, but it must be a thing, because every woman in the group is donning similar outfits —except Manuela, who's in a soft knit sweater and comfy sneakers that definitely don't look like they're apt for hiking or even any sort of sporting activity. But somehow, she looks like she belongs here more than any of them. "You'll survive."

"I'm not built for this terrain," he insists, huffing and puffing by his girlfriend. Nicole rolls her eyes but smiles at him nonetheless, like she's completely charmed by his foolishness. "I'm a man of the city."

"You're from Connecticut," Cash throws over his shoulder.

I catch Manuela's smirk beside me. She's walking behind Elle and a few steps ahead of me, her sunglasses pushed up on her head, hair tied in a loose bun. Her small backpack is tiny —maybe purely decorative?—and I'm guessing it holds a protein bar and a phone. Still, she's holding her own on the trail, and every so often she glances over her shoulder like she's checking to see if I'm still back here.

I am.

We pass through a narrow stretch of trees that opens up to a ridge overlooking the valley. The tip of a lake glitters in the distance, and somewhere below, I can hear bells on cows or goats or whatever charming livestock lives here. It's the kind of view people use as screensavers or desktop wallpapers. Completely unreal.

"I promise, you guys, this looked shorter on the map," Elle says, pausing to check her phone. "The wedding coordinator said it was only a three-kilometer walk, so I assumed that should be quick, right?"

"It *is* short," Sterling says, not even winded. "You people are soft."

Cash claps him on the shoulder. "Easy, man. You're, like, ninety percent protein powder."

"Elle, honey," Jack says, dropping his voice just enough for those of us nearby to hear. "Are we sure about this?"

"Babe," she replies, flipping her long hair over one shoulder and speeding up the hill. "Follow me."

We keep walking.

The farther up the mountain we go, the more sunlight appears and the warmer it feels. Within the trees it feels damp and slightly chilly. Eventually, the trail levels off, leading to a clearing with big flat rocks and a few wooden benches that look like they've seen better decades. Right behind it, a large yellow building shines in the sun—its mostly outdoor space wraps around it, and there are a few patrons already sitting on the side that faces the valley.

"See?" She turns to face her fiancé, who scoffs at her but pulls her in for a kiss. "Ye of little faith."

"Where is the waterfall?" Hannah says from behind us. She's moving in circles on the clearing and squinting her eyes in every which way. She's always been my favorite of the guys' girlfriends—no nonsense and doesn't take herself too seriously. I see her smile and roll her eyes, then walk in the direction of her boyfriend. "Babe."

"Wait a minute," Elle says, pulling out her phone again and scrolling furiously through it. "Are we in the wrong place?"

A beat of silence.

Then Jack groans. "No, babe. No, no, no."

"Okay, but..." Elle starts, already doing that thing where she talks fast when she's spiraling. "I swear this is what the email said. It had a photo of the train station and the trailhead. There were rocks and trees and a freaking waterfall. This is all of those things."

"Is it though?" Hannah mutters, pointing to the sad little trickle of water sliding down a mossy rock wall about thirty feet away. "Because that looks like someone left the tap on uphill."

Cash holds up his phone and zooms in. "Yeah, no, this is a seasonal fall. Like, it only shows up after major rainfall or snow melt."

"Why does Switzerland even have seasonal waterfalls?" Elle snaps, waving her arms around like she's been personally victimized by an entire nation.

Hannah and Amelia are doubled over laughing now, hands braced on her knee. "I'm sorry," Amelia wheezes, "but we climbed a hill for two hours for a glorified leak?"

Jack looks at Elle with a soft smile, like he finds the whole thing charming. "Still builds character."

She glares at him. "Your *character* is about to be tested."

"Why don't we just go to the restaurant and get lunch, babe?" Jack says, hugging his bride and slightly pulling her in the direction of the building a hundred yards away. "You get grumpy when you're hungry."

Manuela snorts and smiles, sliding her sunglasses on her face. We walk the rest of the way there, Banks complaining about how he's dehydrated and needs to sit down and eat or he will *simply perish.*

The restaurant—which happens to be a hotel at the top of this specific peak—ends up having a private dining area on the side that resembles a traditional Swiss chalet. Wooden beams, native flowers in window boxes, tables set outside with checkered cloths like it's trying to mirror a Pinterest board. But the view is unreal. Mountains in every direction, clean air, and enough sun to make the whole thing a reward for surviving the hike.

We get seated at a long table by the floor-to-ceiling windows on the side, which give us unobstructed views of the valley below. Everyone starts peeling off layers and setting phones down and debating what kind of cheese they want melted on bread or potatoes. Sterling is already pointing at the menu like it's a negotiation.

"C'mon, babe, if I get the rösti and you get the fondue, we can—"

"I'm not sharing with you," Hannah says, stealing his menu. "You hoard the good bites."

Jack and Elle are locked in their bubble at the far end of

the table, heads leaned together, whispering about the wine list and the overlap with the ones they selected for their upcoming nuptials. Cash is trying to order in French, which would be impressive if we weren't in the German-speaking part of Switzerland.

And across from me, Manuela is running her fingers through her hair. She's flushed from the hike, freckles visible now in the sunlight, and there's a quiet glow to her I don't remember seeing before.

It hits me out of nowhere.

That feeling like she belongs right here. Not in the *surrounded by finance bros in Europe* kind of way, but just—here. Existing. Effortlessly next to me.

She catches me staring and raises a brow. "What?"

I shrug. "Just surprised you made it up the hill in those sneakers."

She snorts. "Please. I'm from a mountain town. I was pacing myself. Not my fault the rest of you went full Everest on the first incline."

"Banks cried," I whisper.

"Twice," she adds with a grin.

A waitress comes by with bottles of water and a few charcuterie boards and sets them on the table.

"Oh my god," I whisper, leaning toward her. "I'm positively dehydrated. Thought I was going to have to start drinking from the stream."

She rolls her eyes, but I see the corner of her mouth twitch. There's something in the air between us now. Lighter than last night but still charged. Like we're both aware of it, just not naming it.

Everyone orders—plates of traditional potatoes, grilled sausages, soups I can't pronounce. The food takes a while, but no one is in a rush, especially since the day is warming up and the slight bite in the air is practically gone, even at this altitude.

I glance at my watch and notice that it's almost two.

"Remind me what time the train leaves?" I ask, mostly to Elle.

"Five sharp," she calls down the table. "If you miss it, you're staying here with the cows and the tiny waterfall."

CONNOR

By the time we leave the restaurant, the group's energy has shifted. The air is cooler, the sun a little lower, and the promise of warm baths and wine is pulling everyone back down the trail at a decent pace. We're walking in loose formation, half listening to Jack and Banks argue about elevation gains and who's in better shape.

Some of the women are at the front of the pack, very much in conversation with Elle about some of the wedding details. For a woman who plans no less than fifty parties a year, she's being vague about the particulars—maybe to make sure that everything is a surprise for her guests.

I stay toward the back, walking beside Manuela, who keeps glancing down like something's bothering her. Sure enough, a few minutes into the descent, she stops and crouches.

"My shoelace is driving me insane," she mutters, fingers

fumbling with the knot. "I think I double knotted it earlier without realizing, and it's way too tight."

"Isn't that the best way to avoid them coming loose?" I say, leaning against a tree.

She doesn't even look up. "You'd be surprised."

The others keep going, their voices fading into the trees. No one seems to notice we've stopped. It's not that far behind, but the trail's narrow, and the sound of leaves underfoot carries weirdly.

By the time she stands up again, we're alone.

She glances down the trail, then back up. "Did they turn?"

I squint. The trail splits ahead. "Pretty sure they went left."

"Okay," she says and continues down the path, no hesitation. "Let's go left then. Worst case, we're five minutes behind and we can find our way to the station."

The path is quieter, less trampled. It doesn't look like people have come this way recently, but what do I know? The trees thin out in patches, letting in the last of the warm sun. I was expecting a little bit of heat this early in September, but I guess that mountain air behaves differently.

"Do you hear that?" she says, slowing down to a halt in the middle of the path. There is a faint sound of water coming from our right, covered only slightly by the sound of a few birds chirping in whatever is left of the tree canopies. "I think that's the waterfall."

We're halfway down the slope when she speaks again.

"Have you ever noticed how group trips like this one work best when everyone knows their role?"

I glance over, studying her. Her cheeks are flushed again, and she has a faint sheen of sweat covering her face. Not sweaty by any means, but something that makes her glow. "What do you mean?"

"Like, someone's the planner, someone's the comic relief, someone's the one who smooths over drama before it explodes."

I tug at the strap of my bag. "Jack's family has always kind of operated that way. Big gestures. Big expectations. Everyone slots into a part, whether they want it or not. That is one of the reasons why I think Elle and my cousin are such a good fit."

Manuela tilts her head, curious but quiet.

"His dad and mine are brothers," I offer. "So technically, I've known him my whole life, but it's always felt... like their world was a little shinier than mine." I huff out a breath, not quite a laugh. "My family's more... traditional? Reputation matters a lot, but it's quieter. All whispered impressions and carefully curated dinner parties. Jack's side wants to dazzle a room. Mine just wants the room to nod in approval and go home thinking we're the most respectable people in attendance."

She doesn't say anything at first, instead keeps walking beside me, matching my pace. The descent isn't as steep as when we got in, and my knees are grateful.

"You'd think it'd be easier, you know?" I add, laughing

softly to myself. "Coming on the trip without Athena, without anyone. But it's not."

"Why'd you come, then?" she asks inquisitively.

"I don't know," I admit. "Obligation, maybe. Guilt? Jack asked, and I said yes. Figured I'd show up, blend in, do the thing."

We round a bend in the trail, and the noise hits us first. The sound of water swells around us, filling the space: big, echoing, alive.

Then the trees open, and there it is. The waterfall.

A proper cascade, cutting through the rock like it's been doing this forever. Mist floats in the air around it, catching the late afternoon light. The whole clearing smells like pine and river and something faintly metallic.

Manuela stops walking. "Oh."

"Yeah," I say.

We stand there for a second.

"I feel like we were supposed to find this," she says, almost to herself.

"Me too."

We sit on a boulder near the edge of the pool at the base. The sun is slanting hard now, warm and bright and low in the areas where it cuts through the leaves. I should be thinking about my inbox, about the dozen emails waiting for me back in New York, but for the first time in months, I haven't checked. Not once since we landed. And right now, staring at the water, I don't want to. The quiet feels like a luxury, a peace that I didn't realize was missing from my life.

Eventually, Manuela leans back on her hands and sighs. "I really don't want to get up."

"We should probably head back soon."

She nods, but neither of us moves.

When we finally do stand and retrace our steps, the light has changed again. Dimmer and cooler. We follow the hill down to the base, but when we emerge near the train station, it's empty.

No one is waiting. I pull out my phone, thumb moving with a practiced motion. No service and a blank screen where the bars should be.

Manuela walks ahead, checking the board. Her shoulders drop.

"What does it say?" I call, already knowing what she's going to reply.

She turns around. "The last train was at five. There's not even another connection to a different town. Maybe we can catch an alternative method of transportation."

I check my phone, just to make sure. 5:12 p.m.

We look at each other, and she sighs again, louder this time. "Switzerland and their punctuality, darn it."

I try not to laugh, but I can't help but chuckle a little.

"Connor, we missed the train," she says flatly.

"I noticed."

"And no one thought to text us?"

"Maybe they assumed we were on the train? Like, a different carriage?"

She runs a hand through the front of her hair and paces

in a small circle, then stops and looks up at me. "You think they'll come back for us?"

I glance at the board again. "Not unless they're taking a helicopter."

Her mouth twitches. "You're telling me we're stuck?"

"Seems that way."

She groans but then, surprisingly, laughs. "Okay. Fine. Great. *Fuck*. Okay. I think we can figure this out, right?"

I smile, letting the weight of it sink in. "Sure."

"I mean... *puta madre*, why do these things happen to me?" She groans again and then pulls out her phone. "This is a first world country. They must have, like, an app for a ride share. Right?"

She starts furiously tapping the screen while muttering under her breath. I step beside her, peering at her screen. No signal, just like me. She tilts it to the sky like that might help.

"Anything?" I ask.

"Besides rage? No."

I laugh. "Looks like we're walking to the nearest town, then."

She exhales, then shoves her phone into that tiny backpack she's been carrying all day. "Okay. Adventure, part two."

We start down the road, the trail turning into cobblestone as we near the edge of the village. The sun's dropped lower now, casting everything in a golden light I haven't seen in months. Quiet and cinematic.

She glances at me, and her mouth twitches again. At least

she's finding this amusing. If this were Athena, everyone and their mother would have heard her, and we would have probably gotten out of here by now. One of the locals feeling sorry for me and offering us a ride to another train station, maybe. "If we end up sleeping on a park bench, I'm blaming you."

"We won't have to sleep in a park, Manu," I say, and I can't help my smile. "Let's just find a store and ask for directions to the nearest train station. I'm sure there's another service that can take us back."

Manuela sighs dramatically. "Why do you have to be so logical?" She rolls her eyes, and I catch the grin before she turns her head, and we follow the road to what I hope is a town nearby.

11

———————

MANUELA

"No luck."

"Connor, there's no freaking way no one speaks English," I say, stomping my foot like a child. It's getting late, and we haven't had any luck finding someone who can tell us where the nearest train station—not the one we should have been at hours ago—is. I was hoping that maybe we could get to a different one, served by a different train, and that would connect us to our stop, but I can't figure out the train systems and the language is so complicated. Even as a bilingual person, German is nothing like Spanish or English, even both of them combined.

"I already tried Uber," he says, holding his phone up so I can see the app frozen on the screen. "The closest car available is forty kilometers away."

"Jesus," I mutter.

"Let's try one more spot," he says, dragging me by the

hand to the end of the street. We walked for about fifty minutes south—according to Connor's compass app—and ended up in a charming town with approximately four streets. It's a miniature version of Tres Fuegos, which has been, consistently, the smallest town I've ever been to. "There's a neon sign on that window, look."

The restaurant is small and quiet, dimly lit with amber wall sconces and a few tables scattered around. In a corner, two patrons are engaged in conversation, their plates empty but their drinks topped up. It's the only table with people, but this town seems sleepy, so I'm not surprised.

It smells incredible, like melted cheese and warm bread, and honestly, I could cry just from that.

A man in a burgundy wool sweater stands behind the counter. He looks up as we walk in, drying a glass with a white towel.

Connor steps up to the bar, that easygoing smile of his already in place. "Hi," he says to the stoic man in front of us. "Do you speak English?"

The man nods once. "A little."

I exhale through my nose, somewhat dramatically, because I'm relieved. "We're trying to get back to Lucerne. Is there any chance the trains or buses are still running?"

He makes a sound that could be half laugh, half sigh, and shakes his head.

"No more trains. Last one left at seventeen."

Connor leans in slightly. "Five p.m.?"

"Exactly."

I glance at the clock on the wall. It's almost seven. I think we both know we missed our window, but hearing it out loud makes it real.

The man gives us a small smile. "You could try the Ubers, but I don't think you will have... eh, how you say? Any luck."

My eyes widen. This was absolutely not in the plan, but I guess I'll have to go with it. Part of the adventure, right?

"Next train comes in the morning."

"Well," Connor says, turning to me, "looks like we're staying."

I tilt my head at him. "So when you said, 'Let's try one more spot,' this was your grand plan?"

"No," he says, and the corner of his lip lifts slightly. "But we really have no other options, do we?"

The bartender gestures toward the tables. "You want dinner?"

Connor looks at me, eyebrows raised.

My stomach answers for me, growling just loud enough to make us both laugh. "Yes, please," I say.

"Fondue?" the man offers, already reaching for menus. "Very traditional."

Connor flashes a grin. "If we say no, do we get kicked out?"

The bartender chuckles. "Fondue is good."

We settle at a table near the window. Outside, the streets are dark, with only a few lights on inside the homes across the street. It's quiet and intimate and familiar somehow, even if I've only just started to get to know the man across from me.

Connor shrugs off his coat and hangs it behind his chair. He stretches out like someone who's not sure if they're allowed to relax yet. Measured and controlled.

I peel off my sweater and sit on my hands for a second, warming them. "I can't believe the trains stop running at five."

He lets out a low laugh. "Switzerland's got boundaries, apparently."

"I should text Elle," I say but get distracted the moment the bartender returns with a steaming pot of fondue, a small basket of bread, and two short glasses and a chilled bottle of white wine. He sets everything down with practiced efficiency and nods once.

"Let me know if you'd like potatoes."

My eyes flick to Connor. He doesn't reach, just says a polite thank you before the man disappears again. I'm not sure what is going on in his head, but his expression is more curious than concerned.

I busy myself with pouring the wine, reading the label carefully. "Well. This wasn't in the itinerary."

He grins, resting his forearms on the table. His hair is ruffled slightly after the walk, and for a second, I remember the version of him I used to glimpse at parties years ago— always impeccably dressed, posture tight, scrolling on his phone or nodding along as Athena dazzled the room with her stories. He'd hover behind her like an afterthought, like he was trying to make himself smaller.

Now, he just... takes up space. Easily, like he doesn't have to ask permission first.

"I don't know," he says, a smile tugging at his mouth. "Feels very... me."

I snort. "What, getting stranded?"

"No," he says, picking up a fork. "Things not going according to plan."

The wine slips down easily, and the fondue smells amazing—sharp and creamy with hints of something herbal. My stomach growls again, and this time I don't even try to hide it.

"Go for it," he says, motioning to the red pot at the center of the table. "I think we earned it."

I stab a cube of bread, dunk it carefully, and take a bite. It's too hot, but I pretend otherwise.

He watches me for a second, then copies my motion. "Okay, yeah," he says around a mouthful. "I take it back. This was definitely the plan."

I laugh hard, and Connor makes a face, tilting his head to the side in confusion. It makes him look like a puppy, with those brown eyes and ruffled brown hair that is longer than usual. His lips twitch like he wants to say something else but doesn't. Instead, he leans back in his chair and looks around the restaurant. It's empty now, the other table having left at some point while we ate. The only sound is the soft clatter of dishes being cleaned somewhere in the back.

"I thought you'd be more annoyed," I say quietly. "About missing the train."

He looks at me, eyes warm but unreadable. "I'm not."

I nod, unsure what to do with that.

Outside, it starts to drizzle, so fine it's barely visible against the light of the lone streetlight a few yards away. The glass fogs up slightly, the way it does when a place is warm inside and cold out. I lean toward the fondue again, trying to stay focused on the food.

"This is really good," I say, mostly to fill the silence. The food, the wine, his presence—it softens the edges of a hard day.

He dips a piece of bread into the pot and swirls it around slowly. "It is. I didn't expect to be this into melted cheese, but here we are."

I grin. "You say that like it's not a lifestyle."

He chuckles, shaking his head. "I don't think I've ever had fondue before. Do you think Swiss people eat this regularly or it's just one of those tourist traps that definitely got to us?"

"That's a great question." I laugh, then take a sip of wine, letting the warmth settle in my chest. "We could ask."

Connor smiles at that, like he knows we've been duped. "What about you? Do you eat steak every day back home?"

"I mean, in this economy?" I say, twisting the fork with a piece of bread into the cheese mixture. I feel the bread fall off the fork and spend an exorbitant amount of seconds trying to fish it out. "I do not. But in Argentina? I would say yes. Everyone eats beef in some style of preparation at least three times a week."

"That actually sounds kind of amazing."

"Can I tell you a secret?" I say, leaning into the center of the table, almost conspiratorially. I think the wine is finally hitting my system because I feel loose and relaxed. I would never, ever own up to any of this so freely—except maybe with Martina or my other close friends back in Argentina—so I'm taken by surprise by my candor. "I'm a little homesick."

He pauses, fork halfway to his mouth.

I nod. "Yeah. I know. You would never guess."

Instead of laughing it off, he sets his fork down and studies me. "That makes sense," he says quietly. "You changed the whole rhythm of your life. That's not small."

The words feel like permission, like someone finally validating what I've been carrying. Of being here but not fully, afraid to say it out loud. Of dodging calls from my sister or my mother because one mention of home can break me open like a dam.

I swirl my glass gently, watching the wine catch the dim light from the lamp overhead. "New York feels a little... much sometimes. You know?"

He nods like he gets it. "I grew up there, so I thought I was immune to it. All the noise, the pressure, the never stopping. It just becomes a background hum after a while. But somewhere along the way, I stopped noticing everything else too." He stops himself abruptly and takes a sip of his drink. "It's so loud, right?"

I glance over at him, the glow from the table lamp casting

shadows across his face. There's a quiet honesty in the way he says it, like he's not putting on a mask for anyone in our friend group like usual. Not even himself.

"You're allowed to think that," I say gently.

He gives me a small smile, one that feels like it belongs just to me. For a moment, it feels like we're both suspended in something neither of us wants to name. Then he drums his fingers lightly against the table, a small grin tugging at his mouth, and the moment loosens its grip. The rain is falling harder outside, and the condensation on the window is forming irregular paths on the glass. "We should probably figure out where we're sleeping."

I blink, thrown off by the shift in topic. "Right."

We finish the last of the fondue, letting the conversation trail into something soft and quiet. When the man comes back with the check, Connor looks at him and asks, "Is there a hotel nearby for us to stay the night?"

The man, who hasn't shown any emotion all night, puts on a devilish smile. "I thought you'd never ask."

12

CONNOR

THE MAN POINTS us next door, through an open-air courtyard to a semi-attached building that looks exactly like the one we're standing on. I assume it's part of this restaurant, maybe a small inn with an independent entrance. "They are expecting you at the front desk."

The light drizzle of an hour ago has turned to full-on rain. We pause at the restaurant's entrance after paying, watching the water fall in steady sheets.

"We should run for it," Manuela says, as if the distance were large enough to get us wet.

"To what?" I say over the sound of the rain. "The entrance is ten feet away."

"It feels more dramatic if we run."

She opens the door with a crooked smile. "After you."

We sprint, laughing like idiots, into the rain.

We make it two steps before she veers off course. "Where are you going?" I shout over the rain, turning back.

Manuela just laughs and runs the long way around the courtyard, cutting a wide, unnecessary arc past a fountain and under the tree dripping with golden leaves. Her shoes splash through shallow puddles, her arms lifted like she's trying to fly. Her body is loose, a little wilder than usual, wine still warm in her system.

It's ridiculous.

I follow.

By the time I catch up to her at the entrance to the bed and breakfast, we're both soaked, breathless, and grinning like idiots.

"Very dramatic," I say, pushing the door open for her.

"Thank you," she says, stepping past me into the warmth of the lobby. "I love committing to a bit."

The front desk is barely more than a counter with a bell. A man in his fifties who looks suspiciously like the man at the restaurant looks up from behind a wooden partition, already holding a key.

"You are the one from the restaurant, yes?" he asks in accented English.

"Yep," I say.

He checks something on a clipboard and nods once. "Only one room available tonight. Twin beds."

Manuela nods. "Perfect."

We exchange glances. I keep my face neutral. This is fine.

Not ideal, of course. But manageable as two grown adults in their mid-thirties.

"Do you have a toiletry kit?" Manuela asks, leaning on the counter. Her hair is plastered to her face, and some loose strands are slowly dripping water. "Like toothbrush and toothpaste?"

"In the room, yes."

"Thank you," she says, turning to look at me.

The room is on the second floor, past a narrow spiral staircase and a corridor lined with old photographs of the town—black-and-white prints of snow-covered roofs and fishermen by the lake. The waterfall during the four seasons, clear indications of each one by the trees surrounding the pool at the bottom.

At the end of the hallway, I unlock the door. Manuela steps in first.

And stops. "Oh."

The "twin beds" are here, alright—pushed together like a single queen bed, dressed in one enormous white duvet. No space between them. Zero separation.

"Oh," she says again.

I run a hand through my damp hair. "I'll go back down. See if the man can pull them apart."

She kicks off her wet shoes and peels off her sweater. The long sleeve tee she's wearing underneath is damp, especially in the shoulder area, and sticks to her body. "Okay."

"It'll take two minutes."

"Nothing ever takes two minutes." She laughs, soft and

buzzed, making her way to the tiny bathroom by the door. I hear the shower turn on and stand there like an idiot, waiting for my body to react to what is happening. "I don't mind, just don't steal the covers."

"Okay, then," I say. But even as I head for the door, I know I don't love the idea of crawling under one blanket and pretending the lack of space doesn't matter. She might not mind, but I do. Not because of her, but because of me. Because two weeks in close quarters with her is already dangerous, and one bed pretending to be two feels like a line I shouldn't be so quick to blur. "I'll be right back."

By the time I get downstairs and back—after ringing the bell three times and getting no answer and then making my way to the restaurant to find it locked—she's out cold. Fully under the shared duvet, limbs sprawled diagonally across both beds like it's her birthright.

I stand in the doorway, staring at the scene like a fool, again.

Maybe if I can find another duvet, I can make a bed on the floor. There are enough pillows for me to be able to sleep semi-comfortably. Admittedly, I haven't been camping in decades, and even then, it was much more luxurious than just a sleeping bag on the floor.

Manuela shifts in her sleep, murmuring something into the pillow. Her hair's still damp and curling along her neck. She looks... soft. Uncomplicated. Like someone who could sleep through anything.

I toe off my shoes, peel off my wet shirt, and hang it in

the closet in the hopes that it dries overnight. I lie down on top of the duvet and use the throw blanket at the foot of the bed to cover myself, keeping a respectful distance from her and trying not to breathe too loudly.

My phone lights up when I check it one last time. There are a handful of missed messages stacked in the group thread. I type quickly:

ME

We missed the train. Found a place for the night.

Don't worry, we'll catch up tomorrow.

I hit send, drop the phone on the nightstand, and exhale.

Outside, the rain keeps falling in rhythmic sheets.

I close my eyes and let it settle in.

This is nothing. Just two people stuck in a small town. Two beds, kind of?

But it doesn't feel like nothing.

Not even a little.

———

THE RINGING BELLS WAKE ME. They echo through the window in low, even chimes, distant but clear, like sound carried over water. I blink into the soft morning light, unsure of where I am for a second—until I see the pale wooden beams overhead, the white duvet tangled around my legs, and the bare curve of a shoulder just inches from mine.

Right. Right, right. Yes.

Manuela's hair is spread across the pillow, golden and messy, one arm draped over my chest. Her bare leg is hooked around mine, and when did she get rid of her leggings? At some point during the night, we must've both shifted closer, too I had been intent on keeping a respectful distance over the duvet, covered only with a decorative blanket.

I don't move.

The room is quiet, and the outside seems to be slowly waking up. It reminds me of lying awake in New York in the middle of the night, when the city is finally asleep. There's no traffic, no footsteps or people moving around, just the occasional creak of old wood and those church bells ringing out again. Like they're giving us a second chance to wake up.

Her breath is warm against my neck, and my heart kicks in response to her proximity.

I should shift. I know this, logically. I should roll over and create some space, make this less—

But she shifts first.

Her nose nuzzles into the hollow of my throat, and her fingers graze my ribs. Lightly, but it lights me up like a fucking switch. I try to hold my breath and exhale slowly, like keeping my heart rate even might help.

I think that she's half-asleep. Eyelashes resting on her cheeks, mouth parted slightly. Her thigh presses against my body in a way that feels entirely intentional, even though I know it isn't. My cock is impossibly hard but definitely not because there's a beautiful woman plastered to the side of my body. It's an absolutely natural response to waking up.

Yes, that's what it is.

She murmurs something into my collarbone, but I can't make out the words. Her voice is low and raspy, laced with sleep.

"Morning," I say, quieter than I mean to.

Manuela stirs again, her eyes fluttering open, and for a moment, we look at each other. Her hand is still on my chest, and I'm convinced she can feel my erratic pulse, my heart hammering like it wants to leave my body.

There's a flicker of recognition in her eyes, then something else—the realization blooming slow and warm.

"Oh," she says. But she doesn't move away.

Neither do I.

"Do you sleepwalk?" I ask, trying for a joke, but my voice comes out hoarse and charged.

She huffs a laugh. "You're the one wrapped around me, dude."

I glance down and realize, albeit a little too late, that she's not wrong. One of my arms is curled behind her back, my hand resting above her hip like it belongs there and she's mine.

"I thought I stayed on my side," I murmur.

"You did," she says, eyes narrowing but still not moving, "until, like... the middle of the night? Then you started hoarding the blanket."

"That absolutely does not sound like me."

"Uh-huh. Sure."

The bells toll again, softer now. There's a faint sound farther away, like the even cadence of the train running over the tracks. Somewhere downstairs, a door opens and shuts, and loud voices float up and linger between us. Her fingers twitch slightly on my chest.

It would be so easy to kiss her.

It would also be the most terrible idea.

Her leg brushes mine as she shifts again, finally pushing off the covers and flopping onto her back. The duvet slips low, revealing the soft curve of her stomach where her tank top has ridden up.

I look away. I'm not a monster. But...

She stretches with a quiet groan, eyes still half-lidded. "I need coffee. And possibly a new set of legs. My age is betraying me. I don't think I can manage another of these hikes again."

"This bed is criminal."

"Speak for yourself. I slept like a baby."

"Yeah," I say under my breath. "You looked like it."

She throws me a lazy glare, then swings her legs over the side of the bed and stands up, hair wild, still half-asleep. I watch her cross to the bathroom, bare legs carrying her across the room, the waistband of her underwear riding low on her hips. The fabric clings just enough to make me look away before I start thinking more things I shouldn't. She pauses at the door and looks back, and something about the way she holds my gaze—casual, like we didn't just spend the night tangled together while half-naked—knocks the air out of my lungs.

"You coming?"

I blink, brain short-circuiting. "To the bathroom?"

She smirks. "To coffee."

"Right." Obviously.

She disappears behind the door, and I exhale, rubbing a hand down my face.

Good lord, I'm well and truly *fucked*. These are going to be the longest two weeks of my life.

13

MANUELA
WEDNESDAY

By the time we get back to the house, it's late morning. The sun is out, the sky is a clean, cloudless blue, and the gravel crunches under our shoes as we walk up the hill from the train station. The return trip was uneventful, really, just like I assumed it was for the larger group the day before. But my thoughts weren't.

My skin hasn't stopped buzzing since waking up next to him.

Elle spots us before we even make it up the steps to the front door. She comes barreling down the walkway in a pair of linen shorts and oversized sunglasses, all dramatic flourish and toned legs, blonde hair in a messy braid. She throws her arms wide like she's rehearsed this moment, whether for real or in her head—drama all around.

"There you are!" she calls, loud enough for birds to scatter from a nearby tree. "Do you have any idea how worried I've been? Even with Connor's little midnight text, we were this close to calling the police." She crushes me in a hug, then pulls back, scanning me head to toe like she's checking for injuries. "Do you know the scenarios I was making up in my head?"

I let her hug me, laughing into her shoulder. "We missed the train."

"Cliff fall, ski-lift collapse, kidnapped by rogue Swiss bandits. I don't know, maybe the Italian mafia—"

Connor raises an eyebrow behind her. "That escalated quickly."

Elle waves him off, still gripping my arms. "I mean it. You check in once, and then nothing? Not a single follow-up? Amelia and I were spiraling!"

Nicole appears in the doorway, arms crossed, tone sharper than Elle's. "It's called a *phone*. Works in the morning too."

"Sorry," I say, feeling scolded. "We found a place to stay, had dinner, slept well." I leave out the part where we shared a bed and found ourselves tangled into each other half the night. Totally accidental, of course. Still, the memory flashes through me now, hot and distracting, and I have to blink it away before it shows on my face. "Promise, we're fine."

Her expression softens. "Glad you're alright. But next time? A text from you would be nice. I mean—Connor vanished? Fine, he's a grown man. You? I worry about."

"Noted," I say with a sheepish smile.

Inside, the house is humming again. Doors are opening

and closing upstairs, and voices echo down the stairwell. There's low jazz playing from speakers I cannot see, probably hidden in the walls in the latest European technology. Everyone seems to be getting ready for another group hike.

But Elle's nursing a headache—which I take to mean she's still hungover from last night, and Nicole has zero interest in "sweating uphill for views you can Google." Which is how the four of us—me, Connor, Elle, and Nicole—end up staying behind, lounging on the back terrace overlooking the lake while the rest of the group traipses into the mountains again.

After a quick change of clothes, I come downstairs to Elle stretched out on a cushioned lounger, legs crossed, sipping something with cucumber and mint. "So," she says, eyes hidden behind those massive sunglasses she always sports outside, rain or shine. "What'd you two get up to while you were stranded?"

Nicole perks up, not even pretending to be subtle. "Yeah, do tell."

Connor is sitting under the umbrella at a table, scrolling on a tablet. Occasionally, he types something out, but it doesn't really look like he's working. Probably catching up to the news or social media. At Nicole's words, he leans back in his chair, arms crossed. "We watched the rain. Ate very good fondue. Slept, then took the train back."

I shrug like it's nothing. "The town was small and charming. We stumbled into this family-run place with wood-paneled walls and mismatched chairs and a super cozy feel."

Elle smiles. "Sounds kind of romantic."

Nicole raises an eyebrow, and my stomach churns. She's friends with Athena; *they all are.* They grew up together, this tight little circle that feels impossible to slip into, and it's strange that she's not here, stranger still that no one has mentioned her. I wonder how much they know about the breakup or if they're just pretending for Connor's sake. Either way, the air feels heavier. I clear my throat. "Not at all. But we did find the waterfall."

Connor adds, "The real one. Not just the little drip we saw at the top of the mountain with you all."

Elle gasps and claps once, delighted. "Shut up. You two found *the* waterfall?"

Connor nods. "By accident. It was pretty majestic, honestly. That's why we missed the train."

Nicole looks impressed. "That sounds like the most successful detour of all time."

I can't tell if they're teasing or interested. Probably both. I take a sip of my sparkling water and look out at the lake to avoid eye contact.

A beat passes, and the breeze flutters the linen napkins on the table. Nicole sets her glass down with a sigh, her tone just casual enough to sound rehearsed. "Such a shame Athena won't be able to join."

Elle hums in agreement. "She always did love these group trips."

My head tilts before I can stop it. Always? Did love? The wording makes me pause. I glance at Connor, waiting for him to explain, but he doesn't. He just smooths a hand down his thigh, posture tightening, eyes on the lake.

"Maybe next year," Nicole adds too brightly. She doesn't look at me—her gaze is fixed on Connor, like she's daring him to say otherwise.

He doesn't but instead nods once, nothing more.

I force a small sip of sparkling water to cover my discomfort. Everyone at this table clearly knows more than I do, and yet no one is saying it out loud. The silence feels loaded, like I've stumbled into a script I don't have the lines for.

Connor lets it play out and doesn't flinch or correct them. He doesn't say a single word to untangle whatever assumptions are tightening around this table like vines. Part of me wants to kick him under the table. A bigger part just wants to know why he won't simply say that they've broken up.

"When is George getting in?" Connor asks about Jack's brother, his tone light, trying to steer the conversation somewhere safer. "I thought he'd be here by now."

"Oh, right, you missed the conversation last night," Elle says, standing to grab something from the far end of the table. "He got held up in New York. Some last-minute work thing. He's flying in Sunday."

Connor nods, his gaze dropping back to the tablet in front of him. "Got it."

Nicole doesn't look up from her phone, her scrolling steady and a little too pointed. There's a flicker of tension in the air. It's quiet but present. No one says anything about

Athena again, and I start feeling like I can relax and breathe. Even though I have done nothing wrong. It just feels weird, to be monopolizing this man's time.

One of the staff members sets down a fresh plate of roasted vegetables between us, and the conversation drifts toward safer territory. Lunch, the boat ride next week, the wedding wine list.

The breeze of the lake picks up enough to rustle the cloth napkins, and everything looks golden filtered through sun and vacation vibes.

Across the table, Connor catches my eye.

He doesn't say anything but holds my gaze for a beat longer than usual, like maybe he's still thinking about this morning.

I look away, pretending I'm focused on the food, but the flush creeping up my neck says otherwise.

14

———

CONNOR

THE HALLWAY UPSTAIRS IS QUIET. There's movement downstairs as the staff prepares the house for dinner, but otherwise, everyone else is in their rooms—showering, dressing, touching up their makeup or recharging their social batteries. I should be doing the same, maybe changing into something less wrinkled and warmer for dinner out on the terrace. But instead, I'm leaning against the doorframe of the sliding glass door in my room, half watching the lake through the open window and half hoping she'll walk by.

The thought takes me by surprise—the whole point of this trip was to reset, regroup, and figure out what's next for me after years of working myself to the ground and walking away from something that should have been permanent but never felt right.

The last time I traveled internationally was five years ago, a trip Athena had planned down to the last minute. I spent most of it holed up in a hotel room, trying to put out a fire for a client who panicked about his portfolio. She gave me the silent treatment for months after that. It should've been a red flag. For both of us. But I let it slide, the way I let too many things slide.

This time feels different. I've got an out-of-office reply running, my phone is stripped of work apps, and for once I've promised myself I'll actually be here. Even if "here" means watching everyone else—including the groom—float around in their happily paired-off lives while I sit on the sidelines.

My phone buzzes on the nightstand, the screen lighting up with *Mom*. I almost let it go, but years of conditioning win out. I swipe to answer.

"Connor, son," my father says without preamble, "have you given more thought to that proposal from Joe?"

I pinch the bridge of my nose. "Not now, Dad. I'm—"

"It's a good opportunity," he presses, voice clipped like a verdict was already handed down.

My mother cuts in before I can respond. "We'll see you next week at the wedding, darling. It'll be so nice to have you there, looking settled."

The word lands with a thud. *Settled.* Like that's the metric. Not happy. Not present. Just... squared away, box checked, correct on paper.

I hang up, the echo of their voices still in my ear, and let the phone slide face-down on the nightstand.

I don't know why the word grates me so much, like nails to chalkboard. *Settled.*

I don't have time for dating, anyway. I'm still buried in a demanding job and trying to figure out what comes next. And it hasn't even been that long since Athena and I walked away from each other. Long enough for the dust to settle but not long enough to forget.

So why the hell am I standing in my room, glancing over my shoulder every two minutes, half hoping Manuela will walk by?

"Are you hiding?" She slows by the door to my room, her hair still damp at the ends, and a soft sweatshirt is slung loosely over one shoulder. She's wearing no makeup and is barefoot, even if temperatures have decreased since we spent the day soaking up the sun on the back deck.

"Definitely."

Her smile is faint but it's there, curling at the edges. She takes one step into my room, then another. "Mind if I join you?"

"Not at all." I close the slider and turn, waiting for her next move.

Inside the room, it's warm and golden from the setting sun. She sits at the foot of the bed on a very stiff leather bench that really ties the whole vibe of the room together. She crosses her legs so naturally, like she's done it a hundred times before while having a conversation with someone who has been friend-adjacent for years. Her fingers pick the bottom of her lounge pants, running over the stitching in a back-and-forth motion.

"So," she says lightly, "do you think Nicole suspects we got stranded on purpose?"

I smile. "You mean because we definitely didn't?"

"Right. Complete accident."

She laughs softly, then goes quiet. I let the silence stretch between us for a beat. The movements in the house soften the hard edges of whatever the fuck this is between us. I'm ready to cut this shit open with a knife, spill all its guts out.

"You didn't sleep much last night, did you?" she asks, still not looking at me.

I shake my head. "Not really."

"Me neither."

She finally glances up at me, and that's when it shifts—everything. It's like the floor beneath my feet gets removed from under me, and I swear I can feel my heartbeat in my throat.

Her voice is softer now. "I kept thinking you were going to pull away."

"I didn't want to."

Another pause.

Neither of us moves, but the energy is unmistakable now. If someone were to walk into this room right this minute, they would definitely see it. It's a golden current, a hum under my skin that has my fingers twitching by my thighs.

"I've been thinking about it all day," she says, her voice barely above a whisper.

"What?"

"That bed. Beds." She laughs lightly and shakes her head. "The way you..." She exhales, eyes closing briefly. "You know what, never mind."

I cross the room and stand in front of her, close enough to see the flush blooming across her cheeks. I reach for her hand.

"Tell me," I say.

She looks up, and for a moment, I think she's going to deflect again. But she doesn't. "I didn't want to stop touching you."

My breath catches.

And then I bend down and kiss her.

It's not rushed or desperate. It's a steady pull—like gravity, like something we've been avoiding for days, since two nights ago on the couch when we were both slightly buzzed and relaxed after a nice dinner.

Manuela's hands slide up my chest, around my neck. She leans in, deepens it, and the way she moves against me makes my thoughts scatter everywhere.

I pull her up gently from the bed, and I stumble backward with her in my arms until I feel the mattress at my knees.

She laughs into my mouth, breathless. "God, this is so—"

"Terrible idea," I mutter, kissing down her jaw. "Absolutely awful."

Manuela sneaks her hands under my shirt, her warm

fingers touching the skin of my back. The movement makes my shirt lift. "Then stop me."

I don't.

Her sweatshirt goes next, soft fabric pulled over her head and tossed somewhere near the nightstand. I press her back against the bed and follow her down. We kiss like we're starved, hands everywhere, mouths open, breathing fast.

I tug my shirt over my head, breathless, just as there's a knock at the door.

We both freeze, but Manuela is stifling a giggle and hides her face against my neck.

Then Elle's voice, sing-song and completely unbothered. "Connor, darling, dinner's ready. If you're not downstairs in five minutes, we're starting without you."

Silence.

Then Manuela groans and drops her head against my chest, but there's a smile on her face. "Are you fucking kidding me?"

I laugh, still catching my breath. "I don't think she is."

She sighs, then looks up at me, her expression caught somewhere between exasperated and amused. "I was just getting to the good part."

"We can revisit it," I say, brushing my thumb across her cheeks and trying not to sound too eager. "Soon."

We lay there for another minute, catching our breaths, then slowly start to untangle.

Before she sits up fully, she pauses. "Hey."

"Yeah?"

"Would you... Like to..."

"Would you like to what?" I say, a smile tugging at my lips as she struggles with the words.

"This doesn't have to be a thing," she says carefully. "I'm not expecting anything. But we can if we... want to keep doing this. While we're here. You know, so we're not lonely."

I blink because I can't make sense of her proposal.

"Like, a no-pressure pact," she says. "To help us relax."

I nod, my voice quiet. "Yeah. Okay."

"Okay," she says, and she gives me a big smile that reaches her eyes. "I'll see you downstairs."

I grab my shirt from the floor and turn to follow her, but she stops me with a hand on my chest. "You need a minute."

I look down at the front of my pants and decide that yes, I definitely need a minute.

When the door clicks shut behind her, I sit back on the edge of the bed, running a hand through my hair. My pulse is still hammering, my shirt still wrinkled on the floor, and all I can think is: what just happened? This trip was supposed to be a clean break, a chance to clear my head and keep things simple. Instead, it feels like I've stumbled into something bigger than myself—something I can't quite name but don't want to let go of.

I tug my shirt back on, exhaling slowly. Maybe this isn't a distraction. Maybe it's exactly what I need. A no-pressure pact with her.

15

MANUELA

"A no-pressure pact?" I mutter to myself as I go down the stairs. "What kind of fucking idiot suggests something like that? God, not like you're in your mid-thirties or something."

The words sound even louder out loud. A no-pressure fling. With someone I *barely know*. I mean, sure—we get along. There's chemistry. There's definitely attraction. He listens when I talk. He makes me laugh. He looked at me like I was the only person in the universe last night and again five minutes ago when his hands were halfway under my shirt.

But this?

During this trip?

Too many eyes. Too many questions. And I've never been the type to do this, to hook up on a trip, let alone with someone in the same friend group. I've dated, sure, but it's always been deliberate, slow, something with labels and expectations. Maybe I'm just touch-starved and it's making me delusional. That's what it is.

I reach the bottom step, slow my pace, try to smooth the flush from my face with my palms. I make it two feet into the hallway before Nicole appears out of nowhere like she's been waiting to corner me.

She's holding a wineglass and wearing a gauzy linen set that probably costs more than my entire wardrobe. There's a glint in her eyes that I can't place.

"Oh, hey," she says, voice light and friendly in a way that makes all my instincts stand on edge. "You missed *aperitivo.*"

"Lost track of time," I say, keeping my tone breezy.

She sips her wine. "Connor too?"

I blink. "Sorry?"

"I just assumed," she says with a small smile, tucking a strand of blonde hair behind one ear. "Since you two seem to have synched schedules lately."

There's nothing in her voice I can *technically* call out. No accusation or sharpness. But instead, there is a sugary glaze that feels put on too thick, intentional. I smile, even though I want to roll my eyes. "I think he was reading or something."

"Mmm," she says, letting the sound stretch. Then: "It's nice that he's so... relaxed, you know? I always got the impression Athena keeps him on a tight leash."

My spine stiffens just enough for her to notice.

I want to say *what the fuck is that supposed to mean,* but instead I just smile tighter. "I'm sure they have their reasons for how they work."

Nicole's eyes sparkle. "Of course. Every relationship has its rhythm."

And just like that, she takes another sip and walks away, humming to herself.

I stand there for a second too long, trying to shake the interaction off and trying not to read too much into it. It's expected that she's defensive of her friend, especially a friend that was in a relationship with someone for so long.

A few minutes later, after a quick stop in the bathroom to calm myself down, I step onto the terrace where the large table is set for dinner. My cheeks are still hot, and my skin is still buzzing like I haven't fully returned to my own body. The table is already filling; Elle and Jack are at one end, Amelia taking a sip of wine from a very elegant glass in a deep purple color.

I take the only open seat left next to Amelia. Connor is across the table, directly in my line of sight. He glances up just as I do, and the corner of his mouth lifts. It's small, private, and totally devastating. My face flushes hotter. Amelia offers me a sunny smile. "We were starting to think you two were going to skip dinner entirely."

Before I can respond, Nicole cuts in from across the table. "Maybe they were just finishing the last of that fondue they had last night."

There's a chuckle or two, but it's not exactly a joke, and I know it. My stomach knots.

Connor just raises an eyebrow and says, "Are you jealous of our culinary detour, Nicole?"

She lifts her wineglass with force, the liquid sloshing slightly off the rim. "Deeply."

Conversation shifts back to the wine list and the spa treatments scheduled for tomorrow, but the undercurrent is still there. Tense. Watching. Everyone pretends not to be paying attention to who looks at who and for how long. I can feel it in the way Nicole's eyes flick toward Connor every time someone says his name, in the way Elle keeps her tone light like she's trying to smooth something over, in the way Hannah studies me like she's still deciding if I should be at this table at all.

Amelia turns to me as the servers come out and begin setting plates in front of us. "You know," she says lightly, with her usual easy smile, "I was surprised Athena didn't come. Trips like this are her *thing*."

I blink. "That's what I've heard."

"She probably just needed a breather," Amelia adds, tone gentle and almost conspiratorial, like she's offering reassurance. "They've been... figuring things out, I think. It can be good to take a little space."

There's no malice in it—just casual kindness—but the words catch in my chest.

"And I'm also surprised that Connor joined. Athena always said that he would *never* do one of these big group events again. Said he wasn't the type."

I glance at Connor before I can stop myself. He's looking down at his plate, jaw tight, as if the comment slid straight under his skin.

I clear my throat. "Well, you know, things change."

"Sure," she says brightly, turning back to the breadbasket as if nothing about what she said could possibly be news to anyone at the table.

Connor doesn't look up. And neither do I.

The tension pulls tighter than a rubber band. Like everyone knows *something* is happening, but no one's naming it. Not directly. They just keep poking at the edges, and it makes me very uncomfortable. More than normal.

I reach for a piece of bread I don't want and chew slowly, hoping the food gives me an excuse to stay quiet. The thing is, Athena's always been part of this group—louder than me, more polished, the kind of woman people naturally gravitate toward. I've spent years on the edges, watching her command every dinner, every trip, every moment. And now she's not here, which feels strange for everyone. Maybe that's why it feels like all eyes shift to me when Connor laughs or when his gaze catches mine.

Across the table, Connor finally looks at me again.

No smile this time but instead something careful and watchful. Like he's trying to figure out if I regret everything already.

I don't. I just didn't realize how many eyes would be on us the second we came back down.

No pressure, I said.

But pressure is *everywhere.*

THE SERVERS clear dessert like they're on a mission, working fast and diligently so that they can close the kitchen and probably head home. Chairs all around the table scrape. Someone suggests cards inside. Someone else yells "hot tub," and three people cheer like they've trained for this moment their whole lives.

I stand too fast and pretend it's to help stack plates instead of to stop my hands from shaking.

I'm halfway to the kitchen door when a warm-hued glass appears in my line of sight.

"Water?" Connor's voice is low and soothing, like a salve to my nerves. I don't quite know why I'm so on edge. I was fine when it was just Connor and me, stranded in a small town, anonymous. But back here, under this roof with these people, everything feels magnified. Every laugh, every glance, every pause is another chance for someone to connect the dots. And maybe they already have.

"Thank you." My throat is dry enough that the word comes out scratchy. I sip. I don't look at him. Not yet.

He tips his head toward the kitchen. "Walk with me?"

We cut through the swinging door into soft light and the hum of the fridge. We're at the back of the kitchen, tucked inside a butler's pantry that rivals the size of my bedroom back in New York. Under-cabinet LEDs make everything look prettier than it already is in natural daylight. The bowls they used to serve dinner are stacked on a drying mat, and although it's messy, it looks incredibly aesthetic.

The terrace chatter blurs to a muffled chorus.

"About earlier," I say and then stop because I don't actually know what I want to say. *Sorry I climbed you? Thank you for making that noise I can't stop hearing?* "I didn't expect a welcome committee the second we came downstairs."

He leans a hip against the counter and folds his arms. Sleeves pushed up. Forearms tan. There's a damp ring on his glass from the condensation, and he idly traces the drops with one finger. "I should've seen it coming."

"You did," I say. "You handled Nicole like a pro."

He huffs a laugh. "I've had practice."

"Right." Of course. He's been around these people—he *is* one of these people—for years. I rest my back against the opposite counter so we're parallel, a safe strip of tile between us. "So. The pact?"

One of his eyebrows lifts, barely. "The no-pressure pact."

"Don't make fun."

"I'm not." He shakes his head, eyes steady on mine. "I just want you to know I heard you."

I set the water down. My hands are calmer now. "Okay. Then here are my terms." I count off on my fingers like I'm pitching a client. "No making it a thing in front of the group. No explanations. No... fondue jokes."

The corner of his mouth twitches. "That euphemism was definitely a stretch."

"And we check in. If either of us feels weird, we stop. No resentment. No... emotional hangovers. Discretion is welcome, of course."

He nods once, like he's tucking each into a mental

drawer. "And a rule for me," he says. "If anyone starts taking shots, we vanish."

I blink. "That's... oddly specific."

He glances toward the door, rueful. "Big groups, alcohol, and gossip? Not our sport." He pauses, thumb dragging over the edge of the table. "People get sloppy, and sloppy usually means loud. Too many ears, too many opinions. I've learned the hard way that it's better not to hand them anything they can twist."

Something about the flat honesty in his tone makes my chest pinch.

We let the quiet sit while the sound outside grows louder by the second. I swear I can hear someone chanting "shots, shots, shots," but it's so faint that I can't be sure. If it were the case, then we could, potentially, retreat upstairs while no one is looking.

Connor straightens, like he's about to move away, and then doesn't. "You have, uh..." He gestures to his own jaw, and I touch mine, mortified, thinking, *Mascara? Crumb?*

"Here," he says softly and takes a step. He stops short enough that I can smell the slight notes of citrus from his cologne, lifts his hand, and very carefully tucks a stray lock of hair behind my ear. His knuckles brush my cheekbone, and it's not a big moment, but my whole body lights up like I've swallowed a live wire.

"You're going to get us in trouble," I whisper.

"Probably." He doesn't step back. His gaze flicks to my

mouth and then away, like he's disciplining himself and forcing his body to retreat. "We should rejoin civilization."

"Or we could hide here with the lemons," I say, nodding at the cutting board.

"One more logistics thing."

I groan. "So fucking sexy."

That smile appears again. He moves closer, his mouth barely touching my ear. "You think you can be quiet?"

I gasp, and the question hangs between us like it's carrying extra weight. My pulse jumps so fast I'm sure he can hear it.

I lean back against the counter, casual on the outside, pure electricity on the inside. "Depends. Are you planning to test me?"

His gaze flicks down my body before returning to my face, so quick it could be an accident if he wanted to lie about it. "Just wondering how much trouble we'd get into before someone opened that door."

The hum of the refrigerator fills the space where my answer should go. My brain is doing dangerous math—distance to the door, volume of the group outside, how easy it would be to close that space between us.

"You're terrible," I say finally, but it comes out low, not even close to an accusation.

He tilts his head like he's considering it. "Maybe." Then, quieter: "But I'd behave. For now."

I laugh, softer than I mean to, because I believe him and

also don't. "Good. Because I have a strict no-being-caught-in-the-kitchen rule."

"Sounds like a challenge," he murmurs, stepping aside so I can pass.

When I do, my shoulder brushes his chest, light and intentional. His hand lifts and catches my waist, pulling me back against him in one smooth motion.

My inhale is sharp, unplanned. His chest is solid at my back, his palm warm through the thin fabric of my shirt. I can feel the heat of him everywhere he touches me and in places he doesn't.

"Connor." It comes out more breath than word.

"I love how you say my name." He dips his head, close enough that I can feel the whisper of his breath at my ear again, warm and electrifying. "Still think you could be quiet?"

My brain short-circuits. I don't turn to face him because I don't trust what I could do if I look at his handsome face.

"Guess we'll never know," I say, forcing lightness into my tone that doesn't match the way my heart is hammering inside my chest.

His hand lingers long enough to make it clear he's in no hurry, and then he lets go, fingers dragging lightly over my hip before he steps back. The absence is absolutely dizzying.

I push through the door, cheeks hot, and rejoin the noise outside. But I feel him behind me for a long time after, that smile still pressed against the back of my neck.

16

CONNOR

THE VILLA'S finally quieting down after a long night of card games, more drinks than I can count with both hands, and copious amounts of local chocolate. Laughter finally thins to a low murmur behind closed doors and the clink of glasses against marble countertops.

I've been lying on top of the covers on my bed, staring at the ceiling long enough to know sleep's not happening tonight. Just like eighty percent of the nights the past few months. My phone is face-down on the nightstand, buzzing every so often with the reminders I keep ignoring—two missed calls and three texts from my parents, all variations of *call us back* or *don't forget to meet with so-and-so in Zurich before the wedding*—their most recent attempt to line up a bigger and better job offer that will give me a bigger and better status.

I can't. Not right now. I'll see them in a few days at the

wedding, and we'll go through the usual performance—me nodding, them criticizing, everyone pretending that being passive-aggressive is something normal. For now, I want quiet.

From my window I can see the edge of the pool—flat and dark except for the soft blue wash from the lights. And her.

Manuela is on a lounger, legs stretched long, a towel under her and her hair down from that messy bun she was wearing after dinner. Someone left three stubby candles on the little table; they gutter and throw short shadows across her calves. She tips her head back and exhales like she's trying to breathe the day out.

Like finally being alone relaxes her. It's worse now, I think, the way her body betrays her and gives all the signs of her being uncomfortable. She's been the same way since I met her at the engagement party—sitting at the edge of the conversation and simply watching, a polite smile slapped on her face.

I tell myself I'm going down for water. My feet already know better.

The deck is warm through my socks. I keep it casual—hands in pockets, slow steps.

"Couldn't sleep?" I say.

She turns her head and gives me a lazy smile. "Not even a little."

I sit on the chaise lounge beside her. Close but not crowding her. The pool filter hums. A breeze lifts the edge of her towel and drops it again.

"These days are... long," she says, eyes on the water. "Not bad long. Just, like... a lot, you know? And I know we still have, what, ten more?"

"Something like that," I say, resting my arms behind my head and looking at the starless sky. It feels cool, the breeze bringing in a slight mountain chill. "Feels like we've packed a week into forty-eight hours."

She huffs, amused and tired at once. "You okay after dinner?"

I lift a shoulder casually. I don't know what she's asking of me—if I'm okay after having to endure that much or if I'm okay after that little scene in the butler's pantry, hidden in plain sight from the other people in the group. "I've had worse. You?"

"We mainly talked about the outfits everyone is wearing for the next few days." She tilts a hand. "I'll survive."

Silence settles. Not awkward—I don't think it's ever been awkward around her. But it definitely feels charged, like maybe we are both thinking about the same thing and pretending not to.

"The kitchen—"

"Manu," I say at the same time.

Her mouth curves, and she shifts on the chaise, moving slightly backwards but facing me. We grin at the same time. It breaks the tension and tightens it.

I shift closer. "You sure?"

"Yes," she says, like it's obvious. "But, umm..."

I don't wait for her to finish her thought, and instead, I

kiss her. Slow, first, like we're easing into a pool. She sighs against my mouth and slides a hand to the back of my neck. The second kiss is not slow. She opens her mouth for me, and I forget all the reasons to pace myself.

"Someone can definitely see us," she murmurs, not moving away. She smiles against my mouth, like the thought is egging her on or even amusing her to no end, so I press closer. "If I can see the pool from my room, the others can too."

"We'll be quiet," I say, already failing at being rational.

"Promise?" It's teasing and a little not.

"Try me."

We tip sideways onto her lounger. It's narrow, so we have to contort our bodies to make ourselves fit; one of her legs wraps around my hip, and my hand finds her waist to pull her closer against my body. She makes a sound I feel all the way down to my hardening cock. I kiss the corner of her mouth, the edge of her jaw. She tangles her fingers in my hair and pulls, gentle, like she wants me exactly where I am.

I breathe her in: mountain air, shampoo, and the faintest trace of her perfume from dinner. The villa lights throw soft stripes over her collarbone, and I choose to put my mouth there as she tilts her chin up, a generous move that gives me more to work with.

Manuela's hand finds the front of my shirt and fists. The other drifts lower, over my stomach, resting there for a beat like she's asking without words. I hold her gaze and nod once.

Her palm slides under the waistband of my sweatpants—slow, steady, like she plans to take her time with me. My breath stutters, and she smiles against my mouth, an indication she's loving this.

"Shh," she says, barely there. "You're going to get us caught."

"You started this," I whisper.

"Did I?" Her fingers wrap around me, sure now. My head tips back, and I bite the inside of my cheek to try not to swear loud enough to wake the whole villa. She kisses me while she strokes, long, teasing passes that make staying quiet a losing game. I anchor my hand on her thigh, squeeze when she swirls her wrist, and I almost forget where we are.

"Manu," I try to say, but instead a needy fucking whimper comes out, and she gasps. She's definitely on to me, how desperate I am for touch—for *her* touch.

Upstairs, a door slides. Voices. Her hand stills but doesn't move away.

She looks at me, and there's mischief all over her blue eyes. "Tell me if you want to stop," she whispers.

I should. God, I should. My whole body is one live wire under her hand, but there's a voice in my head, louder than the risk or the want, that says I don't want this to be just about me.

I catch her wrist gently, just enough pressure to make her pause. Her brows pull together, like she's trying to read me.

"I don't want to stop," I say, and I mean it. "I just..." My voice comes out rough. "Let me."

She blinks, surprised, but she eases her hand back, resting it over my chest like she's grounding me there. I slide mine down her thigh, fingers curling under the edge of her swimsuit bottoms. The heat of her hits me instantly, and my pulse kicks harder. She's warm and wet and ready, and suddenly, I feel so ravenous, hungry for more.

I lean in, my forehead brushing hers. "You have no idea what you do to me," I murmur. It's not a line. It's by far the truest thing I've said in a while.

Her lips part, but whatever she was going to say dissolves into a gasp when I touch her clit. I keep my eyes on her face, memorizing every flicker, how her lashes lower, her mouth goes soft and open, how she bites her lip like she's trying to keep quiet but can't manage it entirely.

"You need to be quiet, baby," I whisper in her ear, and there's a whole body shiver that runs through, head to toe. "Can I use my fingers?"

She nods.

Every shift of her hips against my hand pulls me deeper into her rhythm. I want to be inside her so badly it's a physical ache, but there's something about having her like this, falling apart under me with my fingers, that's undoing me in a way I didn't plan for.

"Are you going to come for me, pretty girl?" I kiss her forehead, her temple, and down her cheek until I get to the corner of her mouth, waiting there for her to give me more.

Her breath hitches, her nails curl into my shirt, and I feel her starting to lose control. I kiss her to muffle the sound, swallowing it like it's mine to keep. She comes with a sharp, quiet gasp against my mouth, her whole body going tense before melting into me.

I pull back just enough to drag my fingers slowly past my lips, tasting her deliberately, letting her see me do it. Her eyes go wide, her chest still rising and falling in quick bursts. The flicker of want that flashes across her face nearly undoes me.

I should stop here. I should breathe, regroup, let her have this without taking more. Maybe drag her into my bed and keep her there, warm and boneless against me. But I'm too far gone to be able to do any of that. Watching her like that, feeling her like that, has me right on the edge.

I keep my hand at her hip, holding her close, while the rest of me tips over. No stroke or touch from her but the intensity of being here with her, the taste of her still on my tongue, the sound of her breathing unevenly in my ear. Heat slams through me, and I bury myself against her neck, biting back a groan as I come hard in my pants.

We stay tangled there, breathless. My heartbeat is in my ears, hers is under my palm. I press my mouth to her shoulder, not kissing but... lingering.

When I finally pull back enough to see her face, she's smiling in this soft, almost shy way that kills me. Like she knows exactly what just happened but isn't going to say it out loud.

"Connor," she says, a breathless laugh threatening to come to the surface. "Did you...?"

"Worth it," I answer, and it comes out like a vow.

17
———

MANUELA
THURSDAY

I SINK DEEPER into the lounger in the spa's indoor pool area, the white fluffy robe puffed up under my neck, warm and heavy in a way that makes my eyelids dip. It's nice and humid here, and it's a perfect day to be inside since the weather turned and it cooled down compared to yesterday. Storm clouds threaten in the distance—dark gray and approaching fast, like they do in Tres Fuegos in the summer.

Somewhere behind me, the whirlpool churns steadily, and there's the occasional splash from the indoor pool where a couple is laughing out loud and messing around, something about playing mermaids that has the woman giggling like a little girl.

The spa smells like eucalyptus and salt, I think? I don't know what salt smells like, but this is what I imagine when someone says something has notes of Himalayan pink in it.

Nicole stretches beside me, her legs a perfect tan. "So,

Manuela," she says like she's been waiting for this precise moment of perfect quiet to pounce. "What do you do in New York?"

The question shouldn't make me nervous, but it does. I thought everyone knows I work with Elle, but I guess maybe they don't know the details. And I know I'm already on edge —still replaying last night over and over, every glance and every too-long pause feeling more loaded in my head than it probably is—so her tone grates at me.

"Oh, I work with Elle at the agency," I say, lifting one shoulder casually. "But we're on different accounts."

Elle smiles from across the circle of loungers. Her head is tilted back, and there are slices of cucumbers over each of her eyes. Really, if you were to look up "relaxed woman at over-priced spa," this is what you would find.

"She's underselling it," she says, blindly going for her cup of lemon water on the side table next to her. "Manuela is the most requested strategist at the agency, and she fucking rocks."

"Not true," I protest.

Amelia leans in, her robe slipping off one shoulder. "It's a little true, isn't it? You practically run your accounts, especially since that fucking boss you guys have is a good-for-nothing asshole."

I smile like it's no big deal, but my stomach tightens. I've been pretending their praise still fits, that this job still fits, even as I keep replaying the email from my old boss in Buenos Aires asking if I'd ever consider coming back. I haven't answered her. I'm not even sure why. Maybe because saying yes—or no—would make it real.

Nicole tilts her head in the direction of Elle. "Wait, James? I hate that guy. We went to prep school together, and he was always such an asshole."

"Yes, he has his moments," I say, keeping my tone light. "But I really like the job, most days. And the city."

"Oh, that's true," Nicole adds, and I catch the faintest flick of a smile. Maybe it's harmless, but it's leaning towards not. "You're not from around here."

"No," I say, tucking my feet up under the robe. "Argentina, originally. Buenos Aires before New York."

Hannah glances over, expression unreadable. "That's... quite the jump."

"It was. Still is sometimes," I admit. "But Elle made it so much easier."

Elle lifts her head from her lounger again, eyes warm, like she's remembering those first months too. "She's being modest. She handled the move much better than most people who've lived in the city their whole lives. And she learned the subway faster than I did."

"That's debatable," I say, grinning. "I got so lost my first week that I ended up in Queens when I was supposed to be in Midtown."

Amelia laughs. "Oh god, I could never take the subway."

"She texted me in a panic, and I sent a car to pick her up," Elle says. "The benefits of having a car service on speed dial, honestly."

"Yeah, and I haven't really taken the subway alone since," I say with a faint smile on my face. The idea terrifies me. I know that I should learn how to navigate the city but... "I gave up and started walking to work every day. About thirty blocks one way."

Nicole's brows jump. "That's... commitment."

"Completely out of necessity," I say, smiling. "But then I realized I liked it—taking different routes every day, finding new thrift stores, and seeing shop windows change with the seasons. There's always something to look at."

Elle points a finger without opening her eyes. "See? This is why she fits in. She actually *looks* at New York instead of just rushing through it."

"That's actually how I discovered this tiny little antique shop in the Lower East Side that has the best vintage jewelry. I've been working on my bangle collection since I moved here."

Nicole's gaze flicks up at that, softer than usual, like she wants to admit something but thinks better of it. The moment is gone as quickly as it comes, her glass tipped back toward her lips.

Hannah hums like she doesn't quite agree. "Guess I've never thought of walking as fun."

"Different perspectives," I say, settling deeper into the lounger. "That's half the fun of moving somewhere new."

The conversation drifts on, the storm clouds outside drawing closer. I let their voices swirl around me—some warm, some cooler—feeling both part of and separate from the group. Elle's presence is an anchor, though, her occasional smile or squeeze of my knee reminding me I'm not entirely adrift.

———

BY THE TIME our treatments are over, the rain has started in earnest, fat drops streaking the floor-to-ceiling windows in uneven trails. The indoor pool area is busier now, steam curling above the water and blurring the edges of everything.

We pad out from the changing rooms, hair still damp from the showers, robes cinched tight. The air is warm and humid, the faint chlorine tang mixing the citrusy smell coming from the juice bar. This definitely looks like any upscale New York gym, except make it *heavily* European.

Elle spots the guys first—Jack, Connor, Sterling and Cash—sitting at one of the low tables tucked under an overhang in the lobby. Jack is gesturing animatedly with a glass of something bright green, while Cash scrolls his phone with the single-minded focus of someone avoiding small talk.

Connor is the only one who looks up as we approach.

And it's more than a glance. It's a slow shift, his attention narrowing until it lands squarely on me. His hair is darker wet, pushed back carelessly, a few short strands falling loose to his forehead. There's the faintest shadow along his jaw, like he hasn't shaved since yesterday, and his brown eyes are fixed on me in a way that feels too deliberate to be casual. They flick down—quick, almost imperceptible, to the rolled cuffs of my robe before coming back to my face.

"Still in your robes?" Jack says, getting up to kiss Elle's cheek. "How was it?"

"Amazing," Amelia says, reaching for the bowl of mixed nuts on the table and moving slightly to sit on Cash's lap. "Except for Nicole almost drowning in the plunge pool."

Nicole snorts. "I did *not* almost drown. It was *cold*. Where's Banks?"

Elle and Jack fall into their own side conversation, and Cash starts talking about what the men did for their part of the spa day to both Amelia and Nicole. I overhear something about Banks enjoying the sauna a little too much—whatever that means—and heading to the house earlier to take a nap.

Somehow, I end up standing across from Connor, the table between us, and the rest of the group drifts around us like background noise. It's ridiculous, but the second our eyes meet, my brain cues up last night again—his voice low in the dark, the warmth of his hand when it brushed mine, the way I'd gone to bed with that stupid restless hum under my skin, my heart thumping nonstop in my chest.

"Good massage?" he asks, voice pitched low enough that it doesn't have to compete with the others.

"Very," I say, matching his tone. He's wearing a white linen shirt, unbuttoned halfway down his chest, and preppy looking swim trunks—little lobsters peppering the light blue background. "I might be too relaxed to walk back to the house."

His mouth tilts, slow, like he's enjoying a joke only half-formed in his head. "They do have those golf carts."

"Will you drive me?" I tease, tilting my head, my robe sleeve falling to my elbow just enough to show a sliver of my wrist.

"Only if bribed," he says, leaning back in his chair. His leg hooks around the one beside him and drags it closer with an easy scrape across the floor, a silent invitation.

I drop into the seat, and my knee brushes his under the table. A small thing, perhaps, but it lingers longer than it should. Neither of us moves it away.

"So," he says, picking up his glass and nodding toward mine, "did you try the green juice yet?"

I glance at the swamp-colored liquid. "No, because I have taste buds and a will to live."

That gets a quiet laugh from him. "It's not bad. Kinda... sweet."

"Wow," I deadpan. "Really selling it."

He leans in a little, lowering his voice even though there's no reason to. "I could tell you what I actually think it tastes like, but..." He lets the sentence trail off, smirking in a way that feels unfair.

I raise a brow. "Is that one of those fondue euphemisms?"

"Maybe." His eyes hold mine a beat too long. "Maybe not."

We talk about nothing important—how the rain might cancel tomorrow's hike, whether the plunge pool was really cold—but there's a rhythm to it that feels like we've done this before. Little pauses. Glances that last a beat longer than necessary. A faint tap of his thumb against his knee, close enough that I could pretend to brush it by accident if I wanted to.

When Jack calls for everyone to head out, I stand, tying the robe tighter. Connor looks up at me, eyes catching the shifting light from the water feature's reflection a few yards away.

"Guess I'll see you later," I say, careful to keep it casual, even though something in my chest pulls at the words.

"I hope so," he says, quiet but clear over the sound of water and voices.

It's absolutely nothing. A completely polite response to a normal greeting.

But it doesn't feel like nothing.

18

CONNOR

THE SHUTTLE'S SLIGHTLY CHILLY, the windows fogged up from the earlier rain and the body heat inside. Jack is leaning forward in his seat, chatting with the driver in rapid, confident English that's somehow still peppered with very Swiss-sounding names. Cash has one of his earbuds in, his eyes locked on the screen to something that looks like a replay of an economic summary of some sort. Maybe a news segment specifically on an IPO? I can't tell. And I also don't care.

I sit by the window, and even though the weather is terrible outside, the views continue to be stunning. My reflection stares back at me, faint over the blur of green hills and gray clouds breaking apart overhead.

The road curves, and I catch a flash of light over the vineyards—rows and rows of vines rolling toward the horizon and down to the edge of the lake, damp from the storm, the sky still moody enough to make it all feel like a painting. It's the kind of view people take out their phones to memorialize. I don't.

Because my brain is too busy thinking about Manuela. Like a fucking creep, I might add.

The robe she wore at the spa, cinched tight, but not tight enough to keep me from noticing the bare skin of her collarbone. The way she leaned in over the table, teasing me about the golf cart like it was a private joke just for us. The sound of her laugh when I deadpanned about the green juice.

It's ridiculous. I've known her for a few years, but since then we've had maybe a handful of interactions.

Jack points to a sign as we turn into the drive for the vineyard. "Best wine in Switzerland, I'm telling you," he says animatedly, eyes shining with excitement. Like everything he does, this is grand. I'm guessing we have the whole space to ourselves for the rest of the evening, with a catered dinner and a selection of wines to get very, very drunk. "This place wins awards every year."

"Looking forward to it," I say because it's easier than pointing out I'm not really here for the wine. We step out into air that smells fresh and sharp from the rain, the faint mineral scent of wet stone rising from the gravel path. The vines stretch out in every direction, leaves heavy and dark, the fruit almost ripe for harvesting.

Far off, the sky's still holding on to its last streak of gray.

Inside, the sommelier is waiting, smiling like she already knows Jack. She leads us to a long wooden table under an open overhang—gleaming glassware, plates of cheese, thin slices of cured meat, little bowls of olives lined up in perfect symmetry.

"Welcome, everyone. Mr. Paul," the sommelier says with a heavy French accent. Banks and Sterling are already sitting at the table, slices of warm bread halfway to their mouth. "We will start with some light appetizers, followed by a distillery tour, a walk of the vineyard, and finally, a wine tasting. How does that sound?"

Jack's smile grows as he takes the seat at the head of the table and nods. The sommelier exits, and a few seconds later, a handful of servers appear with what looks like soup and additional plates of cured meats and cheeses. I see a sliced pear and grapes on one plate and berries on another.

Sterling is already halfway through pouring himself a glass before the cork is even set down on the table next to the bottle. Jack raises his eyebrows but says nothing, instead reaching for the bread while egging his buddy on.

It takes me a second to register what's been nagging at me since we sat down: the girls aren't here. Elle mentioned earlier that they'd opted out of this excursion in favor of a cooking class, and now the absence feels almost too quiet. I catch myself wondering what Manuela's doing right now—if she's rolling out pasta dough with flour on her fingers, humming to herself without realizing it.

I pick up the wine but don't drink right away. The glass is cold in my hand, and it immediately makes me think about last night—how the chilly night breeze enveloped us by the pool, her sounds, the way she tasted after coming on my fingers. The look in her eyes like we were standing on the edge of this thing we decided to do just for the heck of it.

"Athena would love this," Banks says, mouth stuffed full of a cheese that tastes like flowers. "I'm surprised she let you come on the trip without her."

I pause with the rim of the glass halfway to my mouth. Keep my expression easy, neutral. "Yeah. She's got... a lot going on right now."

It's vague enough to pass, and it does. They nod like they half expected that answer, already reaching for more food. I don't add anything else. Not here, not with this group who still thinks of her as one of them.

And maybe they suspect the truth. I'm sure Athena has told some of their girlfriends what happened, but I'm not ready to let them name it out loud.

Sterling gives a low whistle. "Guess some people just don't know how to prioritize." He grins like he's joking, but the comment lands heavier than I want it to.

Normally I'd let it slide. They all work the same brutal hours I do—if anyone should understand, it's them. But with Athena gone, it feels less like a shared truth and more like a reminder: she would've shown up. She always did.

Jack jumps in to talk about the vineyard's awards, and I let the conversation slide off me, focusing instead on the way the rain-darkened vines stretch down towards the lake. At some point, the owner of the winery comes to talk to us, telling us about how September is harvest season in Switzerland and a lot of the vineyards open their doors to locals to support the yield.

Eventually, the owner and the sommelier lead us into the distillery, all cool stone and the sweet tang of fermenting grapes. My friends are eating it up, asking questions about yield and barrel aging. I hang back, trailing my fingers along one of the massive casks, thinking about how Manuela would probably ask, low and only for me, if they let people taste right from the tap and if Banks would be the first to volunteer as tribute.

When the tour shifts outside, the chatter swells again, everyone buzzing about the "harvest experience." Shears are handed out, baskets passed down the row, instructions given. I'm there, moving with the group, but my head's somewhere else. The grapes are cool and slick in my palm, their skins so taut they almost snap, and I catch myself wondering what Manuela is doing right now—if she's still lounging in that robe, if she's telling the girls some joke about me, or if she's simply observing like usual.

By the time we're seated back inside for the formal tasting, the sky has cleared to a pale gold. Five small courses arrive in order, each paired with a different wine. I go through the motions: smell, swirl, sip. But my attention keeps drifting. The rosé that is paired with a creamy tomato tart reminds me of the flush on her cheeks last night as she—

"And finally," Cash says, looking around and focusing his gaze on Jack. "To the groom!" Everyone around the table lifts their glasses, and I'm lost in what is happening, having been so focused on dirty thoughts of Manuela that I missed what was being said around me.

Dessert is poached pears over cream, served with a late-harvest wine that's so sweet it sticks to my teeth. Jack is talking about shipping bottles home, Banks and Sterling are arguing over which pairing was best, and I'm nodding at all of it while thinking about the drive back to the house later. About whether she'll be there in the kitchen or by the pool. And if her eyes will still have that look.

19

———

CONNOR

FRIDAY

"You're staring again."

I look up from the coffee table to find Manuela watching me, head tilted, one eyebrow raised like she's caught me red-handed. A blush threatens to form on my cheeks, as if I were caught staring at *her*.

"I'm strategizing," I say, even though my last play earned me a measly eight points and no one is buying that excuse; it's extremely obvious I suck at this game.

Elle snorts from where she's curled into the corner of the massive sectional, a blanket wrapped around her like a cocoon. "You're losing because you're too busy trying to figure out how to beat her without making it obvious you're trying to beat her."

"Not true," I say with a laugh, though she's not wrong.

The rain's been coming down steadily since lunch, the kind that distorts the view beyond the glass doors until the lake and the mountains are just smudges of gray and green. The sliding doors are shut, but the sound of it—soft, constant—fills the quiet spaces between words. The living room smells faintly of the espresso that was served earlier post lunch, a dark roast that Jack insisted was "better in this weather," and there's a plate of tiny butter cookies between us that's already down to crumbs. Our whitewater rafting excursion got cancelled due to the weather, so instead we are enjoying a lazy day inside.

Jack is sprawled out in the armchair, one arm stretched, hand curling around Elle's foot as he massages the arch. He's watching the game like he's a sports commentator. "You're doomed, bud. She's been killing us since round one."

Manuela smiles without looking up from her tiles. "Big talk from someone who just played 'cat' for six points."

"I was setting up for my next turn," Jack says, and Elle snorts in response.

"Sure you were, babe," Elle says, tossing a stray cookie crumb at him.

The Scrabble board between us is a mix of long, fancy words and short, desperate ones. Manuela is ruthless. She lays down "zenith" on a triple word score, and the little sound she makes while tallying points is pure satisfaction.

"It's the bilingualism, Connor," she says as she looks up, a cheeky grin forming on her face. She flips her hair and adds, "We learned all the big words first."

"Yeah, alright," I say, pulling my letters, but I smile at her cheekiness. We both reach into the bag at the same time, and my fingers brush hers, just enough to notice but not enough to make it weird. Except my brain apparently wants to make it weird because now I'm aware of the heat of her skin and the faint lavender smell from whatever lotion she used after her shower. Last night, when we got back for dinner, they were still out in town—a cooking class that turned, allegedly, into a rowdy girls' night that had them all waking up right around lunch today.

I focus on my tiles like they might spell out an escape route. They don't.

"Zany," she says a minute later, setting down the tiles and claiming another ridiculous amount of points.

"That's not even a word," Jack says.

"It is," she replies, her voice calm, almost amused. "A man who is a stupid, incompetent fool. Look it up."

"Oh babe," Elle says, making starry eyes at her partner. "You're so handsome."

Manuela shrugs, but there's a flicker of a smile in my direction because she knows I'm enjoying this more than I should.

By the time Elle "accidentally" plays a made-up word and somehow gets away with it, the game's devolved into mock arguments and Jack declaring himself morally opposed to two-letter plays. I'm not winning, but I don't care. Not when Manuela laughs like that—soft but sharp at the edges, like we're sharing this secret.

When we finally pause, Elle stretches and emerges from her cocoon, standing up quickly like she suddenly perked up after her mandatory resting period. "Okay, let's take a break before someone flips the board," she says, eyeing her fiancé with slits for eyes. "I'm ordering pastries from the resort. Any takers?"

"I'll make more coffee," Jack says, already standing. He wraps an arm around Elle's waist as they head toward the kitchen together, leaving the two of us in the living room with the rain and the steady hum of quiet around us.

I sink back into my chair, trying not to look too obviously at Manuela as she pulls the blanket off the back of the couch and drapes it over her legs. She tucks her feet under, knees angled toward me. She doesn't say anything, simply lifts her gaze slowly until it meets mine.

The look lingers. Long enough that I have to clear my throat.

"Comfy?" I ask, my voice rougher than I want it to be.

"Very," she says, tilting her head, eyes flicking toward the empty seat next to her. "But you're over there all by yourself."

My pulse stutters. She didn't say I could join her, but that's what it sounds like. I've been so out of practice that every word has me second-guessing myself.

I lean forward, elbows braced on my knees. "Is that a hint?"

"Maybe," she says, a soft laugh in her throat. She tugs the blanket higher, but her legs shift slightly under it.

The smell of coffee drifts in from the kitchen. Rain taps harder against the glass. Everyone else is out of sight, and it feels like the house has shrunk to this small corner, just the two of us.

I stand and cross the short distance to the couch, heart thudding harder than it should for something as simple as sitting down. The cushion dips under my weight, and the blanket shifts when I brush my knee against hers.

"The rain reminds me of summer storms back home," Manuela says, looking out the window.

"Yeah?" I ask like a dumbass who apparently has forgotten how to even hold an adult conversation. But she makes me nervous in the best of ways, and being around her is becoming a very welcome distraction. "Tell me about it."

"I'm from a super small town in the mountains," she says, gesturing with her hands. "Almost like this but not as fancy, *obviously*. Very middle class."

I watch the way her fingers move, painting the picture in the air. She doesn't even realize she does it. It's the kind of detail that makes me want to lean in closer, to catch every word coming out of those lips.

"What's it called?" I ask.

"Tres Fuegos." She says it with that easy lilt, like fire and music rolled into one. The tone of her voice changes as she says it in Spanish, and I wonder if she has a different personality when she's back home. "Tiny place. Everyone knows everyone. When something happens, the whole town knows before your family does."

I laugh quietly. "Sounds like a nightmare." But also sounds like my family and friends.

"Sometimes it is." Her smile curves, though it doesn't reach her eyes. "But also... safe, in a way?"

Safe. I roll the word around in my head, glancing at her profile. There's a part of me that envies that. My family knows me too well in ways I'd rather they didn't, but safe isn't a word I'd use. Expected, maybe. Bound. But not safe.

"What do you miss most about it?" I ask. There's a faint knock at the door, and I wonder if it's the pastries being delivered. Elle and Jack haven't come back from their excursion to the kitchen, but the smell of coffee lingers in the air like there's a pot brewing there.

She pauses, considering. "The mountains. The slow, steady rhythm. Knowing everyone, even if that could get suffocating sometimes." A small smile flickers, then fades. "But it was too small for me. I always wanted more, daydreamed with my best friend Martina about leaving. I ended up in Buenos Aires for university, then New York." Her voice softens, the last words slipping out like a confession. "I'm sure it's a universal immigrant experience, and I'm not the only one who feels like this occasionally. A lot of the time I wonder if I'll ever belong anywhere."

I lean forward, needing to close the space between us. My hand stretches of its own accord and tucks a lock of hair behind her ear. "You do. You will."

She gives me a look, not exactly skeptical but more like she doesn't trust herself to believe me.

And because I can't leave it there, I add, "I minored in

Spanish in college. Thought I'd go to Argentina for a semester abroad. Ended up in Chile instead."

Manuela's whole face lights up, her laugh breaking the tension in the air. "Chile?" She says it like it's the punchline to a joke. "Why would you do that to yourself?"

I grin, glad she's laughing, glad it's me who caused it. "It was cheaper, I think? Or maybe the program filled up? I don't know. I regret it, though. My buddies that ended up in Argentina had a blast."

"As you should." She tugs the blanket higher, smirking now. "Chile is fine, but... come on. You picked wrong."

"Guess I'll need a local guide if I ever want to fix that mistake," I say before I can stop myself.

Her eyes flick to mine, sharp and amused. "Maybe. If you're lucky."

The blanket shifts again, her knee brushing mine, and I don't move away.

20

———————

MANUELA

THE HALLWAY CREAKS under my bare feet. The house is mostly quiet, except for the muffled sound of rain sliding down the windows and a laugh or two drifting from behind closed doors one floor below. I clutch my phone against my chest like it's a valid excuse for what I'm about to do, heart hammering way too fast for something as innocent as needing a charger.

Connor's door is closed, but there's a thin stripe of warm light from under it, and I wonder if maybe he's asleep. I stop, turning back around to head back to my room, but then change my mind again.

Something about never being this forward with men flashes through my mind. In Buenos Aires, dating was easy—messy, sometimes, but familiar. Two longish relationships, a handful of casual things that burned bright and quick. There was always someone to go out with, to laugh with, to text late at night.

But when I moved to New York, I stopped. It never felt like I could risk the distraction when I was barely keeping my head above water. Everything there still feels temporary, like I'm borrowing the life I've built and might have to give it back at any moment. Dating means letting people see you, and I've never been sure I'd be staying long enough for that to matter.

And suddenly, here I am in the hallway of a Swiss villa in the middle of the night. It feels reckless. Especially so because this is someone from the friend group, and what's the saying? Don't shit where you eat?

Maybe I'm rusty. Maybe I don't know how Americans do this—if this even is a thing people do outside of movies. For all I know, he's going to laugh, hand me a charger, and send me back to bed.

I knock softly.

"Yeah?" His voice is low, rougher than usual.

I push the door a little. He's sitting on the bed, propped against the headboard with his laptop open, shirt stretched across his chest. His hair is damp, like he showered after dinner, and a knot of nerves coils low in my stomach. Not regret, exactly—just the sharp awareness that whatever happens next could change everything.

"Sorry to interrupt your..." I hold up my phone. "Do you —uh, have a charger?"

"Not interrupting. I was catching up on the news." He

arches a brow, mouth tilting. "That's the excuse you're going with?"

Heat floods my cheeks. "What, I can't need to charge my phone?"

Before I can blink, he's off the bed, across the room, pulling me inside. The door clicks shut softly behind me, and then my back is pressed against it with urgency. His body is close, his hand braced beside my head.

"Tell me the truth," he says, voice softer now, eyes dark.

I can't. Or maybe I don't want to. Instead, I smile and lift my chin slightly, forcing all the confidence I left in the hallway. "I need a charger."

That's all it takes. He kisses me hard, like he's been holding himself back since that night on the terrace. His mouth is warm and insistent, tasting faintly of toothpaste and whatever wine they opened after dinner. My mouth parts on a soft sound I don't mean to make, and he swallows it like he's been starving. His other hand slides down my side, palms my hip, and my knees threaten to give out.

He eases the kiss slower, then slower still, like winding the dial back on purpose. A press, a pause, a drag of his lower lip. It turns me inside out, and I'm ready to climb him, drop this phone, and forget there are people outside in this same house.

"Hi," he murmurs, barely pulling back. His forehead rests against mine. His breath ghosts my mouth.

"Hi," I whisper, my voice not entirely reliable.

His thumb sweeps along my jaw, patient. "Can I tell you

a secret?" His voice is so soft against my ear, a low grumble coming right from the center of his chest. "I hoped you needed that charger last night."

I chuckle and look into his eyes, and he smiles in return. That feeling of uncomfortableness I had the second I knocked is swept away by the appearance of his dimple.

Connor kisses me again, slow enough to make my toes curl, and his hands are thorough like he's finally able to learn me by touch—waist, ribs, the slope under my shoulder blades, the back of my neck. My fingers have their own agenda; they sneak under the hem of his T-shirt to find warm skin and a steady hum of muscle. He shivers, almost imperceptibly. I feel stupidly victorious.

"Tell me if you want to stop."

"I don't." The answer finds me before the question is even finished.

"Bed," he says against my mouth, and I nod because walking sounds complicated and very dangerous. He guides me there with one hand at my waist, never quite breaking the kiss. The mattress dips, sheets cool against the back of my bare knees. He stands to push the laptop and sets it aside, then looks down at me like he's trying to decide where to start.

"Everywhere," I say, surprising the both of us. The honesty of it makes my cheeks heat.

His smile is small and wrecking. "Okay."

He peels my shirt over my head, slow, careful of my hair. The air touches my skin and tightens everything. He doesn't rush. He watches, like that first day on Elle's rooftop, quiet and introspective. His hands slide up my stomach, under the band of my lace bralette, then back down like he's teasing himself as much as me.

When he finally unclasps it, he breathes out with a quiet, reverent "god," and the sound shoots straight through me.

I tug his T-shirt up, and he lets me—arms raised, obliging —and then it's tossed somewhere I don't care about. He's warm under my palms, smooth. I mouth along his collarbone, taste clean skin and a hint of salt, and he mutters something that could be my name, or maybe it's a curse word. In any case it makes my skin break out in goosebumps and my spine tingle.

We take each other apart like this for a long time—hands, mouth, breath, that slow slide of patience that makes everything sharper. He kisses down my sternum, the center of my stomach, the sensitive place just above the waistband of my shorts where I swear I feel sparks.

"*Por favor*," I hear myself say, and I don't even know what I'm asking for. Just... more.

He slides his hand under the elastic and slowly works my pajama bottoms down with the soft scrape of his knuckles against my thighs, and then his mouth is on me through the thin cotton of my panties, deliberate. I arch into him without meaning to. He hums, pleased, and the vibration drags a whimper out of me I try, and fail, to swallow.

"Quiet," he whispers, not unkind. "You'll get us caught."

"Then don't—" I can't finish my sentence. He hooks his

fingers in the edge of the fabric and eases it aside, breath warm where I ache. The first slow stroke of his tongue against my clit blanks my mind. My hand finds his hair on instinct, fingers tangling, not pushing him but instead anchoring myself to something that isn't floating.

He takes his time, maddening and generous. Slowly, he tilts me backwards so I'm lying in the middle of his bed as he maps me. He learns what makes my hips chase his mouth, what pulls a sharp breath from my lungs, what unspools me without warning. He doesn't rush past any of it. When he slips two fingers inside, I clamp my legs around his head, my eyes falling shut.

"Look at me," he says, voice low.

I do. His eyes are dark and steady, and his mouth is slick with me, his hand moving in a rhythm I can't fight. He looks like he's exactly where he wants to be. Something tight coils low in my belly, and I try to hold it, and then he curls his fingers just so and I break—jaw slack, breath stuttering, the world narrowing to white noise and him in between my legs. I come with a strangled sound into the crook of my arm, trying to remember how to breathe, how to keep quiet, how to exist in a body he's turned upside down and backwards.

He kisses the inside of my thigh once, a soft little stamp of heat, and crawls up over me, bracing himself on his fore-arms so his weight is a promise, not a crush. I kiss him because I don't know how else to say thank you. I taste myself and him, and the combination makes my head spin.

"I've wanted to taste you since the rooftop," he admits into my mouth, words rough and unguarded.

Something in my chest kicks hard. I don't let myself think too hard about what that means—not now, not with his mouth this close—but it lodges somewhere deep, humming through my body.

"Me too." It feels like jumping and finding ground beneath my feet.

He reaches to the nightstand, finds a foil packet, pauses. "Okay?"

I blink at it, then let out a small, startled laugh. "Do you just... carry condoms with you?"

His mouth tilts, sheepish and amused all at once. "No. Jack."

"Jack?"

He nods, sliding the packet between his fingers. "Apparently he thought I might, you know... get lucky? His words. Not mine."

I cover my mouth with my hand to muffle the laugh that bursts out. "That's the most ridiculous thing I've ever heard. What kind of cousin sets up a condom stash for you like a care package?"

"He did it for all the guys. Even though everyone's in a committed relationship." Connor lifts his shoulder casually, though the curve of his mouth betrays him. He leans closer, voice dropping into something conspiratorial. "You cannot tell him I am very, very grateful for his care package."

That does me in. I laugh again, softer this time, and tug him closer by the back of his neck.

"So…"

"Yes," I say, and it's the easiest yes I've ever given.

He tears it open with his teeth, quick and practiced but not detached. When he settles between my thighs again, he doesn't push right away. He hovers over my body and looks down at where we meet, then up at me again, like he's giving me another chance to change my mind. I don't.

The first press of him makes my breath catch, stretch and heat in one long, patient push. My hands fly to his shoulders, then slide up to frame his face because I need to see him. His eyes flutter shut, a curse breathed into the space between us.

"Tell me if it's too much," he says, jaw tight like he's on a cliff edge.

"It's perfect," I hear and then realize it's my voice.

He moves like he's listening: small adjustments, a shift in angle, a deeper stroke that drags along nerves that haven't been touched in so, so long. The bed creaks in soft protest. The rain patters against the balcony floor, but I can't focus on anything else but Connor.

He keeps kissing me—mouth, jaw, the very corner of my lips, as if to anchor me to something. As if he needs the anchoring too.

I wrap my legs around his waist, and the change in depth rips a cry from my throat that I barely smother.

"You need to be quiet, baby," he says, whispering in my ear. "Fuck, you're so hot."

He swears, lowers his forehead to mine, and the next roll of his hips is deliberate and devastating. The pleasure builds again, impossible and fast and slow all at once, and I cling to him like that will slow it down. It doesn't.

"Manu," he warns, a little broken, voice gravelly and low. "I'm—"

"Yeah," I say, exhaling. "Please."

Everything in my body tightens, dissolving once I climax and the world tilts bright and breathless. He follows on a ragged groan, his movements stuttering as he shudders above me, buried deep. For a second, we're both suspended there, held up by nothing but the aftershocks and the way we're still clinging to each other.

Silence, except for breathing and rain.

The faint, clean smell of laundry beneath us.

A soft click somewhere outside the door.

He rolls to the side, careful, and immediately drags me with him, tucking me against his chest like he's not ready to let any part of me go. His skin is hot under my cheek, and his heartbeat is a steady knock against my ear. He presses his lips to my forehead once, again, a third time like a habit he's testing.

I stare at the slope of his collarbone, the tiny constellation of freckles there I didn't notice before. My body hums.

"Hey," he says after a while, voice gone soft at the edges. "Are you okay?"

I nod, then realize he can't see it. "Yeah. Yes." My voice comes out wrecked. I clear my throat, softer. "I'm great."

He exhales, something like relief loosening his hold.

I don't know how long we stay like that—long enough for him to disappear into the bathroom to clean himself up, for me to go pee right after. For Connor to tuck us under the covers and wrap his hand around my waist, holding me against his chest.

I trace a line over his bicep with the tip of my finger, and it exhilarates me, a quiet thrill that comes from touching without asking permission every time.

"Connor," I whisper, turning to face him. His hand plants against my hip, and I can feel his skin still slick with sweat.

"Yeah?" he replies, sleepy but pulling me closer to him.

"I actually do need your charger."

A laugh slips out of him, small and surprised. "I have an extra one in my backpack."

I smile to myself as he drifts to sleep, and a few minutes later, I sneak out of his room, charger in hand, to my room down the hall. In the morning, everything is going to feel loud, so this is the safest way for this to work. This no-pressure pact that I so foolishly suggested.

21

———

CONNOR

SATURDAY

THE BOAT HUMS low beneath our feet, slicing through the water in one smooth motion. Rain lingers at the edges of the sky, but for now the clouds are lifting, and faint strips of sunlight catch the ripples in the water, making it look a deep blue I've never seen before.

Jack, of course, has made the whole thing into an event. A private chartered boat with cushioned seats, blankets folded neatly in case anyone gets chilly. He's standing near the bow with a captain's hat on, pointing out landmarks along the shoreline like a man who's already adopted this corner of Switzerland as his personal kingdom.

I'm sitting toward the middle, window cracked, the mountain air sharp with the scent of pine and lake, if that's even a thing. Cash is scrolling on his phone again, and his girlfriend Amelia is napping, head on his shoulder. Somewhere else, Banks and Sterling are swapping stories about some ski trip from years back, the kind of conversation that loops around and around without ever going anywhere.

And then there's her.

Manuela sits across from me, head tilted toward the window, strands of hair caught by the breeze. Her posture is lightly tense, but she laughs at something Elle says from behind her, soft and low, and the sound makes me ache in a place I didn't realize was hollow until a few days ago.

I don't even try to join the conversation. Instead I watch her fingers toy with the edge of her sleeve, watch the way her mouth curves when she smiles. I shouldn't be staring, but the problem is I don't want to stop.

Jack claps his hands together. "Alrighty, folks, we're almost there. Who's excited for some chocolate?"

"Dangerous," Manuela says, shaking her head with mock seriousness. "I'll have to be rolled out of there."

"Same," I say before I think better of it. Our eyes catch. It's a flicker—half a second too long—and I swear her face changes, like she knows exactly where my head went: last night. Her taste still on my tongue, the sound of her falling apart under my hands.

My throat tightens, and I glance out the window like the scenery has suddenly become riveting.

"And to your right," Jack bellows above the wind that has suddenly picked up. He gestures with his whole arm, playing tour guide. "See that white house? That is Tina Turner's residence."

Manuela nods her head a few times like she's impressed,

but then I catch her slipping her phone from her purse. She thumbs something in quickly, lips moving silently as she reads the screen. Fact-checking him. I'd bet money on it. Or maybe googling who Tina Turner even is.

Her focus is sharp, brows furrowed in that way that makes her look like she's solving something important, like when we were playing Scrabble. I imagine leaning across, brushing my lips to her ear, teasing her about it. Whispering the words just for her. The picture in my head is so clear I almost feel the warmth of her skin.

I press my coffee cup harder against my knee. Jesus. I need to get my shit together.

"Connie, hello?"

The nickname grates, snapping me out of the daydream. I blink across the boat—Banks is staring at me like I've missed something.

"Sorry, what?" My voice is rougher than it should be, so I clear my throat. "Spaced out."

He smirks. "Clearly. I asked you if you think Athena would've hated this little field trip or loved it. Can't decide which."

My chest tightens.

The group chuckles, harmless, but it lands like a weight anyway. Everyone's looking at me now, waiting. My fingers tighten around the cup, the remnants of heat biting into my skin.

"I think she'd..." I pause, then take the easy way out. A shrug. "Depends on the day."

That earns a round of nods, a few laughs, and the spotlight shifts away, the conversation rolling forward.

But across from me, Manuela is no longer reading. Her phone rests in her lap, and she's watching the water, jaw set. The muscle ticks once, sharp.

I want to say something—anything—to cut through the tension. But I don't. Not here. Not with all these eyes and ears.

So instead I sit there, pretending to sip my drink, staring out at the blur of lake and shoreline like it holds answers I don't have and wait to disembark.

———

"HOLY SHIT," Banks says beside me. He's rubbing the palms of his hands together like a child in a candy store. The factory is all polished wood and glass, pristine white floors that look almost out of a modern Wonka movie set. The air is thick and heavy with chocolate, and it's overwhelming, to say the least.

We're led through a private entrance, past a wall-sized fountain of molten chocolate that has my cousin grinning like a kid. I mean, everyone is, because this is just a level of extra that lots of money can buy.

Employees dressed in crisp white outfits and chef hats press tasting squares into our hands at intervals: dark with hints of orange, milk filled with praline, white flecked with crushed freeze-dried raspberries. The group chatters about favorites, tosses out jokes, compares notes.

Manuela takes a bite of one of the squares and closes her eyes. "This should be illegal."

"Probably is somewhere," I say, watching the way her tongue darts out to catch a smear of chocolate at the corner of her lip. I force my eyes away before I do something stupid like wipe it with my thumb.

We follow the sommelier-like guide through the atrium, Jack bouncing on his heels like he's about to offer to buy the whole factory as a wedding present to Elle. The guide, a stern-looking woman with perfect posture and an even more perfect British accent, is talking about the process at the front of the group, but I can't focus on anything but Manuela.

She walks just ahead of me, hair tucked behind her ear, tilting her head at the displays we're passing as though she's cataloguing details no one else sees. Her fingers trail lightly along the edge of a glass case filled with wrapped truffles, her nails painted the faintest neutral pink. I want to reach for her hand and lace my fingers with hers.

"This is the heart of our process," the guide explains, straightening her spine as she stops around a wide window where a chocolatier pours melted chocolate into molds. "Precision and patience. The Swiss way."

Patience. The word almost makes me laugh. Last night, with her pressed against my door, patience didn't stand a chance.

Jack elbows me. "Remember when you guys swore off chocolate for that keto thing?"

My jaw tightens. "Yeah," I try to say lightly, forcing a smile. "Didn't last long."

Eventually, we are led into a long hallway with multiple doors on either side. Sterile white walls are lined with old black-and-white photos of men in chef's hats pouring chocolate into massive molds. The air grows sweeter the deeper we go until it's almost overwhelming. At the end of the hall, double doors open into the tasting room for lunch: high ceilings, rows of wineglasses glinting in the light, and platters of chocolate arranged like jewels on marble stands.

"Too much?" I murmur.

She startles, then glances at me, her lips parting like she wasn't expecting me to speak so close to her ear. For half a second, her hand brushes the edge of my sleeve—barely there, but I feel it like a jolt.

Her smile flickers. "Depends. You mean the sugar or the theatrics?"

"Both," I admit, tipping my head toward Jack, as he's already hamming it up with the sommelier, trying to out-charm her accent.

She huffs a laugh, soft, private. Her eyes drop to my mouth, and I feel it in my stomach, an immediate tightening that has me catching my breath before I can stop it. "Definitely both."

We sit, and the first course is served—tiny portions of cheese, pears, and chocolate paired with a dry Riesling. The guide explains notes and origins, and Jack and Elle ask questions. Hannah and Amelia are sitting at the end of the table, snapping photos of the dishes as they come, and the more we get into the meal, the more chocolate is served with the food.

The meal is long, just like that first day, everyone enjoying the conversation and the drinks.

Once, under the table, our knees knock and neither of us moves, and I'm tempted to place my hand on her thigh, possessively, like she's mine.

Finally, what feels like hours later, we're shepherded down another long corridor towards the demonstration kitchen for coffee. The group surges ahead, drawn by the smell of caramelizing sugar and the promise of truffle samples. Manuela lingers, pausing by a display of antique molds shaped like flowers. I stop beside her.

"They're kind of creepy, right?" I whisper, leaning in.

She tilts her head, a grin tugging at her lips. "My grandmother had one like that one, see?" She points at one in the far corner. It's rusted and old and looks like a Thanksgiving cornucopia. "My sister always thought it was creepy. And no one seems to know where it came from."

"Was it haunted?"

"Maybe, but she baked the best cakes in it, so I'm not complaining." Her laugh is soft, caught in the low hum of the ventilation overhead. She shakes her head but doesn't move away. And that's all the invitation I need to shift closer, just enough that the warmth of her arm grazes mine.

"Connor," she says, warning in her voice, though the corner of her mouth betrays her with a smile.

"You weren't in my bed this morning." My hand hovers at her waist, careful, waiting for any sign I've gone too far.

Manuela's eyes flick toward the hallway, where the rest of the group's voices echo faintly. Then back to me. "Do you want to get caught?"

I shake my head, leaning in just a fraction. "No. But I hate pretending I don't want you."

Her expression flickers, just for a second, like she wasn't expecting this level of honesty. She presses a palm to my chest, firm but not pushing me away. Her eyes spark, amused and sharp, and they drag all the way down to my lips. "Well, I care. No one needs to know our business, Connor."

Something about the way she says it, low and deliberate, makes my pulse spike. Like she's not shutting me down, just reminding me of the line we're toeing and of the temporary nature of this arrangement.

And the worst part? It looks like she believes that.

I dip my head, brushing my mouth close enough to hers that I feel her sigh.

"One kiss," I murmur.

Her hand lingers where it is, then relaxes just slightly, and that's all the permission I need. My lips find hers, quick and hot, stealing the taste of her laugh before the sound of footsteps jolts us apart.

She smooths her hair like nothing happened, stepping out of the alcove ahead of me with a sneaky smile on her face.

I drag a hand through my hair, trying to school my expression before I follow. And realize that I'm fucking done for.

22

MANUELA

"God, I love European towns." Amelia sighs as she stops in front of a boutique window. A mannequin in a floaty white dress stares back at us. "Everything looks like it belongs in a movie."

The cobblestones are slick underfoot, still damp from this morning's rain, even with the sun shining bright in the sky. The town looks like something out of a postcard—rows of white-and-cream buildings with flower boxes hanging from every window, the scent of fresh bread drifting from the corner bakery. After getting back from the chocolate tasting, the men stayed at the house and we drifted lazily into the small town by the resort, going in and out of shops all afternoon.

Elle loops her arm through mine, tugging me along. "You just want an excuse to buy that dress and claim it's practical for winery hopping."

Amelia grins, unbothered. "Wouldn't you?"

We duck into the boutique, bells chiming over the door. Inside, racks of silk blouses and sundresses line the walls, the air perfumed with lavender sachets. Nicole is towards the back, flipping through hangers with quick, practiced fingers, while Hannah drifts toward a display of handbags, her expression unreadable as always.

After a few minutes of casual browsing, Elle drifts toward a table of colorful scarves near the door, fingers trailing absently over the silk. I wander after her, grateful for the momentary lull and the fact that everyone else is otherwise entertained.

"You're so quiet," she says, glancing up with that perceptive tilt of her head I've come to know too well. "Are you having fun?"

I laugh softly, touching a red scarf with my fingers. "Of course. It's been great."

She narrows her eyes, like she doesn't quite buy it. "I feel like I've been the worst host. Always pulled in ten directions with Jack and the others." She pouts. "I thought I'd have more time with you."

"Elle, stop. You don't have to babysit me," I say quickly, and I mean it. "I'm having fun. You've already done so much, and the trip has been amazing. Truly."

Her shoulders ease a little. "You'd tell me if you weren't, right?"

I nod, smile. "Right."

She squeezes my hand before drifting back toward the counter.

And I stand there for a beat longer, letting the noise of the shop swell around me—Nicole's laugh, Amelia's mock gasp at a price tag, Hannah's flat, unimpressed hum.

"Find anything good?" Amelia appears at my side, sunglasses pushed up into her brown hair, a soft smile on her face.

"Just admiring," I say. "Everything's beautiful."

"It is," she agrees, eyes sweeping the shop. "It's also a little... much, isn't it? All of this."

I glance at her, surprised. "You think so?"

"Sometimes I wonder if we all like the performance more than the actual stuff." Her smile tilts, conspiratorial now. "Don't tell Elle I said that."

I laugh under my breath, the tension in my shoulders loosening a fraction at the unexpected vulnerability.

"Anyway," she adds lightly, "I'm glad you're here. It's nice having you around. I really enjoy spending time together."

The words catch me off guard, enough that I almost forget to answer. "Thanks. That... means a lot."

She shrugs easily. "Just the truth." She gestures toward a display at the front of the store. "Come on. Help me decide if that bag is actually cute or if I'm just bored," Amelia says, and I follow her towards the window, smiling despite myself.

"Oh my god," Elle exclaims, turning as she clutches a piece of glossy paper to her chest. I pause mid-browse through a stack of watercolor mini prints, all etched with the familiar views from around the resort. "Ladies."

Her grin is contagious, even if I have no idea what she's scheming. There's the signature gleam in her eye, the one she gets when she's suddenly *obsessed* with something, most likely fueled by a wild idea. "Look at this."

She lifts the flyer in the air and giggles, shaking it like she just won the lottery. From where I stand, I can barely make out the words—it's for a nightclub in town, it seems. The paper promises "Retro Night: all '80s hits, all evening." It gives off *locals only* vibes.

"Please tell me you're in," Elle says, eyes sparkling.

Amelia snatches it from her. "God, yes. Who doesn't want to dance to Madonna with actual Europeans?"

Nicole tilts her head, scanning the flyer. "We already have dinner plans."

"Early dinner," Elle corrects as she tucks her phone in her tiny crossbody purse. She's grinning, her smile so big her eyes crinkle at the corners. She looks much more amused than at the chocolate factory earlier today, that's for sure. "Then this." She grabs another flyer from the counter and waves it again like a flag. "Come on, when are we going to get another chance like this?"

My heart gives a little leap. A night of dancing sounds like exactly the kind of reckless thing I came here for. And, if I'm being honest, the thought of Connor in a dim, crowded club—close, hidden, maybe touching me the way he did on the terrace—sends a flush straight through me.

Hannah gives a noncommittal shrug, though I catch the faintest twitch at the corner of her mouth. Nicole takes longer but finally says, "Fine. But I'm not dancing. I hope they have good drinks."

"Liar," Amelia sing-songs, looping her arm through Nicole's as we head for the door.

Elle leans close to me, voice pitched low so only I hear. "Tell me you're ready to blow the roof off a Swiss nightclub."

I laugh, shaking my head. "I can't even imagine what that looks like."

"Guess we'll find out," she says, slipping the flyer into her purse.

———

THE DANCE HALL doesn't look like much from the outside. It's a squat concrete building with a hand-painted sign that has seen better days, and all the flowers on the boxes hanging from the window are on the verge of death. Inside, though, it's a different story.

Colored lights spin lazily from the ceiling. A disco ball glitters halfheartedly, and the first beats of a very eighties song thump through the speakers. Suddenly, I'm sixteen again, sneaking into my older sister's parties over the summer back home in our small town.

She used to throw them in our backyard—music blasting from borrowed speakers, fairy lights strung haphazardly between the lemon trees, and half the town's older boys showing up just to orbit her. Agustina was loud and dazzling, always at the center of everything, and I wanted so badly to be part of it. I'd slip in unnoticed with Martina, weaving through her group of effortlessly cool twenty-somethings, trying to keep up with their jokes and pretending I wasn't giddy just to be allowed near them.

Those nights convinced me that life could be bigger than whatever small box I was living in. That I could be bold too—that if I just pushed past the fear, I might find my way into rooms that glittered like that backyard once did. I think that's what's kept me moving all these years, from Buenos Aires to New York: the hope that somewhere out there is another night like that, waiting for me.

The place is half-empty when we arrive. Older folks cluster near the bar, leaning on stools, nursing beers. The dance floor yawns wide open, polished wood that looks extremely clean and shiny under the rotating lights.

Elle and Jack are the first ones out there, of course. Amelia drags Nicole with her, laughing when Nicole protests, and Cash heads for the bar, muttering something about "liquid courage."

I hover near the edge, looking around and adjusting the strap of my dress. It's nothing fancy, just a black loose-enough-for-comfort mini, but Connor's eyes catch mine from across the room. A slow, deliberate pass, like he's checking me out without any apology.

Heat blocks in my chest, and I pretend to study the drink options behind the bar a few feet away from me.

"Do you dance?" His voice comes low behind me.

I turn and find Connor close to me, the warmth of his body stretching in my direction. No one is watching us, I think. His brown eyes are darker in the neon light, and his delicious forearms are on full display.

"Not well," I say, shrugging.

"Perfect." His mouth tilts, and before I can argue, his hand slides down my arm to catch my fingers. "Come on."

For the first twenty minutes, the dance floor feels ridiculous. Couples move in clumsy circles, and the women in our group are the loudest ones, their laughter rising above the music unapologetically.

But when Connor pulls me closer, one hand at my waist, the ridiculousness fades into background noise.

"I thought you hated this kind of thing," I tease, leaning in to be heard. "Being like this at the center of things."

He dips his head, his lips brushing close enough to my ear that I shiver. "I don't hate it when it's with you."

I roll my eyes, but I can't fight the smile. "That's a terrible line."

"Yeah." He smirks. "But it worked, didn't it?"

We move to the beat, awkward at first, then easier, like our bodies already know the rhythm. My hair sticks to my cheeks; his hands steady me when someone bumps past us.

When a song I don't recognize starts pulsing, the floor fills up.

Somewhere between the last chorus and now, more people have trickled in without me noticing—slipping through the doors, shedding jackets, letting the music pull them straight into dancing.

Elle twirls under Jack's arm, and he dips her low, planting a kiss on her mouth that has them both laughing loud. The space shrinks, bodies pressing in, and suddenly Connor and I are tucked into the far corner, half-hidden by shadows.

The corner isn't part of the dance floor, exactly. It's a narrow strip of wall between the edge of the bar and the DJ booth, partially concealed by a stack of chairs that towers over us. From here, the crowd looks like a single moving organism, a blur of limbs and glittering lights.

"Manu," he murmurs, his hand tightening at my hip.

My breath catches. "Hmm?"

The beat thrums through the floor, up my calves and through my ribs until it feels like my whole body is vibrating. Connor's mouth is hot on mine, one hand firm on my lower back, pulling me tighter against him. My body presses into the rough wall, lights flickering over us in dizzy spins of pink and blue.

Everywhere else is chaos, but in this corner, obscured, it feels like the world has shrunk to just Connor's lips and the relentless beat of the music.

"Connor," I murmur against his mouth, my fingers curling into his hair, tugging just enough to hear the sound he makes. The half groan, half laugh runs through my body and settles low in my belly.

"Manu," he whispers again, low and rough, like he's

unraveling. His hand slides lower, from my waist to my thigh, thumb pressing through the thin fabric of my dress.

I should one hundred percent stop him. I should remind him there are people ten feet away, on top of the group that knows us on the other side of the room. But then his lips trail down my jaw, finding the place just under my ear, and my knees actually buckle.

"Someone could see," I manage, though my voice is already betraying me.

"No one's looking," he murmurs. His hand slides higher, fingers brushing the edge of my dress. "And no one needs to know our business."

The words hit low in my stomach, and my pulse jumps. I grip his shoulder harder, torn between pulling him closer and shoving him away.

And then his fingers skim up under the hem of my dress. My breath catches so hard I almost choke on it. His palm anchors on my thigh, sliding slowly and deliberately, until his knuckles nudge the edge of my underwear.

Heat floods through me, sharp and dizzying. My head tips back against the wall as the bass rattles my bones.

"Fuck," he hisses, then kisses me again before I can say more. A moan threatens to spill out of my mouth, but before I can manage to take in some air, he's swallowing the sound and keeping it between us. His hand stays right there, not moving but in a way that makes every nerve ending light up. "Let me touch you where anyone could see and no one would know."

The crowd surges closer as the DJ shifts into "I Wanna Dance with Somebody (Who Loves Me)." The music is so loud now I can't even hear my own thoughts. I can only feel his body pressing me against the wall, his thumb on my clit and his mouth stealing every breath.

"Tell me to stop," he says, voice ragged against my lips.

I don't. I kiss him harder, nails digging into his shoulder, silently daring him to keep going.

And he does.

His other hand moves to catch my leg and lifts it to his hips. It involuntarily wraps around his body, and he moves closer. "You're going to make me ruin these pants if you keep pushing me closer to you, baby. Is that what you want?"

His fingers press firmer, circling once, just enough to make my hips jerk. I bite down on his lips to stifle the sound that wants to rip out of me.

Someone nearby shouts in laughter, so close that we both freeze. My pulse hammers so hard I swear the whole club can hear it, even through the thundering sound of the music and seemingly every patron singing along to the lyrics.

Connor pulls back just enough to look at me, chest rising hard against mine, eyes dark like he's memorizing every inch of this moment. His hand drifts down my thigh again, slow and deliberate, fingertips grazing my skin like a warning.

"Later," he murmurs, his voice wrecked and low, the single word landing like a promise I can feel all the way down to my toes. He eases back, adjusting himself with a rough tug, and then—because he's shameless—he brings his fingers to his mouth, tongue dragging over them as his eyes hold mine.

My stomach drops, heat rushing through me so fast I have to grip the wall to stay steady. And I nod because my voice would give me away.

When Elle appears out of the crowd, flushed and laughing, Connor's already taken a step back, casual, like he's been leaning against the wall this whole time.

And I... I'm trying to remember how to breathe.

23

———

CONNOR

"There you guys are!"

Elle's voice cuts through the haze of bass and neon as she weaves her way toward us, cheeks flushed, hair a little wild. She's got the loose, happy look of someone who's just taken one shot too many, her hand waving like we've been hiding on purpose.

Manuela's spine snaps against the wall, and she tugs her dress down like maybe it'll erase what just happened between us in the shadows. My body still feels like it's on fire, and I'm praying to any god up there that it's dark enough to disguise the obvious problem pressing against my zipper.

"She isn't feeling so good," I say quickly, stepping in before Elle can say more. "I was going to walk her home if that's cool with you."

Elle squints at Manuela, tilting her head. "You do look

flushed," she says and then grins, sloppy and sweet. "Take care of my girl, okay?"

"Always," I say before I can stop myself.

Elle throws us both a wink and disappears back into the crowd, where Jack is waiting for her with one hand splayed out to continue dancing.

The crowd swallows her up, but my pulse is still racing. Manuela's eyes flick to mine, then to the exit. No words needed. We're already moving.

———

EVERY STEP of the short walk uphill to the house feels like winding a coil tighter and tighter. The night air is crisp and chilly, and it smells faintly of the rain we had this week. Manuela walks just ahead of me, the hem of her dress swaying against her thighs, and I swear I'm two seconds away from losing it right here on the street.

The villa is dim and empty, the only sound the low hum of the refrigerator and the pool jets outside. We go inside, and once we reach the stairs, she pauses with her hand on the banister, like maybe she's about to say goodnight.

Not a fucking chance.

I crowd into her space before she can get the words out, pressing her back against a door to a closet. Maybe it's a closet, I don't care. Her lips part on a sharp inhale, and then we're kissing—hungry, reckless, too far past pretending restraint is possible.

Her hands fist in my shirt, dragging me closer until I can feel every line of her body against mine. My tongue sweeps into her mouth, and she tastes like gin and lime, like something I could drown in if she let me.

"Upstairs," she murmurs, breaking just enough to breathe. Her normally blue eyes are dark, daring.

The climb is frantic, almost clumsy. I trip over the last step and laugh against her mouth, breathless and too far gone to care.

Inside my room, the door barely clicks shut before she pushes me against it. Her mouth finds mine again, desperate, hungry. My hands go to her hips, sliding up, tracing the zipper of her short dress.

"Slow," I rasp, though I'm not sure if I'm saying it for her or me. My pulse is everywhere—throat, fingertips, cock straining against my pants.

Her lips graze my ear. "Then make it slow."

The zipper gives way inch by inch, revealing warm skin, the strap of her bra, the dip of her spine. She shivers under my hands, and I bite back a groan because I don't think I've ever wanted anyone like this.

She turns, tugging me with her toward the bed. When she falls back on the mattress, blonde hair spilling wildly across my pillow, it steals the air from my lungs. I climb over her, not touching yet, just looking, memorizing the curve of her smile, the rise and fall of her chest.

"You're unreal," I murmur, and it slips out before I can stop it. Like my tongue is finally relaxed around her and I can actually say what I think, the moment I think it, instead of what is expected of me. This is what she does to me.

Her laugh is breathless. "Less talking, more fu—"

I cut her off with a kiss, slower this time, dragging it out until she arches up into me. My hands run through her soft skin—thighs, waist, ribs, the swell of her perfect tits through the lace of her bra. She moans softly when my thumb brushes her nipple, and I swallow the sound like it belongs to me.

Her hand slides down, tugging at my belt. "Connor," she whispers, urgency in the way she says my name.

I cover her hand with mine, pressing it to my chest. She has to feel what I'm feeling, how my body is out of control for her, heart thumping around my chest ready to take flight. "Not yet," I say as I breathe her in, that floral scent still stuck to her hair. "I want to take my time with you."

I move to push her down into the mattress, determined to taste her again, but she resists, firm palms against my chest. For a second, panic jolts through me—I've misread her, gone too far. But then the corner of her mouth tilts, and it turns into a full-on smirk, lighting up my every nerve ending as she pushes me back instead.

"My turn," she says, and the word comes out clumsy, drowsy, and thick.

She straddles me for a moment, kissing me like she owns every breath in my lungs, before rocking her hips a few times over my erection. I know if I looked down now, I would see a wet spot on my jeans, and that turns me on even more. She starts slipping lower, her lips trailing down my throat, over my chest, each press hotter than the last.

By the time she reaches my waistband, I'm half wild and impossibly hard, my hands fisting the sheets and my hips threatening to buck up before I can stop myself. She glances up at me through her lashes, a spark of mischief in her blue eyes as she lowers the zipper and starts removing my clothes.

I can't stay quiet. A groan rips from my throat, rough and broken, and I shove a hand over my face to muffle it. The moment her mouth is on me—the wet heat of her tongue and the sure slide of her lips over the head of my cock—my vision blurs. She takes her time, torturing me with every slow pass, every swirl that makes me whimper like a man starved, finally given what he's been craving for too long.

"Do you think you can be quiet for me, baby?" she says, and I know she's mocking me because her tongue flattens and drags all the way down to the base of my cock and then back up. Her eyes are shining, and I see the hint of a smile even as she sucks when she reaches the tip.

"Fuck, Manu," I choke out, my free hand tangling in her hair. She hums around me, and the vibration nearly unravels me on the spot. I'm panting now, sweat beading at my temples, fighting to hold on to some shred of control while she undoes me piece by piece. "You're going to ruin me."

She pulls back just enough to smirk up at me. "I don't know, maybe that's the idea." Her voice is husky, her mouth steady, and then she takes me deep again like she's proving a point.

My hips jerk despite my effort to stay still. I squeeze my eyes shut, then open them again, because watching her enjoy this is better than any fantasy I've ever had.

"Fuck," I whisper, half pleading. "Do you have any idea how good you look right now?"

Her free hand slides down over her own stomach, fingers sliding under her panties. I see it. I feel it, the shift in her breath, the faint tremor in her shoulders as she touches herself. The sight makes my whole body seize with want.

"Oh my god," I choke out, sitting forward slightly, one hand braced on the mattress. "You're touching yourself while you—" The words break off into a groan. I can't finish the sentence. My head tips back, and I bite my lip, desperate not to come too soon.

She hums low in her throat, the vibration wrecking me. Manuela pulls back again, licking her lips deliberately slow, her eyes locked on mine. "You like that?"

My laugh is broken, needy. "You're evil." I reach down, cupping her cheek, thumb brushing where her mouth glistens. "Beautiful and fucking evil."

Her grin is pure challenge. "Don't hold back on my account."

That's it.

My restraint cracks.

But instead of giving in to the way her mouth is undoing me, I bend down, scoop her up with one arm, and drop her on the bed. She lets out a surprised laugh that turns into a gasp when I open her legs and spread her knees apart.

"Con—" she starts, but I'm already on my knees, dragging my hands up her thighs slowly. Goosebumps erupt all over her skin, and her lashes flutter. I can see her pulse fluttering on her neck, and my hand drifts there, touching the softness right below her jaw.

"No one," I mutter against her skin, kissing the inside of her knee, "no one should look this fucking good."

Her breath stutters. "You probably say that to all the girls," she says with a laugh, and I know she's mocking me again, especially given that conversation we had the first night here.

"God." My voice comes out rough, and a smile starts to form on my lips. I remove her underwear slowly, dragging my hands slowly down her legs as I go along.

I kneel on the floor, settle between her legs, and lower my mouth to her. The first taste of her makes me groan against her clit, the sound vibrating into her body. She fists the sheets, arching up, and when I glance up, her head is tipped back, lips parted, eyes squeezed shut.

"Connie," she gasps, saying the nickname I hate so much. But from her lips, it has the potential to destroy me.

"Shh," I murmur, licking slowly, savoring her like we have all the time in the world.

Her hips roll against my mouth, small, helpless movements she can't seem to stop, almost like she's on autopilot. I anchor her with my hands on her thighs, greedy for every sound she makes. She moans, and I swear it shreds me in the best way possible.

I'm so hard it hurts, but I don't touch myself. I don't need to. Just the heat of her thighs trembling around me, the slick taste of her, the way she's coming apart in my hands—it's enough to push me right to the edge.

When her moans break into a sharp cry and her whole body goes taut, I come. Hard. No touch or hand or relief except the brutal, blinding release that tears through me just from giving her everything.

I collapse forward, forehead against her thigh, trying to breathe. She's still shaking, one hand in my hair, tugging gently like she knows exactly what just happened.

And she's smiling, wrecked and soft all at once, when I finally lift my head to meet her eyes. My chest heaves against the end of the bed, and the thought comes uninvited, unstoppable: I could get used to this.

I could get used to her.

24

———

MANUELA

SUNDAY

"Who the fuck is *we*?" I hear Jack say to Elle at the foot of the stairs. I'm slowly making my way down from my room, listening for any indication that what happened with Connor last night was witnessed by everyone. I'm still buzzing, still walking on air, still sore in places I didn't think I could be sore from simply being touched. From being wanted.

I slipped back to my own room before sunrise, careful as a thief, but my body hasn't gotten the memo. My lips still tingle from Connor's kisses, and my skin feels branded where his mouth was. I tell myself to pull it together, to walk down to breakfast like nothing happened, but the truth is written all over me. I feel it in every step.

"I thought he wasn't bringing someone," Jack continues, and I struggle to understand who he's talking about. "Apparently *their* suitcases took a while to come out of the baggage claim?"

"Jackie, babe, keep your voice down," Elle says. She's wearing her massively oversized glasses inside the house, and her hair is up at the crown of her head in the messiest bun I've ever seen from her. She definitely looks like she had a wild night out. "You're being too loud."

"Sorry, baby," he says, kissing her temple as he drags her into his body. "It's just a classic move. For all I know, it's someone he picked up on the plane. Jesus, my parents are going to be livid."

Elle sighs into her fiancé and wraps her hand around his waist. "We expected something like this from your brother." She looks up at Jack, and he pushes the hair off her face before cupping her cheeks. "At least we're prepared and it's not that big of a surprise."

The last step creaks as I make my descent, and both of them look up from their bubble at me. "Good morning," I say, but my voice comes out rough and weary, and I feel my cheeks instantly flush at the prospect that I've been messing around with someone from the friend group right under their noses.

"Oh, honey," Elle coos at me. She takes a few steps in my direction as I head towards the living room. "How are you feeling?"

I furrow my brow, and it takes me a few seconds to realize that was the excuse we used last night to get the hell out of that club and into this house. "Much better, thanks." I try to laugh in a light way, but it definitely comes out forced. "I think I had a little too much to drink with dinner."

Elle laughs and hooks her arm around mine, dragging me with all her petite force in the direction of the food. The dining room is lively already, and there's just a sliver of sunlight pouring through the glass doors. Storm clouds hover in the distance so similar to the past few days. The table is set with fruit and baskets of pastries, and there are three servers walking around taking personalized coffee orders.

Elle heads toward the end of the table and starts chattering about whatever happened last night, and Jack, who follows her, is laughing at everything she says. A few of the women and Banks are draped dramatically across their chairs, probably too hungover to function.

I slip into a seat, smiling when Elle beams at me from her spot, but my eyes betray me almost instantly. They find him.

Connor is across the table, early as usual, hair damp from a shower. He wears a simple shirt, nothing special or fancy, but he looks unfairly good in it. His eyes meet mine just for a second, no more, but it's enough to make my stomach flip. My fork trembles when I reach for a slice of melon.

Get it together, I scold myself. *No one can know.*

But the memory of last night is relentless. His mouth between my thighs. His voice rasping my name like he'd been starving. My own shamelessness, the way I'd given myself over to him with zero hesitation.

I sip coffee to hide my face, and the thought barges into my mind at full speed: I'm falling.

So dangerous because this was supposed to be a temporary pact. Just a little fun—and boy, has it been—tryst during our vacation. To get the edge off. To fully relax.

But he hasn't told anyone here about Athena, and to them, she's still his girlfriend. Although she's his ex, I have to remind myself constantly and sharply that she's still an invisible presence during this trip. And if anyone found out what we've been doing... it would be a mess. Worse, it would make me a villain. Not just to Connor, but to this entire group I've been quietly trying to be a part of for years at this point. One wrong move, and I could become a story they tell about the girl who ruined Elle's wedding.

The thought lodges in my chest, sharp and cold.

And what if this is just sex to him? What if it ends as quickly as it began?

And what about me? Do I even want more? I don't know if I'll stay in New York, if I'll go home or move elsewhere, if I'll stay anywhere long enough to risk my heart.

The tension in my chest loosens when Connor makes a quiet joke about the espresso being too strong, and Elle laughs, tipping her head back. He's good at this, sliding into the rhythm of the group. I'm the one off-balance, it seems.

I'm about to focus on my food when the front door slamming echoes down the hall. The room stirs, voices pausing at the abruptness.

"Honey," someone yells from the entryway. The steps start growing closer, and Jack's brother George glides out.

His dark blonde hair is tousled and shorter than what I remember from the last time I saw him a few months ago.

"Jesus," Jack mutters under his breath, shoving back his chair. "Of course."

George drops a backpack on the floor and stands, arms akimbo, studying the scene before him. His grin is wide, a little too self-satisfied, and he spreads his arms as if he expects applause. "We're home."

"You couldn't just walk in like a normal person?" Jack's voice is sharp, but there's a flicker of resigned affection underneath. "Always with the drama."

Whoever is standing behind him—a woman, by the looks of it, but I can't quite make her out—snorts at the comment. George claps his brother on the back, unfazed.

"What's life without a little spectacle, huh?"

And then, casually, almost as an afterthought, George steps aside.

Camila appears behind him, shoulders back, smile poised, like she knows the spotlight is about to swing her way.

My stomach drops, and the chair under me screeches as I lurch to my feet, napkin sliding uselessly down to my feet. "Camila?"

Her eyes widen just a fraction, and then she recovers, flashing that calm, composed grin she uses when we bump into each other in the kitchen after work, trading quick comments about groceries or laundry before heading back to our separate rooms.

"Manu." Her tone is light, but her gaze snags mine with razor-sharp intensity.

The room buzzes—Nicole's phone clatters to the table, and Amelia is leaning forward like she's watching a *telenovela* unfold.

"Everyone," George says, beaming at Camila next to him. Her smile drops a tiny fraction, almost imperceptible as he places his arm around her shoulders. "Meet my wife."

The word "wife" detonates across the room, and there's a collective gasp that is almost comical. Jack's jaw tightens. Elle blinks once, twice, and if she's sure she misheard.

"Since when?" Elle whispers under her breath, but it's easy to make out in the silence of the room.

I move toward her, fast, my pulse thrumming in my ears. She waves politely to the group, cheeks flushed like she knows how outrageous this reveal is.

"What the hell?" I whisper, low and harsh, the sound swallowed by the rising chatter around us.

Camila's hand brushes my wrist in warning, quick and subtle. Her smile never falters. "Later," she whispers, almost inaudible. "I'll explain later."

25

____

MANUELA

THE GONDOLA SWAYS as it lifts off the platform, the thick cables whirring overhead. The cars are painted red—-just like every train we've been on since arriving in Switzerland—with wide windows that promise panoramic views. My stomach dips at the jolt, but it's not the height that unsettles me. It's the way we're packed in, knee to knee, every word or sigh or laugh magnified in this cramped glass box.

Jack sits forward, elbow on his thigh, jaw tight. His gaze is pinned on a peak in the distance, already powdered with snow even though it's still technically summer. He hasn't loosened up since George and Camila's grand entrance this morning.

Meanwhile, George has taken on the role of unofficial tour guide. He gestures dramatically at the ridges and valleys below. "Best view in Switzerland, right here, people."

"Jesus," Jack mutters, loud enough for Elle to swat his knee. "Always with the performance."

Elle leans into him, resting her chin on his shoulder. "At least he's enthusiastic." Her laugh is soft, but her grip on Jack's arm is steady, like she's still absorbing the shock of her future brother-in-law showing up married. To my roommate.

I'm absorbing it too.

Across from me, Connor stretches out his legs, and the denim of his jeans brushes mine. He doesn't glance over, doesn't acknowledge the touch, but his thumb taps once against his knee. A nervous habit I've already memorized. He did it the first time we met on Elle's terrace, tapping against his glass, the same look on his face that he wears now—calm, unruffled, like nothing gets to him. Not even George's theatrics. Or Camila sitting across the gondola, perfectly poised, nodding along politely at George's droning narration.

"Stop manspreading, Connie," Nicole calls from the corner by the door, sipping from a water bottle I would bet anything isn't filled with water.

The group laughs, the sound bouncing off the glass walls. Connor leans back, smooth as ever, and says nothing. But his knee doesn't move from mine.

I shift slightly, tugging at the sleeve of my coat to disguise the smile threatening to give me away.

The crunch of our shoes on packed snow fills the silence as we step off the gondola and onto the ridge. The air bites instantly, sharp enough that I pull my jacket tighter around me even though it does nothing against this kind of cold. My breath fogs in front of me, curling white and fleeting. It reminds me so much of Tres Fuegos in July—those bitter, dark winter nights when the only light was the streetlamps and the glow of our own breath as we hurried home, past curfew and still giggling after a few underage drinks.

The entrance to the ice tunnel looms ahead, its archway carved smooth into the glacier. Blue light glints off every curve and angle, almost otherworldly, like we've stepped into some winter fairy tale. The short walk leads us deeper, the temperature dropping with every step, until our noses sting and my fingers ache even through the thick pockets of my coat. At the end, glowing warmly against the cold, is a door that opens into a tucked-away restaurant, wood-paneled and golden, the kind of cozy Alpine place you'd never find unless you knew someone.

George whistles under his breath. "You rented this whole thing out?"

"Of course he did," Nicole mutters, tugging at her scarf. "Wouldn't be Switzerland if we didn't have a private lunch at a glacier restaurant."

Elle squeezes Jack's hand, looking around with wide eyes, and for once George doesn't say anything, just beams like the king of surprises. Camila slips off her gloves beside me, her expression calm but her shoulders pulled straighter than usual, like she's bracing for every glance that lands her way.

I fall into step beside her, my voice low. "What the fuck is happening?"

Her laugh puffs out in the frosty air. "Surprise."

"Cami—"

"It's not what you think," she cuts me off lightly, smile still plastered on like she's taking it all in stride. "Paperwork stuff. I'll explain later."

I arch a brow, biting back everything I want to ask. "You could've given me a heads-up, you know. Just a little 'by the way, I'm marrying the groom's brother' text?"

She bumps my shoulder, conspiratorial. "I didn't exactly have time between city hall and the airport. Tonight, I promise. Over wine."

I should be annoyed, but the corners of my mouth twitch. We've been roommates for a while now, and in that time, I've never seen her bring anyone home except her friends, but that doesn't mean she hasn't been dating.

"It's a huge surprise, that's all," I say, walking in pace with her as we follow the rest of the group. "I didn't even know you were dating anyone."

Camila huffs a little laugh, breath fogging in the air. She drags her fingertips through the ice wall as we walk and shivers slightly as we get deeper into the cave. "That's because there wasn't anyone to tell you about. Not in the way you think, at least."

My brows lift. "Cryptic much?"

She shoots me a sly look, cleaning the tips of her fingers on her jeans. "Manu, just... don't worry. It's not what it looks like. George has his... reasons. And I have mine."

That only makes me more curious, but before I can push further, George turns around midstep and bellows some fact about the glacier's age, and Camila straightens like she's been caught whispering secrets. She gives me one last conspiratorial glance, quick and sharp, before slipping into her perfectly poised smile.

We step fully into the restaurant, and the sudden warmth makes my cheeks sting. The group fans out toward the long wooden tables, but Connor slows near one of the icy alcoves that branch just off the main tunnel, his shoulder brushing mine.

"Cold?" he murmurs, low enough that it doesn't carry.

"Freezing." My laugh fogs between us. "I can't feel my nose."

"Here." He tugs his red scarf loose and drapes it around my neck, fingers grazing my collarbone. The wool is still warm from his skin, and the gesture feels far more intimate than it should.

I tug it tighter, pretending to fuss with the ends. "You realize this makes us look like a couple in a Christmas card, right?"

His smile curves, subtle but deliberate. "Wouldn't be the worst look."

The words land too heavy in my chest, like he didn't just toss them off casually. My pulse stutters. "You're ridiculous," I whisper, trying to laugh, but it comes out thin.

Connor tilts his head, studying me, and for a second, I think he's going to say something more—something reckless. Instead, he leans in and presses a kiss to the corner of my mouth, so quick I almost doubt it happened until his breath ghosts against my cheek.

"Connor," I hiss, laughing under my breath, though my voice betrays me with how shaky it sounds. "We're going to get caught."

His grin is wicked, lighting his face in the dim glow.

But he doesn't move right away. His thumb lifts to brush the wool near my jaw, a touch that lingers longer than the kiss itself. Voices carry down the tunnel, louder now, the scrape of chairs and clatter of plates echoing from the restaurant.

"Connor," I whisper again but softer this time. Warning, plea, all mixed in one.

Instead of answering, he glances down the hall, then back at me, and in the next second, he catches my hand. Before I can react, he's tugging me into a side alcove where the tunnel curves, shadows swallowing us whole.

"Connor—"

He silences me with his mouth. Not careful this time. His kiss is hot and consuming, his body crowding mine until my back presses into the cold ice wall. The shock of chill against my shoulders makes me gasp, and he swallows it, his tongue sliding against mine like he's been waiting all day for this exact moment.

"Jesus," he mutters against my lips, his breath fogging in the air between us. "Do you know how hard it is not to touch you in front of them?"

He always looks unbothered, smooth, like nothing fazes him. But right now, with his voice rough against my lips, I finally see the crack in his composure. And it thrills me to no end.

The words unravel something inside me. My fingers fist in the front of his sweater, pulling him closer until I feel every line of him, solid and real. My pulse races so fast it drowns out the distant voices.

"We'll get caught," I murmur, though I'm not pushing him away.

"Then let's make it quick," he whispers and kisses me again, deeper, like he has no intention of stopping. His hands skim down my sides, firm and sure, before he finally drags them back up, cupping my jaw, framing me like I'm something he can't let himself lose sight of.

When he finally pulls back, we're both breathing hard, foreheads pressed together, the world outside this alcove feeling too far away to matter.

"We should go," I manage, though my voice is wrecked and my lips are tingling.

He smiles, quick and wicked. "Lead the way."

My chest is tight with laughter and panic both. We're walking back like nothing happened, but the taste of him lingers, sweet and dangerous, and I know I'll never get through lunch pretending I'm unaffected.

26

CONNOR

"DON'T LOOK DOWN."

The mountain air cuts colder out here, sharper than in the ice tunnel and hitting my skin like tiny little knives. It hits the back of my throat like glass shards as we spill onto the ridge, the group funneling towards the modern-looking suspension bridge strung between two peaks over the largest cliff I've ever seen in my life.

They talked about it on the way here, and I half listened while Banks rattled off fun facts. I was too focused on the way Manuela looked—her hair down around her shoulders and a mustard-color cardigan loosely draped on her body under her coat. I should have been paying more attention to the words because now I'm paralyzed at the edge, unable to move one single step forward.

"Connor." I vaguely hear my name being called from behind me, but I can't turn to look. Her voice threads through the roar of wind, steady and low, and it's the only thing keeping me from bolting back into the restaurant and parking my ass on a table far from here. "Connie."

Every sway of the cables shudders through me like aftershocks. My stomach knots, hard and fast, and I have to lock my jaw to keep myself from showing my panic. George bounds first, stomping his boots on the slats, making them jump.

"See? Rock solid."

He bounces once more for good measure, his laugh echoing across the gorge. Nicole and Hannah giggle behind him, both phones pulled out and recording his shenanigans. I should follow. I know I should, my brain knows it should. Easy—one foot, then the other. Pretend like it's nothing.

I can't.

"Hey." Manuela's voice again, closer. Her shoulder brushes mine as she eases in right next to me, her body slotting into the small space I've made by freezing up. "Eyes on me."

I drag my gaze from the drop to her face.

Her cheeks are pink from the cold, her breath fogging soft in the air, strands of hair blowing in the breeze and tangling across her face. She doesn't look impatient or even surprised. She looks steady and anchored right here next to me.

The breath that escapes me is shallow, harsh. "I can't do it," I say, the words dragged out like a confession.

And Manuela doesn't flinch. Doesn't tease me for being a panic-stricken man. "Then we don't."

The relief punches through me so fast I almost sag against her.

She loops her hand around my arm and backs us away from the bridge, angling her body between mine and the others, shielding me like it's second nature. We slip past a railing and toward a wooden bench tucked against the building where we just came from. The crunch of our shoes fades under the whistle of the wind as the group drifts farther out over the gorge, completely unaware of what's happening here on solid land.

I sink onto the bench, my palms slick with sweat as I drag them through my jeans. My heart still thuds like it's trying to break out of my chest, and my knees feel weak. The feeling is so similar to that night I ended up in the emergency department... And the worst part is how fast my body remembers. How quickly the old panic slots back in, like it's been waiting for an opening.

I told myself I'd change after that night. That I'd slow down, take care of myself, draw a line somewhere. That's the reason behind the failed hobbies.

But nothing really changed—not the hours, not the expectations, not the way I keep pushing long past the point my body begs me to stop.

It's not just the work, either. It's how easily I disappear into whatever people want from me. The role. The image.

The version of me that looks steady and untouchable even when I'm crumbling underneath it.

I've never admitted that out loud. Not to my parents. Not to my friends. Definitely not to the people at the office who still joke about how "unflappable" I am.

But right now, my hands won't stop shaking, and for the first time, I wonder if they can see it.

Manuela sits next to me without hesitation, close enough that her knee knocks mine.

"I don't know," she says, eyes sweeping across the horizon where snow-dusted peaks stab through the clouds and green fields are visible down below. "Better view from here anyway."

A shaky laugh works its way out of me. My breath fogs in front of us, breaking apart fast. "I guess I'm not built for dangling off cliffs."

"You don't have to be." She turns her head, lips curved in the smallest smile. "I like this version better."

That shouldn't undo me. It's not really much of a line. Maybe she's just saying that she recognizes I'm a city boy through and through, but it slips under my ribs and lodges deep, making my heart thump harder.

I grip the bench with both hands, grounding myself in splinters and cold, the air so thin it feels sharp in my lungs. I should probably joke back, maybe even relax my face and smooth all of this over with something easy and self-deprecating. That's who I am on the surface—smooth, unbothered, untouchable.

But all I manage is, "I hate not being in control." The words come out raw, scraped from someplace I don't usually let people see, except for maybe that nurse and my doorman.

She doesn't look away. "That's not a weakness." Her tone is matter-of-fact, like she's stating the color of the sky or the fact that we are at a very high altitude. Irrefutable. "Everyone's afraid of something."

I let out a humorless laugh, and she smiles softly in return. "Yeah? What scares you?"

"Not heights," she says and bumps me with her shoulder. "I'm from a mountain town, so this is quite literally just a walk in the park. But water…"

Manuela's smile twitches. She leans back against the bench, tilting her head toward the warm sun like she's debating how much to admit to me. "Deep water. Like, lakes. And the ocean. For a long time, I hated swimming. I wouldn't even get in a pool."

I glance at her, surprised. She shrugs, head still tilted towards the sun, eyes closed. "But then I made myself go back. Little by little. Now I do it, but it's not my favorite thing. And that's okay."

The cold air bites at my face, but her words sink warmly into me. I don't know why it matters so much—that she gave me a piece of herself so easily and that she chose to share it now, or even share it at all.

Her hand rests casually on the bench between us, not quite touching mine. Without thinking, I shift, brushing the back of my fingers against her knuckles. She doesn't pull again, but instead, her fingers turn just enough to hook into mine, not a full hold but enough to steady me more than the ground under my feet.

The bridge groans in the distance, the group's voices echoing back across the gorge. Any second now, they'll turn around, realize we're not with them. This moment won't last. A temporary pact that will be over the moment we step into an airplane and head back home.

And maybe that's why the truth hits me so hard.

Sitting here—my scarf still around her neck, her fingers warm in my hand, her smile soft in a way she doesn't show anyone else—-I know it's already too late.

The bridge terrifies me. But this? This is what's going to undo me.

"Want to get out of here?"

"Please," she says with a rush of breath, like she's been waiting for me to ask.

We fall into step, moving in the opposite direction of the others. The wind howls over the ridge, but the farther we get, the lighter my chest feels. At the gondola platform, the line of cars swings in a lazy rhythm, empty except for one that glides in with the doors yawning open.

Manuela pulls her phone from her pocket, thumbs flying quickly over the screen. "Texting Camila," she says before I can ask. "So she doesn't think we fell off a cliff."

I huff a laugh, more relieved than I should be, and step into the gondola after her. The doors hiss shut, sealing us into a glass bubble that rocks as the cables catch. Then we're moving, the mountain falling away beneath us, the whole valley stretching wide and endless below.

For the first time all day, it's just us. No noise or audience or the chance for eyes to be on us. Just Manuela pressed into the bench across from me. Her eyes lift to mine, and the silence crackles.

I cross the small space in one leap and drop into the seat beside her. She doesn't flinch and watches me with that steady, unblinking gaze that knocks me flat.

"You're impossible," I murmur, my hand finding her jaw, thumb grazing the warmth of her skin.

"Look who's talking," she whispers, and then she's kissing me.

Not cautious, not hidden like in the ice tunnel. This is open, full, the kind of kiss that swallows the air from my lungs and makes the world tilt. Her hands fist in my coat, dragging me closer until I can taste her laughter against my tongue.

The gondola sways, weightless, and for once, I don't care.

Because if falling feels like this—like her—then maybe I never want to stop.

27

MANUELA

THE HOUSE IS silent when we slip inside, our steps hushed even though we don't need to be. Everyone's still up there on the mountain, and it feels like we might be the only two people remaining in Switzerland by the sounds of it.

Here, in this moment, it's just us.

I can still feel the gondola swaying under my feet, the kiss pressed hard against my lips. My heart hasn't slowed since.

Connor glances around the empty living room like he doesn't trust the quiet. Then his grin cracks wide, all dimples and trouble. "We've got the whole place to ourselves."

I roll my eyes, but it comes out shaky. "Are you saying I should be worried?"

"Exactly." He steps closer, heat radiating off him. "You should be very worried."

Long gone is that man that looked terrified up in the mountain, and in his place is a cocky, confident one who drags his eyes from top to bottom, then stops at my lips before bringing his gaze to my eyes. I laugh, but it's cut off when his mouth finds mine.

It's nothing like the quick stolen kiss in the ice tunnel or the frantic one in the gondola. This is open and pressed-up-against-the-wall hungry, his hands sliding over my hips like he can't get enough.

My cardigan slides off one shoulder, half falling to the floor before I shove it the rest of the way. He breaks away long enough to glance down at the heap of fabric, smirking. "Finally."

I swat at his chest, breathless. "Shut up."

But he's already tugging me toward the stairs, kisses stuttering against my jaw, my throat, both of us laughing as we stumble dangerously up the steps. We bump into a door, then another, until he shoulders one open—

And I freeze. I mean, this house is ridiculous, but I was not ready for this level.

The bathroom is huge, probably double the size of the one in my room, warm tile glowing in the late afternoon light, and right in the center is a standalone tub big enough to fit four people. Beyond it, a picture window looks straight out over the lake glittering silver blue in the sun.

Connor glances back at me, smug. "Not bad, huh?"

"You knew this was here?" I demand, still staring. My brain is not computing how over-the-top this whole trip has been.

He smirks. "Of course I knew. It's my bathroom."

I shake my head, laughing as he pulls me inside. "You're annoying."

"Correct." He flashes me a grin, then tugs me forward. Clothes fall in a messy trail across the tile, laughter spilling between kisses. I shove at his jeans when they stick at this angle; he groans dramatically about my "patience issues."

Connor reaches back blindly and fumbles with the chrome tap until water gushes out, hot and loud against porcelain. Steam curls instantly into the air, fogging the glass as the lake outside blurs into smears of light.

"Multitasking," I tease, tugging at his underwear until it's gone.

"Try not to break my neck on the tile while you strip me," he shoots back, voice muffled against my mouth.

I laugh into the kiss, the sound swallowed when he presses harder, hungrier, until we're both half-undressed and the tub is nearly full. He twists the tap off without looking, then scoops me up like it's nothing.

"Connor..." I squeak, clinging to his shoulders as he lowers us into the water with a huge grin on his face. "You're going to flood the bathroom!"

"I don't give a shit," he mutters. The water is hot enough to sting before it soothes, a rush that makes me gasp. It rushes over my skin as he settles between my legs, the length of him pressing against me under the surface. His jaw drips, hair plastered to his forehead, eyes locked on mine like he's starving.

"This feels illegal," I whisper, staring past his shoulder at the massive window and the lake and mountains glittering beyond. His hand slides down, fingers teasing me under the surface, the heat of the water nothing compared to the way my body burns from the inside.

"Connor." My voice breaks.

"I've got you," he whispers, lips brushing the corner of my mouth. His free hand braces at my hip, steadying me as I arch into him. "Always."

The water rocks against the porcelain and sloshes high over the sides of the tub as he sinks his fingers into me, slow and deliberate, until I can't hold back the broken sound that rips from my throat.

"Jesus," he groans, forehead pressed into mine. "You feel—" His voice fractures into a curse that I don't understand, a dozen unintelligible words that make me flush with want.

My fingers fist in his wet hair, tugging him closer. "Move," I whisper, almost begging.

His laugh is low, ragged. "Give me a second, baby." But his fingers keep moving, steady and deep, each curl sending a ripple through the water and a sharper one through me, leaving me gasping.

I clutch his shoulders, nails digging into slick skin. His free hand slides up to cup my breast, thumb brushing lazily over my nipple until I moan.

Connor's breath is hot against my mouth, his rhythm faltering slightly. He pulls back just enough to catch my jaw, thumb dragging along my cheek. "Up," he murmurs, voice hoarse. I can see his pulse fluttering, and I want to lick him so bad. "Stand with me."

I blink at him, dazed, but his hands are already guiding me up. Water cascades down my skin, dripping loud against the porcelain as he straightens behind me. My legs tremble, but he steadies me easily, palms spanning my hips.

Our backs face the window now, and the golden hue of the late afternoon sun is streaking through the pane, casting long shadows in front of us.

Connor presses in close, chest to my back, his lips brushing the curve of my shoulder. One hand keeps me steady at my hip while the other trails up, slow and sure, cupping my breast, rolling my nipple between his finger and thumb.

"God, look at you," he rasps, grinding forward so I can feel every inch of his hard cock against the curve of my ass. "Turned on for me like this."

My hand slaps against the standalone faucet, desperate for something to hold on to. Heat floods my face as he fumbles briefly for a condom, the rip of foil sharp under the sound of water and my breath. He rolls it on with shaking hands, then grips my hip and sinks into me, slow but deep, the angle forcing me to arch back into him. The water ripples wildly around our calves, splashing with every thrust, but I don't care.

"Look," Connor rasps, his hand leaving my hip to tilt my chin toward the wide mirror over the sinks. Our reflections glow in the golden light, steam curling around us, my body bent against his, his body moving with mine, the raw need in his expression—like he's never seen anything so perfect. I'm shaking.

"Oh…" It's half a plea, half a curse.

"Yeah," he groans, biting at my shoulder before dragging his tongue over the mark. "Say it. Tell me you see it."

The words catch in my throat, tangled with moans, but the truth slips out anyway. "I see it. God, that's so hot."

He drives into me harder, and the reflection of our bodies blurs through the steam. His arm wraps around my waist, pulling me against him, his other hand sliding down to touch my clit until I'm gasping again, eyes locked on the image in front of us.

His fingers circle, working me in time with his hips, until I'm whimpering, every nerve sparking like the sunlight burning through the window. My body clenches tight around him, pulling him deeper, sharper, until the pressure crests so hard it's almost unbearable.

"We're perfect like this," he growls, breath hot against my ear. "Fucking perfect."

The words detonate inside me. My vision blurs, the lake and the mountains in the mirror smearing gold and white and green beyond the glass, but I can feel him inside me and against me, everywhere.

He drives in once, twice more before he follows me over, hips jerking, forehead pressing to the back of my neck. His arm tightens around me like he's afraid I'll vanish, like I'm the only thing tethering him here.

We sag together, trembling. "You're unreal, Manu. Absolutely fucking unreal."

"Connor," I choke out, holding on to the arm wrapped around me, breath slowly leveling. For a long moment, the only sound is our breathing, ragged and uneven, the water moving faintly around our thighs.

"I've got you," he whispers again. I sag back against his chest, still trembling, his hand smoothing over my stomach, up to cup my breast, then back down like he can't stop touching me. He kisses the wet curve of my shoulder, softer now, reverent.

My pulse finally begins to slow, but the ache in my chest doesn't ease. This was supposed to be easy. Temporary. A no-pressure thing.

Instead, I'm standing here, watching us in the mirror, my body still echoing with him, my heart hammering like I've just admitted something I can't take back.

28

CONNOR

WE STAY TANGLED for a long moment, water rocking lazily against us. She's holding on to my forearm, fingers tight around the muscle, unwilling to let me drift even an inch away.

Finally, she shifts, skin sliding against mine. "This bathroom is destroyed," she murmurs, her voice hoarse and teasing. Another wave tips over the side of the bathtub, splattering onto the tile.

I huff a laugh and kiss her temple. "Yeah, I'll throw some towels down or something."

I guide her up carefully, steadying her slippery legs as she climbs out of the tub. She's flushed, hair plastered to her skin, and I swear my chest aches just watching her. I grab a couple of white hotel-sized towels from the warming rack and toss them onto the puddles in a half-assed attempt to mop the floor. She snorts at me, wrapping herself in one of her own.

"Impressive cleanup skills," she says, deadpan.

"Finance degree," I mutter, grinning, "and honestly, have you seen my friends? It's like I minored in damage control."

Manuela's laugh is low, warm. God, I want to bottle that sound up and carry it with me everywhere I go, open it when things get bleak and stressful and my life is directionless.

I tug on a towel myself, then pull her into the hallway, our wet footprints streaking across the wood floor. We make it through the obscenely big closet and into the bedroom. The space is warm with late-afternoon light, windows stretched wide across the far wall, the lake glittering beyond them. She hesitates at the foot of the bed, hair dripping down her shoulders, leaving tiny dark spots on the floorboards. I can see the thought flicker across her face—the house is still empty but not for long.

"An hour, maybe," I say, brushing a strand of hair behind her ear. "They'll probably stop somewhere else for drinks before dinner."

She nods once, like she's agreed to some unspoken pact, and then I'm kissing her again, walking her backward until the backs of her knees hit the edge of the bed. She tumbles onto the duvet with a surprised laugh, pulling me down after her.

The shift from the hard surfaces of the bathroom to soft sheets and golden afternoon light feels... different. Quieter. More dangerous.

I settle on my side, propped on one elbow, tracing idle lines over her towel-covered stomach. She looks at me like she's not afraid of what she'll see, and it makes me want to tell her everything I've never said out loud.

"When I was a kid," I hear myself say, "I used to sit out by this, like... pond at the back of my parents' property every summer. My parents were inside, some dinner party going on, or maybe they were working, and I'd just... stare at the water and pretend it was endless."

She turns towards me, her expression soft. "Did you swim?"

I shake my head. "Not really. Just skipped rocks. Climbed trees. Told myself I'd run away but never got farther than the end of the driveway." My lips twist into something that's maybe a half smile. "I liked knowing I could leave. Even if I didn't."

Her hand comes up, thumb brushing along my jaw. She studies me for a long beat as she drags her palm through the stubble there.

"Huh," she whispers. "Funny. I thought leaving would fix everything."

I blink at her and study her face. She looks far away, like she's going back home and thinking about growing up. She mentioned she's from a small town, and I wonder how tight that felt—if it was anything like growing up for me.

"And in some ways, it did. I got my dream job, got to start over. But in New York..." She pauses, eyes searching mine, like she's not sure she wants to admit it. "In New York

I feel invisible. Like everyone else is sprinting past me, and I'm still trying to catch up. And then I come home, and I don't fit there anymore either. Too New Yorker for Argentina, too Latina for New York."

Her honesty twists something deep in me. My chest aches. I brush a wet strand of hair from her cheek, tucking it gently behind her ear.

"I get that," I say quietly. My voice doesn't sound like mine—too raw, too unguarded. "I don't belong anywhere either. I've spent years in a job I hate, chasing numbers I don't care about, pretending to be the guy my family wants me to be. The one who makes partner, gets married, raises kids in the suburbs. But I'm exhausted, Manu. Burnt-out to the bone. I wake up and feel like I'm already drowning."

Most days it's like my body refuses to cooperate. My hands shake when I hold my coffee. I forget to eat. I lie awake until three in the morning even when I'm so tired I can't see straight. And then I get up and do it all again, like a machine that's one tiny inconvenience away from breaking.

Her eyes widen, but she doesn't pull away. She listens, and that makes me keep going.

"I ended things with Athena because she deserves more than me half-present, half-pretending. But without her, without my job... I don't even know who I am. Or what I want... I just know I can't keep going like this."

The words sit heavy in the air but lighter in my chest. Like saying them out loud, finally, to her of all people, has carved out space for something else to grow.

"Guess we're both still figuring out how to stay and how to go," I murmur.

She leans into me, her forehead pressing to mine. "Connor?"

"Yeah?"

"This is going to ruin us, isn't it?"

The question slices through my chest. I should tell her no. I should promise this is just fun, temporary, what we agreed to. But I can't. Not when her eyes are this close and I still taste her on my lips.

"Maybe," I say, my thumb stroking her hip. "But right now, I don't care."

Her breath leaves her in a rush. She kisses me, slow and lingering, not fire this time but something heavier that feels like giving in.

I kiss her back, but the panic coils anyway. She curls into me, soft and certain, and all I can think is that I don't know how to bring her into the life waiting for me. I don't even know if I want to.

Not if it means pulling her into the grind that hollows me out, into the constant proving and performing and pretending I'm fine. Into the version of my life that looks perfect on paper but has never once felt like I controlled it.

So I hold her tighter, press my chin to her hair, and pretend we have more than an hour before the rest of the world comes crashing back.

29

CONNOR

MONDAY

I FEEL her before I see her.

The faint shift of the mattress, the slow drag of fabric as she sits up. For a moment, I think I imagined it, still caught between sleep and whatever dream I was in, but then there's a pause. That hush of someone purposely staying still and holding their breath.

We drifted together last night sometime after the last round of kisses faded, after her laugh went quiet against my chest and our breaths evened out. Her legs tangled in mine, her hand splayed over my heart like it belonged there. I don't know when sleep finally claimed me—just that it was the first time in months I didn't fight it.

And now she's slipping away.

My first instinct is to open my eyes and reach out to her, pull her back down into the sheets, and wrap her in whatever this is. But something in the quiet keeps me still. I let my breaths stay slow and even, like I'm asleep, and listen as she rises.

The room is gray with early light, the mountains just catching the edge of sunrise. Manuela lingers there beside me, the weight of her presence warm. I can feel her eyes on me—the way she's watching me like she's memorizing something she isn't sure she'll get to keep.

My chest aches with the urge to tell her she's wrong. That she doesn't have to go. That I don't want her to.

Instead, I stay quiet, eyes closed, and let her slip out. The soft pad of her feet on the wood floor, the faint creak of the door, the click as it closes. The silence she leaves behind is deafening.

I don't fall sleep again but instead linger in a drowsy state until my alarm rings next to me two hours later.

By the time the sun edges over the peaks, I'm showered, dressed, and heading across the resort grounds. The mountain air bites, crisp enough to shock the fog from my head, and the path crunches beneath my sneakers.

The main building smells like coffee and yeast the second I step inside. Someone directs me downstairs to the kitchen, where stainless-steel counters gleam under fluorescent lights. Aprons hang from hooks, bowls and scales lined neatly in rows. A few other guests file in, already chattering, but I claim a spot at the end of a worktable, hidden in plain sight.

It's not lost on me that I could be sleeping in or joining the others on whatever lazy breakfast Elle has planned for the morning. Instead, I'm here. Signing up for a sourdough class in Switzerland like it's the most natural thing in the world.

The truth is, I've tried a dozen times. Starter after starter, loaf after loaf. All failures—dense, flat, nothing like the crisp, airy crumb I see online. The bag of flour in my pantry at home has a permanent rubber band twisted around its neck like a sad little reminder. My fridge has held more dead starters than meals. Just like all my other failed hobbies—the guitar lessons that I started but quickly quit because I couldn't make them fit in my schedule. The different types of diets and healthy lifestyles I tried, the membership to the luxury gym across the street from my office building.

It's all just been me trying to feel something. Trying to prove to myself that I'm not as numb as I've felt for months.

The instructor—a cheerful woman with hair tied in a scarf—starts explaining ratios, hydration percentages, patience. That last word sticks. Patience.

"Most people try to rush this part," she says as she moves down the workstations, checking our bowls. "But if you push it, the dough pushes back. Sourdough needs time to wake up. Like teenagers."

A few people laugh.

She stops at my station, peering into my bowl. "First time?"

"Not exactly." I keep my tone light, though I can feel the corners of my mouth twitch. "I've... attempted a few times. Usually ends with something closer to a paperweight than bread."

She grins, unfazed. "Then this is the place to redeem yourself."

"Or confirm I'm a lost cause," I mutter, which earns me a quiet chuckle from the guy to my left—a wiry older man with a salt-and-pepper beard and a camera strap across his chest.

"Don't worry," he says. "My first loaf could have doubled as a doorstop."

"Same," the woman on my right adds without looking up from her mixing. "My starter actually *exploded* once."

That pulls a surprised laugh out of me before I can stop it. The sound feels strange in my own mouth, unfamiliar among these strangers.

I measure flour and water, stir slowly, watch the mixture come alive under my hands. And something clicks. Not the bread—it'll take days before this turns into anything edible. But the process. The slowness. The lack of shortcuts.

I think about my job, about the deal chasing and the endless need to deliver faster, bigger, more. About my father's voice on the phone, pushing me toward the next role, the next title, the next version of the man he thinks I should be. Settled. Perfect on paper.

And then I think about Manuela. About how she looked at me in the dark this morning, silent but certain. About how she makes me want to be someone who notices the process instead of just the result.

By the time the dough is resting under a towel, I know two things: one, I'll never hear the end of it if Banks finds out

I voluntarily took a baking class. And two, when I get back to New York, something has to change.

Because if I keep going the way I've been going—if I keep measuring myself against expectations I never asked for—I'll burn out for good.

———

THE SUN IS ALREADY high by the time I leave the main building, the gravel warm under my shoes as I walk the short downhill path back to the house. The paper bag crinkles under my arm with every step, the loaf still radiating faint heat through the thin layers. The front door's propped open with a rock, voices drifting faintly from inside, slow and unhurried.

Manuela's on the steps, one knee bent, phone pressed to her ear. Her voice carries across the quiet lawn, rapid and certain, threaded with a laughter I don't hear often enough. Something in my chest pulls tight before I can stop it.

She catches sight of me as she hangs up and places the phone screen down on the step. "You're up early," she says, her face studying me.

"I felt you sneak out of my bed," I say, letting it come out low, easy. "Couldn't fall back asleep after."

Color creeps into her cheeks, but she doesn't look away. "So you got up instead? It was, like, four in the morning." She chuckles to herself, and the image makes me smile. Her sitting on the front stoop, a faint breeze running through her hair.

"Figured I'd make the most of it," I reply, holding up the crinkled paper bag. "I took a baking class at the resort."

Her mouth curves. "That's... I didn't know you baked."

I lower onto the step below hers, setting the bag on my lap. "I don't."

Manuela laughs, tipping her head back slightly, like this is the most amusing thing she's heard all week.

"I've tried before. At home. They've all been disasters," I continue, wanting to spill all my secrets to her. How I've been trying different things to see if I can find myself again. How nothing is sticking. "Maybe if I learned from someone who actually knows what they're doing instead of trying to copy people from the Internet, I'd finally get it right."

"And?" There's a shine in her eyes and a smile so big that the corners get crinkly, and I think it's the most genuine one I've seen yet.

"Not even close." I let out a breath, leaning back on my hands. "But I don't care. It felt good just doing it, for me."

Her mouth softens, and for a moment, she just looks at me, quiet in a way that feels new. Then her gaze flicks toward the lake.

"Who were you talking to?" The question leaves my mouth before I can stop it. It's not casual at all and doesn't sound like me. Because I never ask things like that. I'm not one to ever want to know more than what people choose to offer.

But with her, I do.

I want to know who is calling her this early, who can make her laugh like that. What her mornings are usually like, what songs she hums when she's distracted, what she reaches for when life caves in. All of it.

She blinks, surprised, like she wasn't expecting me to care. "My old boss," she says after a beat. "From Buenos Aires."

"Yeah?"

"She said there's an opening at the agency. If I want it." She pulls at a loose thread on her sleeve, not looking at me. "It'd be a good move for my career. But..."

The words hang there, heavier than she probably meant them to.

"Do you want it?"

"I don't know," she finally says, her voice low. "Probably not. I like my job in New York, despite my asshole boss."

I watch her, the morning light sharp on her cheekbones, and something twists low in my chest before I can stop it. She draws her knees up, wrapping her arms loosely around them, eyes still on the lake.

Footsteps crunch on the gravel behind us. Someone calls her name—Amelia, judging by the voice—and Manuela stands, brushing her hands down her leggings like she's shaking something off.

"Guess we're officially awake now," she says lightly, offering me a small smile before heading toward the house.

I stay where I am a moment longer, the paper bag still warm on my lap, before I push myself to my feet and follow.

30

MANUELA

"Alright, party people," Hannah says from her seat in the living area. She's wearing a flowy sundress that reaches the floor, and a floppy hat rests on her lap. "What do we think about exploring independently today?

"Our hosts are off brunching with Elle's family, and we're unsupervised children. Thoughts on a village trip?"

"Define trip," Banks says from his lounge on the opposite couch. He's slouched low, ankles crossed, looking like hasn't moved in hours. Late-morning light pools across the living room, glinting off Banks's sunglasses where they sit crooked on his head.

"Casual," Hannah replies. "Maybe some coffee, window shopping. Just into the little town downhill."

"Cash and I are going to sit by the lake all day if anyone wants to join," Amelia says. Her voice is a little hoarse, like the trip is finally catching up to her. I feel the same way—

somewhat exhausted from everything we've done in the past week but also relaxed and loose from the change of pace. Cash perks up from the floor where he's sprawled with a sudoku book, lifting one hand in a lazy wave of solidarity.

"I'm in for going down into town," Nicole says, appearing from the hallway. Her hair is damp, braided over one shoulder, and she's wearing the kind of crisp linen set that somehow never wrinkles. "Could use actual caffeine. Not... whatever Banks got me this morning."

"It was artisanal," Banks mutters.

"It was sludge, babe." She sinks into the empty seat beside him, tucking her sunglasses on top of her head.

"Town it is," Hannah declares, standing and smoothing her dress. "Let's aim for ten minutes?"

The group scatters with varying levels of enthusiasm. Connor passes me on his way upstairs, fingers brushing the small of my back like it's a reflex, like he doesn't even mean to. My heart leaps into my throat before I can stop it. I make a quick change into something a little bit more appropriate than my lounge pants and then head out.

Outside, the air is cool enough that I pull on a cardigan over my dress. We fall into pairs and loose clusters as we start downhill, the path curling through tall pines. The lake glints silver behind us, and at the bifurcation in the road, Amelia and Cash drift off.

Nicole drifts a few steps ahead, talking to Hannah about some new gallery opening in New York. Banks lags behind, complaining halfheartedly about his shoes to Sterling, who is half listening as he scrolls on his phone.

Connor ends up beside me. He doesn't touch me this time, just lets our arms swing close enough that they almost brush.

"You okay?" he asks quietly.

I glance at him. "Yeah."

He nods once, accepting it without pressing, and for some reason that makes my chest ache more than if he'd pried. The conversation we had outside of the house just this morning makes me feel raw.

Because I meant it—what I told him about not knowing where I belong—but I also hated how small it sounded once it was out in the air. Like I was still waiting for someone else to tell me where my life should happen. I hate that I sound like a broken record, but it's definitely the heaviest weight on me right now.

I think that's what unsettles me now: that quiet, steady kind of trust. It makes me realize how much of my life I've spent bracing for pushback, defending my choices before I've even made them.

But here, with him, I don't feel like I have to defend anything.

The roofs of the village peek through the trees as we round a bend—timbered and steep-gabled, standing firm there for centuries and rooted at the heart of this little section of the world. The air shifts, carrying the smell of bread and something sweet.

"Coffee first," Hannah calls over her shoulder, already picking up her pace. "Then shops."

Connor glances at me as the cobblestones come into view. "Coffee first," he echoes, like it's a promise.

We spill into the narrow main street like marbles scattering from a jar. Flower boxes spill color from window ledges, hand-painted signs swinging gently overhead.

Ten minutes later, coffee in hand from a tiny yellow side-window café, our group has scattered, and the cup's warmth hums through me.

Connor glances at me over the rim of his mug. "Want to walk?"

I do. Maybe too much. "Sure."

We drift through the winding streets in an unhurried silence. Cobbled alleys curve off in every direction, each one lined with shuttered windows and overflowing flower boxes. Somewhere nearby, a church bell tolls the hour.

It's peaceful in a way that makes me want to breathe deeper, slower. Like the world isn't rushing anywhere.

Connor stops at a rack of postcards outside a stationery shop, thumbing through them lazily. "These look fake," he says. "Like stock photos."

"They're real," I counter, picking one with a watercolor of the lake and holding it up to the actual view behind us. "See? Perfect match."

He huffs a laugh. "Fine. Real. Still feels like a movie."

At the edge of the square, a narrow path cuts up a gentle hill, wildflowers stippling the slope. Edelweiss cluster low to the ground, pale against the green. A little ahead, Camila and George slip up the trail, their heads tipped close together.

"Want to?" he asks, nodding after them, a smile tugging at his mouth.

"Obviously."

He laughs lowly, like he expected me to say no. The path is barely wide enough for two, so we fall into step side by side, arms brushing now and then. The air smells like grass warmed by sun, and for once, nothing feels sharp or heavy.

"What's the deal with those two?" he asks after a stretch of quiet, nodding toward Camila and George a little way ahead. She shoves him off the path, laughing so hard she nearly folds in half, and he catches her by the waist, spinning her in a circle. Their laughter carries down the valley, loud and wild.

"I have no idea," I admit. "She mentioned something about her immigration stuff, but I don't really know how they even met. Or why. The real why." I pause, watching them. "She'll tell me when she's ready."

"You didn't know she was seeing someone?"

"Not a clue."

"How do you know her?"

"She's my roommate."

He stops midstep, blinking at me like in surprise. "Get the fuck out of here. That seems... statistically improbable."

"Agreed." The smile slips out before I can stop it.

He grins back, shaking his head like he's still trying to

make the math work, and we keep climbing. The slope steepens, and our shoulders knock once, then again.

Halfway up, he pulls his phone from his pocket. "We should prove we were here," he says.

He angles the camera, and I lean in. The screen catches us framed by wildflowers, wind pushing my hair into his face. We both laugh, breathless from the climb.

Connor doesn't move for a moment after taking the photo. Just looks at me like he's still memorizing this—like he wants to keep it.

I swallow, suddenly aware of how quiet it is. How far the others feel from here.

Then he tucks the phone away, brushing his thumb across my knuckles as our hands find each other like it's nothing.

We don't say anything for a while.

The path flattens near the top, spilling out into a small grassy overlook. The village shrinks below us—red roofs clustered like puzzle pieces, the lake glittering just beyond. Bells echo faintly from somewhere on the far side of town, thin and distant, like they're meant for someone else.

Connor lowers onto a smooth boulder and pulls me down beside him. Our knees brush. I let it happen.

A breeze tugs at my hair, and I push it behind my ears, suddenly aware of how still he is. Usually, he's always in motion—tapping a finger, shifting his weight, checking the time like he's bracing for the next thing. But now... nothing. Just quiet, like he's not waiting to be anywhere else.

"Feels like we're a million miles from them," I say, nodding vaguely toward the square far below.

"Yeah," he says softly. "Kind of nice."

The sun warms my shoulders. I curl my fingers more firmly around his, and he lets me.

It's not big or dramatic. Simply... steady. Like he's here, really here, and not halfway in his head the way I've seen him sometimes. And it does something to me. Makes my chest feel both heavy and light at once, like I don't quite know what to do with it.

He glances sideways, the corner of his mouth tilting. "You're quiet."

"So are you."

He lets out a small breath of a laugh, then tilts his head back to watch a bird wheel high overhead. His profile is sharp in the sunlight, but his eyes are softer than I've ever seen them.

"I don't do this," he says after a while. "The... stopping part."

"Neither do I," I admit.

And somehow, that feels like the most honest thing I've said all trip.

We sit there until the wind picks up and the smell of bread drifts up from the town below. The kind of smell that means it's time to move again, even if I don't want to.

Connor squeezes my hand once before standing, pulling me with him. For the rest of the walk down, he doesn't let go.

31

———

MANUELA
TUESDAY

"UGH, LOOK AT IT," Elle says, pushing her large sunglasses up her nose and into her hair as she stares at the view from where we are. "It's perfect."

The path climbs gently behind the house, gravel crunching beneath our shoes, the air so clean, it almost stings. Bells clang faintly in the distance, and I can see brown cows scattered across the hillside like someone—the resort, most likely—placed them there just for the ambiance. Banks veers off to take a selfie with one and yelps when the cow noses at his ear, trying to lick at him.

Of course everyone bursts out laughing. My smile comes a second later, like always.

By the time we reach the overlook, the scene looks curated—tables draped in linen, chilled bottles of wine beading in the hot sun, platters of cured meats, cheeses, figs, olives. Umbrellas cast striped shadows, and the lake glimmers far below, framed by mountains jagged enough to look unreal.

After the rain we had last week, the weather has turned, and it feels like an absolute summer day in the mountains.

I take a seat at the edge, grateful for the space, and watch the group splinter into smaller pockets. Elle floats around like a conductor—directing who should pour, who should sit, where the sun is best for photos.

Connor is across the table, sleeves rolled, hair mussed in the casual way that makes it impossible to look anywhere else. I drag my gaze to the cheese platter, then the lake.

Anywhere but him.

George sits stiffly near Jack, and I catch a piece of their argument slipping between bites of fresh bread.

"What are our parents going to say?" Jack hisses, barely containing himself.

George leans back in his low chair, smirking like he's rehearsed this. "They'll live."

"Reckless, that's what it is. You've outdone yourself this time, brother."

George pops an olive in his mouth and doesn't bother replying. Elle pretends not to notice, but her hand trembles when she lifts her glass. Her expression is a pleasant one, but she's hiding behind those oversized sunglasses again, and I can't read her. The silence that follows is the heavy kind, the one that sticks even when someone changes the subject.

I reach for my water as Camila slides into the empty seat beside me, as poised as if she's walked straight out of a magazine spread. The breeze catches her hair, loose today, softening the sharpness I usually associate with her.

"You knew I was in Switzerland," I say, keeping my voice low. This whole thing with George is still an enigma to me, and I'm trying to understand what is happening here.

Her mouth curves. "I did."

I turn, frowning. "A heads-up would have been nice."

"What are the odds it was the same wedding?" she replies, sipping from her glass. That perma-smile is back on, almost performative, because she knows all eyes are on her. Maybe she's feeling the same way I do on the regular—observed and a little out of place—and the shock is still running rampant through her system.

"What are the odds it was the same country, Cami?"

She tilts her glass toward the lake, watching as the sunlight breaks into shards against the surface. She says nothing, just lets the silence stretch until Nicole calls for more wine and Camila drifts away with a shrug, moving back towards her husband as if our conversation never happened.

Connor moves then, coming up behind me with a plate in hand. He leans close to set it down, his fingers grazing my shoulder so lightly it could be nothing. But I feel it everywhere, an impossible spark that shoots through me.

"Here you go, baby," he murmurs, soft enough that it could pass as casual but not soft enough to miss.

I freeze, smile pasted on, praying no one saw or heard—until Nicole's eyes flick up, sharp and glittering, watching.

My throat tightens, but I laugh at something Elle says,

too bright and too late. Connor catches my gaze and holds it for half a breath too long. It's enough.

For a few hours, plates circle, glasses clink. Banks launches into a story about losing his wallet on the subway, and Amelia nearly chokes on her fig tart, laughing. Elle eggs him on, fanning herself dramatically. The mood lightens, but it feels thin, stretched like fabric that could tear with one wrong tug.

Elle sets her glass down with a little flourish, the sun catching the rim, and claps her hands once. "Okay, new game. No one leaves this table until they share their favorite part of the trip so far. And no repeats, so be creative."

A chorus of groans rises from the picnic table, good-natured but dramatic, the sound drifting out over the wide sweep of sky and down toward the lake. Elle, of course, looks delighted. She waves the complaints off like the benevolent dictator she is. "I'll start," she says, then pauses, eyes sparkling. "Actually, no. I'll go last. Camila, George—you don't get to play. You just got here."

Camila laughs, leaning back on her hands on the picnic blanket next to the table, her bracelets catching the sun. George mutters something low, jaw tight. Jack's head snaps toward him, sharp, his reply too quiet for me to listen to but edged with warning. The tension slices through the edges of the group, a private argument wrapped in hushed voices —*stop making a scene*—until everyone else looks down at their plates and pretends to be absorbed in bread and cheese.

Banks doesn't even wait to be called on. Still chewing, he

raises a hand and points at the spread in front of us—platters of cheeses, cured meats, bread still warm from the oven. "The food. Every single meal. I mean"—he gestures with a hunk of bread—"this is the best picnic I've ever had in my life. No contest."

A ripple of laughter moves through the circle. Amelia leans forward, giggling before she even speaks. "The spa. Obviously. Those facials? I'm still glowing." She fans her cheeks, nails glinting a fresh pale pink. "Also, the shopping." Her grin is wicked, like she's in on an inside joke I'm not privy to.

Sterling stretches out on his elbows, tan arms gleaming in the late-morning light, and smirks. "The hotel gym's pretty great. Haven't missed a single day, thank you very much."

Cash groans, tossing a grape at him. "Of course you'd say that." He waves his phone like proof. "Mine's the Wi-Fi. Strong enough to stream football in the middle of the Alps? That's a gift from the heavens."

The laughter this time is louder, looser, folding into the warm air.

Elle, queen of the circle, points across with a perfectly manicured finger. "Nicole. Go."

Nicole sets her wineglass down carefully, like the moment requires gravitas. "The house," she says smoothly, voice soft and deliberate. "Obviously. It's spectacular. And thank you to our generous hosts." She tilts her chin toward Elle and Jack, gracious, but then her gaze flicks sideways— barely a beat, but enough that I feel it—before returning to her glass. "Feels like the kind of place you'd want to share with someone special, doesn't it?"

The words hang there, sweet on the surface, but my skin prickles under them. I smooth the hem of my dress over my knees, focusing on the fabric instead of her tone.

Elle, unbothered, barrels on. "Connor?"

He shifts slightly where he's sitting, gaze tipped out toward the mountains. "The waterfall." His voice is even, but something in it carries.

A soft hum moves through the group—impressed, curious, maybe a little envious. Elle grins. "Good one." Then her eyes land on me. "Manu, your turn."

The air sticks in my throat, just for a second. I force my voice to be casual. "The fondue. It was... unexpected." My cheeks burn anyway. Out of the corner of my eye, Connor doesn't move, but I see the subtle tap of his finger against his knee, steady and restrained.

Across the table, Nicole scoffs—audible, sharp, meant to cut.

The smile slides right off my face, and my skin burns even hotter. "I'm sorry, did I say something that offends you?"

Her head jerks up, brows arched like she's the one being attacked. "Excuse me?"

"You heard me," I say, voice steady even though my pulse is hammering. "You've been sniping at me since we got here. What is your problem?"

I'm nonconfrontational to a fault, more so since living in the United States, where communication styles are different than what I'm used to—less direct and more... worked around. So my words make my chest tighten, a rush of blood running through my ears, and it's the only thing I can listen to.

Her glass clinks against the table as she sets it down. "I don't have a problem with you. This trip is about Elle and Jack, not... whatever this is."

I laugh, but there's no humor in it. "I've been nice, polite, and tried to fit into your circle ever since I met you, and I can never get the same treatment in return."

A ripple of silence moves through the group. No one looks directly at us, but everyone's listening. From the corner of my eye, I can see Elle's parted lips, her hand flattened on the tabletop.

Nicole parts her lips, shocked, but I don't let her answer. "If you'd actually looked closer, you might have noticed we have a lot in common. Starting with our love of thrifting, of collecting things that feel unique, that feel like they belong to us. But you've been too busy being bitter over who knows what to really see it."

Elle shifts, ready to jump in, but the damage is done.

Nicole blinks at me, stunned for half a second, and then her jaw sets. "Bitter? Don't flatter yourself. You've made this trip about you since the second you got here. And we're supposed to be celebrating our friends."

My chest goes tight, anger flashing hot. "That's bullshit. I've done nothing but try to be included, to show up, to be polite even when you've been dismissive and smug. If that looks like me making it about myself, maybe that says more about you than me."

Her mouth opens, closes, a faint flush creeping up her neck. "I don't know what fantasy you're living in, but I don't go around being rude for no reason."

I let out a sharp laugh. "No reason? You've made it very clear what the reason is. You've decided I don't belong here, so you don't have to bother being decent. But news flash, Nicole: not everything revolves around who you grew up with and who you deem worthy of your approval. Just because I'm an outsider doesn't mean I'm less."

The air feels thinner, every breath catching. No one moves. Elle's smile is frozen, her hand clamped tight around her glass stem. Even Banks has gone quiet.

I push myself to my feet, brushing crumbs from my dress, my pulse a roar in my ears. "If you'll excuse me."

For one suspended second, no one speaks, but I catch a faint twitch in Connor's mouth. Then he is up, too, his chair scraping against the stone. He doesn't say anything, doesn't look at anyone else. Just follows me, leaving the circle behind.

I don't glance back, but I can feel the weight of eyes on us —Nicole's sharp and simmering, Elle's worried, the rest uncertain. Let them watch.

32

CONNOR

THE PATH down from the overlook curves through trees, shaded and cool compared to the sunburn of the picnic. I follow a few paces behind her, her steps clipped and fast as if she were walking the city streets, and her shoulders are squared like she's daring anyone to come after her. She doesn't look back once, but I'm confident she knows I'm right behind her for anything she might need.

My chest is still buzzing from the way she snapped at Nicole. Everyone heard it—the whole table went silent, and not even Banks had a quip ready. And then Manuela stood there, spine straight, eyes blazing, calling Nicole out for what she's been doing to her for who knows how long.

I've never seen anyone do that before. Not with Nicole or anyone in this group, instead taking everything that they're handed with a fake smile on their faces. If passive-aggressive were a picture, it would be the way some of these people interact with each other.

It shouldn't surprise me. Manuela doesn't hide who she is. She doesn't water herself down for the sake of making other people comfortable. I've watched her stumble into this friend circle that was never built to include someone new, and instead of shrinking to fit, she's holding her ground and trying to carve some space for herself.

And it made something in me twist hard. Admiration, yes, but also shame. Because she is right. About Nicole and herself, about belonging. And I've never had the guts to stand up like that, not to my father, not with anyone.

"Manu," I call after her when the trail widens. My voice sounds rough, like I've been shouting, even though I haven't said a word until now.

She slows, not enough to stop, but enough that I can catch up. Her jaw is tight, eyes fixed on the path like this is what finally personally insulted her.

"You didn't have to follow me," she mutters.

"I wanted to."

Her laugh is sharp. "To make sure I didn't set the whole mountain on fire?"

I step in front of her so she has to meet my eyes. "To tell you I'm proud of you."

That gets her. She blinks, the fight in her shoulder flickering and finally relaxing for a moment. "Proud?"

"You said what no one else would. What everyone thinks, but no one's willing to risk saying out loud. You're not wrong, Manu. And you don't need to keep apologizing for simply existing."

Her throat works, like the words caught somewhere between belief and disbelief. She looks away, down at her shoes, scuffing gravel with the toe. "I just... I don't know why I let it get to me. I should've ignored her."

"No," I say, firmer than I mean to. "You shouldn't. You are right. You've been nothing but yourself, and if that threatens Nicole? That's her problem."

Silence stretches. The trees sway overhead, the faint clang of cowbells drifting up from the valley.

She crosses her arms, but it feels less defensive, more like she's holding herself together. "It's exhausting. Always feeling like I have to prove myself. Back home, here, even in New York. Like no matter what I do, it's never enough."

Her words hit low in my gut. Because I know that feeling. Pretending, performing, being the version everyone else expects. The difference is—she just said it out loud. And I've never had the courage to.

I want to tell her that. That watching her fight for herself makes me want to fight for myself too. But the words clog in my throat, heavy with everything I've avoided saying for years.

Instead, I reach out, tuck a strand of hair behind her ear. Her skin is warm, her eyes still lit with the residue of anger, but there's something vulnerable underneath. Something that makes my chest ache.

"You belong here," I say quietly. "More than half of them put together."

Her lips part, but no words come out. Just a breath, shaky and soft.

And before I can stop myself, I lean in and kiss her.

It's not desperate like so many times during this trip, not about hiding in shadows or stealing time. It's steady, grounding, like I'm telling her with my mouth what I can't with words: *I see you. I want you. You belong here with me.*

She kisses me back, arms sliding up around my neck, holding on like maybe she believes me for a second.

But when we pull apart, her eyes are shining in a way that makes my chest tighten. Doubt flickers there for a fraction of a second. And I wonder if it's related to us—what comes next after this trip is over in a matter of days.

And the truth is, I feel it too.

Because no matter how right this feels, I can already sense the walls closing in—the group's eyes, my family's expectations, her fear of never belonging.

And I don't know if we're strong enough to carry all of it.

We start walking again, slower this time, gravel crunching underfoot. She doesn't say anything, and neither do I. But I keep sneaking glances at her, at the way her shoulders have dropped a little, at how she's chewing her bottom lip like she's still replaying every word with Nicole.

I want to tell her again that she was perfect. That she didn't need to explain herself to anyone. That the way she called Nicole out was the bravest thing I've seen in years, from anyone. But if I say it out loud, I'll have to admit how much I needed to hear it myself.

And that terrifies me.

Because if she can face everything head-on, then what excuse do I have for not doing the same in my own life? What excuse do I have for ignoring calls from my parents, for leaving an email unopened because I'm afraid of the weight it carries?

We round a bend in the path, and the villa comes into view below, white walls glowing in the late afternoon sun. Laughter drifts faintly from the terrace, already back to normal like nothing happened.

Manuela exhales slowly, like she's bracing herself.

I want to grab her hand. Tell her she doesn't have to go back in there alone. That if she can stand up to Nicole, maybe I can stand up to my father. That maybe we're stronger together.

But I don't.

Instead, I shove my hands in my pockets, keep my eyes fixed on the house, and tell myself the timing isn't right.

Even though I know it never will be.

33

———

CONNOR

THE VILLA FEELS heavy after the picnic, and it has nothing to do with the excessive amounts of food and wine we've been consuming. Conversation was bright enough on the surface, but underneath it all, something sharp lingered, and now the walls seem to carry it. Doors shut harder than they need to upstairs. Laughter drifts faint and uneven, like people are trying too hard. Even in the kitchen, the clatter of staff resetting for dinner sounds louder, more brittle.

I'm on the terrace, alone, a sweating glass of water untouched beside me. My phone sits face-down on the table, but I can feel it buzzing like an accusation. The vibration carries through the wood, faint but steady, every few minutes.

Missed calls from my father and at least seventeen texts from my mother.

DAD

> Call him back. This can't wait.

> Connor, you need to respond to his email.

> He's giving you an opportunity people in
> your shoes only dream about.

Opportunity. Right.

I drag a hand down my face, tilt my chair back, and stare at the perfect line where the mountains meet sky. Blue stacked on a different hue of blue, endless and serene. Everything I'm supposed to want right now. A vacation in Switzerland. Time to connect with friends. A break from the constant grind of work and obligation.

But the email is still there, unopened. The offer from the man my dad lined up, a friend of a friend who approached me with a job before I even decided I wanted to start looking for something else. It's polished, prestigious, exactly the kind of thing my father's been grooming me for.

I can't even make myself click it and read the details.

"Thought you'd escaped." Jack's voice cuts through the quiet, wry and knowing.

I glance over my shoulder. He's loose in his linen shirt, sleeves rolled, tan deepening from the day even though we haven't purposely set out to do so. George follows him out, already lighting a cigarette, the match flaring orange before the afternoon breeze snuffs it out. He shields it with his hand, gets it going anyway, then leans against the railing with that careless posture that drives Jack insane.

"Escaped what?" I ask.

"Family business talk," Jack says, heading to the bar cart like it personally owes him a drink. It probably does since he's paying for all of this. "Georgie thinks he's reinventing the wheel."

George exhales smoke in a slow stream. "Not reinventing. Building." His smirk is faint but practiced, the kind that's been annoying Jack since they were old enough to fight over who got shotgun. "There's a huge difference."

"The difference is you don't care who you burn in the process," Jack shoots back. His voice sharpens as he drops ice into a glass, the cubes cracking. "You throw money around, make promises you can't keep, and leave the rest of us cleaning it up. Your poor wife."

George doesn't flinch. Just shrugs, inhales, blows smoke toward the sky. "Don't be dramatic. I know what I'm doing."

Jack snorts into his drink. "Sure you do."

I keep quiet. That's how it always goes with them—Jack the moral compass, George the chaos machine. I'm just the cousin who nods and stays out of it. But George's words hit harder than I want to admit. *I know what I'm doing.*

"You'd be an idiot not to take an opportunity handed to you," George adds, flicking ash over the terrace edge. "Not everyone gets those."

Jack glares at him, but I freeze. My chest tightens like he's talking to me, not to Jack.

Because he's right. Not everyone gets those. And I've had more than my share—connections, strings pulled, doors opened without me even knocking. Opportunities I never asked for but that somehow define me anyway.

Jack downs the rest of his drink and mutters something I don't catch before heading back inside. George lingers a moment longer, flicks the end of his cigarette over the railing, then shrugs. "You'll figure it out, Connor. You always do."

He says it casually, like it's a compliment. And it makes me wonder what he knows—if people are talking about this job my father keeps pressuring me into. I'm sure it's not about the part of me that's been unraveling for months. I hope not.

Then he's gone too. Before I even say another word to either of them.

The terrace is quiet again. Only the faint lap of water against rocks and the engine of a boat approaching the dock down below carry up from the lake.

I flip my phone over, finally. The screen lights, the same thread of messages glowing like a neon sign.

DAD

Connor, this is a gift. Don't waste it.

Call him back tonight. He's expecting you.

Your future doesn't wait forever.

My throat tightens.

It should be simple. I should want this—an offer practically handed to me, the kind of role that makes my father beam with pride. The kind of role people like George brag about at cocktail parties. More money than I'll ever need in my lifetime.

But the thought of accepting makes me feel... hollow.

I picture myself in another glass tower, endless spreadsheets, clients breathing down my neck about one thing or another. Late nights, early mornings, nothing but a treadmill disguised as a career. It's everything I know. Everything expected.

And I'm so fucking tired.

The irony isn't lost on me: I'm in Switzerland, mountains stretched endlessly in front of me, and all I can think about is how trapped I feel. How every choice has been mapped for me before I've even considered if I want it.

For years, I told myself that was fine. That was normal. You don't question the path when it's been paved so carefully by people who swear they only want what's best for you.

But then... Manuela.

Her laugh drifts faintly from somewhere inside the villa. Light, low, completely unguarded. It cuts through the tightness in my chest like sunlight hitting water. I close my eyes and let it echo in my head, the sound stubbornly softer than everything else.

She doesn't pretend. Not like I do. She's restless, yes, but honest in it. She admits when she doesn't fit, when she feels invisible, when she wants more but doesn't know how to get there. She makes me want to stop lying to myself.

My phone buzzes again. I don't look.

Instead, I stare at the mountains until my vision blurs, the sharp peaks bleeding into the sky. My pulse beats in my throat.

I can't keep living someone else's idea of a life. But if I walk away, what's left? Who am I without the job, the pedigree, the expectations? Who am I without Athena, without the plan that's been sketched for me since I was twenty-two?

The questions gnaw until I want to scream.

The terrace door slides open. I jerk my head around like I've been caught doing something illicit.

It's her.

Manuela steps out, barefoot, a glass of water in her hand, curls loose around her shoulders. She spots me and pauses, like maybe she didn't expect to find me here. The sun paints her skin gold, warm, and unhurried.

"Hey," she says softly, a little tentative.

I clear my throat, pocketing my phone like it's guilty evidence. "Hey."

She tilts her head, studying me with those eyes that see more than I want to admit. "You okay?"

The question is simple, harmless on the surface. But it lands like a stone in my chest.

I should lie. Say I'm fine and shrug it off. Pretend I wasn't just unraveling under the weight of familial expectations and unread emails.

Instead, I hold her gaze for a beat too long, the words stuck in my throat.

"Yeah," I say finally, quietly. "Just... needed some air."

Her expression softens, like she doesn't believe me but won't push. She moves closer, rests her glass on the table, and sits beside me. Close enough that I feel the warmth of her body. Close enough that for a moment, all the noise in my head finally goes quiet.

34

MANUELA
WEDNESDAY

"Hey. Can I... steal you for a second?"

Late-morning light slides across the floors, catching on abandoned wineglasses from last night and half-finished crosswords someone left on the table. Nicole and Banks are nowhere to be seen, and no one has mentioned them, which makes the air feel sharper somehow—like we're all waiting for the other shoe to drop.

I find Elle in the kitchen, loading fruit into a bowl, phone propped against a mug on the counter. She's in another flawless linen set, looking freshly pressed and dewy like she hasn't spent the last week wrangling chaos.

"Yes, that's Mommy's perfect girl," she coos into the screen, voice all sunshine. "Did you eat your salmon bites? Did Mimi warm them for you the way you like? Oh my *goodness*, you're looking so pretty. Did you get a new bow today?" She pauses, gasping so dramatically it echoes off the marble.

"Is that a *sparkly* bow? My heart can't take this, Fifi. Mommy's heart is exploding. Mommy loves you more than air."

Elle ends the call with a kissy noise and sets her phone down on the counter like it's made of glass. She exhales, dreamy, then pops a grape into her mouth. "She was wearing sequins and a tutu, Manu. I'm deceased."

I smile, nervous, picking at my nail polish. "She's... very loved."

"Obviously," she says, eyes finally flicking toward me. "What's up?"

I shift my weight from one foot to the other. The words taste awkward already. "I just wanted to apologize. About yesterday. With Nicole," I start, fingers knotting in the hem of my shorts. "I shouldn't have snapped."

Elle's mouth twitches—not quite a smile but also not a frown. I think she's amused by it, and I hope she is because everything feels a little like we are a gentle breeze away from everything imploding. "She was out of line," she says simply and then shrugs one shoulder. "Still, thank you for saying something."

"I don't want to make things harder for you," I say quietly. "This is your wedding week."

That gets me a smile. "Manu, please. This group has survived much worse. I mean... George showed up married. At least you didn't do that."

I let out a weak laugh, heat rising to my face.

"Honestly," Elle goes on, plucking a strawberry from her

bowl and taking a small bite of the tip, "you've been great. Everyone likes you. Nicole will get over herself eventually."

She says it lightly, tossed in there so casually, but it lands heavy in my chest anyway. "Thanks."

Elle pats my arm like this whole thing is settled. "Now go do something fun before I'm dragged to another champagne and cake tasting with my parents."

And just like that, she's gone, barefoot down the hall, phone on her ear.

A few minutes later, Camila and I are slipping out the front door. The house is still quiet, sunlight filtering pale and thin through the trees as we pick our way down the gravel path. The hill drops steeply toward the lake, the air growing warmer with every step.

She walks with her coverup tied loose at her waist, sunglasses perched in her hair. For a while, we just listen to the faint hum of insects and the crunch of our sandals dangling from our fingers. Then she says, casually but not really, "Out with it."

I blink. "Out with what?"

Camila's mouth curves, sharp. "You've been looking at me like you want to ask me a question."

Heat prickles the back of my neck. "Fine. I just... George. The whole"—I gesture vaguely, helplessly—"marriage thing. It surprised me, that's all."

"Same," she says lightly. "But sometimes life doesn't need to make sense to work."

"That's it? That's your explanation?"

She laughs, low and soft. "For now." Then, glancing at me from the corner of her eye: "Don't worry, Manu. We accelerated our timeline because of my whole visa issues. You know the struggle."

I huff a laugh, tension easing just a little. "Wait, you've been dating him? You never brought him home."

She bumps her shoulder against mine like she's punctuating it. "It was pretty casual."

The path levels out as we reach the lake. Heat shimmers off the rocks, the water glaring bright silver in the sun. We find a flat stretch near the edge and drop our towels side by side, the air so thick it's like wading through syrup.

———

THE HEAT IS the kind that clings. Not the dry, mountain crispness I expected, but thick and sticky, like the air is wrapping itself around us. Camila and I are drenched in sweat and desperate for an opportunity to cool off. We kick our sandals off to the side and stretch out anyway, both of us sighing at the same time like it's some kind of ritual.

The lake is almost metallic in the sunlight. A boat hums lazily somewhere across the water, but otherwise it's just us and the faint buzz of late summer insects and cowbells.

Camila pulls her sunglasses down the bridge of her nose. "You realize tomorrow I have to meet his parents?"

I tilt my head, eyes closed against the glare. "Like, officially?"

She groans. "Officially. Jack says I've probably already met them at one of those fancy charity galas for work, but come on—seeing them across a room is not the same thing."

I crack one eye open.

"Tomorrow I shake their hands, look them in the eye, and say, 'Hi, I'm the girl your son married without telling you.'"

"That sounds a little terrifying."

Her hand flutters in the air between us. "They're going to eat me alive."

"They won't," I say, though my tone is softer than convincing. Camila always looks composed—perfect clothes, glowing skin, not a hair out of place. But right now there's a tightness in her mouth I don't usually see. "I mean, if the group hasn't, then I think you'll be fine."

We lapse into silence for a while. Sweat slides down the back of my neck. I shift, tucking my arm under my head, and glance sideways at her again.

"What's up with you and Connor?" she says finally, almost like she's been waiting for the exact moment to intercept my thoughts and ask. "What's on your mind?"

I shrug, too casual. "Nothing."

She snorts. "*Por favor.* You've been staring at the same patch of sky for ten minutes."

My mouth opens, then closes again. Because the truth is, my head is absolutely chock-full of him. Long gone is my preoccupation with my job and what my next move might be. Instead, it's full of the sound of his laughter at the picnic.

The way he looks at me across the table, unflinching, even with Nicole's eyes like knives between us. The feel of his hand steady on my waist, brief and too much all at once.

"It's not... him," I say finally, picking at a loose thread on my towel. "Not exactly. It's just... the group. The Nicole thing. Everything feels tense now, and I... Whatever."

Camila hums, not pushing, but I can tell she's not buying my deflection. She never does. There's a glint of curiosity in her face, but she lets it slide, stretching her arms overhead like the question was just idle chatter.

In my head, I add what I can't say out loud: *This won't last. He'll retreat. He'll fold back into whatever life is waiting for him once this trip is over.* And I'll be left with nothing but the echo of all these too-long glances.

The thought lodges sharp behind my ribs. I dig my toes into the warm stones, grounding myself, but it doesn't help. It's been easy to pretend this is all temporary, something light and contained. But the truth is, he's gotten under my skin. And if he walks away—when he walks away—I'm not sure what will be left of me here.

I close my eyes against the glare, swallowing the words before they can get out and ruin everything.

35

MANUELA

Camila flips onto her stomach, adjusting her bikini straps an hour later.

"Don't let them eat you alive," she mutters, face pressed into her towel. I don't know if she's talking about the group or herself. We've been lounging in silence for an hour, absorbing the heat and the sun like it's the last day of the season.

We let the heat press down on us until it's unbearable, the sun turning everything sluggish. My skin sticks to the towel at my back, the stones under it radiating enough to toast bread. I've just about convinced myself to roll into the lake when a shadow falls over us.

"Christ," George mutters. "You two trying to roast your-selves alive?"

I squint up. He's standing above us, shirt unbuttoned halfway, sunglasses perched on his head. Beside him is

Connor. His hair is damp, curling slightly at the edges like he's just showered, his T-shirt clinging to his shoulders in a way that makes my mouth go dry.

Camila props herself up on her elbows, the picture of unbothered glamour even with sweat running down her temple. "What, jealous you didn't think of it first, *honey*?"

George smirks, offering her a hand up. "Come on, *babe*. Let's go raid the kitchen before Elle has the staff hide the good bread again. You get angry when you're hungry."

"It's called hangry, you brute."

"Whatever you say, *baby*."

Camila groans but takes it, putting on her breezy coverup and handing George her towel. She glances at me once—something unreadable flickering in her eyes—before she lets George tug her back toward the path.

And just like that, it's only me and Connor.

The silence stretches. I'm suddenly hyperaware of everything: the sweat rolling down the back of my thigh, the faint buzz of insects in the grass, the way the air feels like it's vibrating between us.

"You're going to get heatstroke," he says finally, dropping his own towel on the ground near mine. He crouches down in the little scrap of shade cast by the tree, close enough that I can smell the faint citrus bite of his soap. "Seriously, Manu, you're flushed."

"I'm fine," I say, too fast. My voice is scratchy from the heat.

His eyes catch mine, steady, skeptical. Then he reaches

out, thumb brushing across my temple like he's testing. The touch is nothing, barely pressure at all, but it sparks across my skin like fire.

"Connor—"

"Too hot," he murmurs, ignoring me, still watching me like I'm hiding something.

I sit up, heart thudding harder than it should from a little heat and a little touch. He doesn't move his hand right away. The space between us shrinks, and suddenly the whole world feels like it's holding its breath.

"You really think I'm going to let you pass out here?" he asks, but his tone is different now. Lower. Rougher.

"I told you, I'm fine."

He huffs a laugh, but it's humorless. "You're impossible."

And then I don't know who moves first. Him, me, both at once. His mouth is on mine before I can think, hot and insistent, nothing polite about it. I gasp, and he swallows the sound like it belongs to him.

The tree shade offers no privacy, not really—other guests of the resort are scattered along the shoreline a ways off, towels sprawled, laughter drifting faintly across the water— but I stop caring. My hand fists in his shirt, dragging him closer until we're pressed together, sweat and heat and all. He kisses like he's been holding back for days—maybe weeks— and I feel myself unraveling under it. Almost like a silent goodbye.

His hand slides down my side, rough palm against over-heated skin, tugging at the edge of my bikini bottoms. My legs part without permission, the towel sliding away from me, forgotten. He groans against my mouth, low and guttural, like the sound has been trapped in him.

"Connor," I moan, breaking just enough to say it.

He pulls back a fraction, forehead against mine, chest heaving. His thumb brushes the inside of my thigh, and my whole body jolts. "Not on the shore," he mutters, voice raw. "The water. Shade of the tree. Now."

The command shouldn't thrill me, but it does. My pulse hammers as he grabs my hand and tugs me toward the shallows, half stumbling across the hot stones. The lake laps cool water around my calves, then my thighs, shock cutting through the heat. The shade from the leaning tree cloaks us in a thin pocket of privacy, branches low, water rippling dark.

I gasp as his hands find my waist, lifting me just enough to press me against the slick trunk at the edge, water swirling around our hips. "Connor—" My protest dissolves when his mouth crushes mine again, rougher, hungrier. His body pins me against bark and water, urgency vibrating through every movement.

Cold seeps into my skin, but he's all heat. His fingers hook my bikini bottoms, sliding them aside beneath the surface, knuckles grazing my thigh. I arch into him instinctively, water rocking, the sound of our breaths too loud in this hidden pocket of lake.

"Fuck," he groans, his forehead dropping to my shoulder. "How are you so wet already?"

I clutch at his wet hair, my laugh breaking into a moan as

his hand moves lower and softly circles my clit, claiming me beneath the waterline where no one can see. The lake hides everything, but the way my body reacts to him is impossible to conceal. My nails scrape his back, and he swallows every sound I make with his mouth, desperate and consuming.

"Connor," I whisper, shaky, clinging to him as the pressure builds. "Please."

"Always," he says before pushing deeper with his fingers, the rhythm steady, relentless. My hips buck against his hand, water splashing quietly around us, branches creaking above like they're the only witnesses.

"You drive me insane," he mutters, voice ragged. His mouth drags across my jaw, down my throat. "You don't even see it, do you?"

"See what?" My voice breaks on the question.

His hand fists in my hair, tilting my head back so I have to look at him. His eyes are dark, burning, nothing like the smooth surface he shows the rest of the world. "The way I can't stop fucking watching you."

The words hit me harder than the heat ever could. My breath stutters, and my pulse thrums everywhere at once.

I kiss him again because I can't not, because anything else feels impossible. His teeth catch my bottom lip, his tongue slides against mine, and the only things anchoring me to this planet are the solid press of his hands and the rough bark of the tree at my back.

"Can I fuck you like this? Right here? I don't think I can wait."

The question splinters through me, hot and terrifying and everything I want at once. His words, his eyes, the raw need in them—that's what pins me in place

"Yes," I whisper, and it feels like stepping off a cliff. "I'm on birth control."

He curses under his breath as he lowers his swim trunks. The water ripples around us, cool and deceptive, hiding the urgency that crackles between our bodies. My hands are shaking when I touch his shoulders, his jaw, anything I can reach, really, like I need proof this is real.

"Jesus," he says as he pushes inside me, deep and all at once, and my gasp echoes against his mouth. He holds me steady, one arm banded tight around my back, keeping me anchored against the tree as he sinks all the way in.

"Jesus," he groans again, head dropping to my shoulder. "You feel—fuck, this feels—" His voice fractures, lost in the rush of water against our skin.

He keeps his thrusts steady but urgent, his mouth finding mine again like he can't bear to be anywhere else. Each push drives me harder into the tree, rough bark and cool water and the burn of him inside me fusing into something that feels like it'll undo me.

He pulls back just far enough to look at me. His eyes are wild, searching, like he's trying to memorize my face, like he's afraid I'll vanish if he blinks. "Do you have any idea what you're doing to me?"

"Yes," I whisper, my voice breaking. "Because you're doing the same to me."

His pace falters for a moment at that. And then he moves faster, rougher, the rhythm impossible to mistake for anything but desperation. My moans are muffled into his shoulder, the world narrowed down to the pulse of water, the scrape of bark, the drag of his body inside mine.

When I come, it's sharp and sudden, my whole body tightening around him, water splashing higher as I cling to his shoulders. He groans, low and guttural, burying his face against my neck as his own release follows, his body shaking with it.

For a long moment, neither of us moves. The lake rocks gently around us, cooling everything except the heat still coursing through my chest. He keeps me pinned against him, breathing hard, his hands refusing to let me drift even an inch away.

Finally, he pulls back just enough to press his mouth to my temple. "You scare the hell out of me," he admits quietly.

My throat is raw when I answer. "Good."

36

———

MANUELA

THURSDAY

THE HOUSE IS a flurry of perfume, heels, and steam from curling irons by the time I finish my makeup. There's at least three people getting Elle ready in the primary bedroom, and everyone is fluttering around with that kind of energy she's only able to evoke. Dresses in different colors swish past the hallway, laughter bouncing between doors and floors, Amelia shouting for another glass of prosecco like it's already a party.

Camila leans against the doorway of my room, slipping in earrings, her lipstick a sharp red that makes her look more glamorous than I've ever seen her. "Are you ready?"

I smooth my palms down the satin of my red dress. "Ready enough."

She glances at me in the mirror, lips twitching. "You clean up nice."

I roll my eyes, but it's true—I barely recognize myself.

The dress I packed for the first official event of the wedding trip feels more like it belongs to someone else, sleek and bright with a flow that makes me self-conscious. New-York-me thought it was perfect. Tres-Fuegos-me wonders if I'm playing dress-up in the Swiss Alps.

The others are already gathering in the entryway by the time we head downstairs. Elle looks like she's floating, her champagne-colored floor-length gown catching one particular bright ray of sunlight. Jack stands, steady at her side, looking very much like a fool in love.

Outside, the air is crisp but not cold yet. It's almost like Elle had words with whoever controls the weather because the temperature is perfect, and the sky is a deep blue I haven't seen in a long time. Guests are walking down the gravel path to the dock, and the air is buzzing with hellos and cheek kisses, and the small talk and different conversations mix in a way that makes me dizzy.

"Boat cocktails," Nicole says, sweeping past in a sparkling green dress, phone in hand. Banks is holding her free hand as she drags him towards the line that's forming to board. "Only Elle would rent a yacht for pre-dinner drinks."

"It's not a yacht," Elle protests from behind the group, though her grin betrays her. "Just... a boat. A nice one."

The group spills toward the dock, laughter echoing as the lake comes into view. The vessel waiting there is lit with strings of fairy lights, its deck already staffed with servers balancing trays of champagne. The water glitters around it, mountains fading violet in the distance.

"This is insane," Camila murmurs at my side.

"Look at your husband in a freaking tux," I whisper back. "I feel underdressed."

She bumps my shoulder. "Not possible."

We queue up on the dock, shoes clicking against the planks and the chatter rising around us. Connor stands near the front with George and a couple of their cousins, his tux jacket cut sharp against his shoulders. He looks unfairly good—hair swept back, bow tie loosened just enough to make it look intentional. He laughs at something Sterling says, dimples flashing, but when his eyes slide toward me, the sound falters.

I swear I feel the world stop moving around me. The sight of him actually knocks the air from my chest.

This morning he was all wet hair and teasing grins, both of us looking at the other across the room. Now, he looks like he belongs on the cover of a magazine, like someone I shouldn't be allowed within arm's reach of. And he looks comfortable in it. Effortless.

My pulse trips hard. Heat rushes through me in a wave so sudden I have to press my hand against my clutch, grounding myself before I give myself away.

As if he feels it, the left dimple hits first, and then the smile—slow, devastating, meant only for me.

I want to look away, but I can't.

"*Ahh, no soy la única con secretos,*" Camila mutters under her breath, low enough that only I hear about how I'm not the only one keeping secrets.

My head snaps toward her, cheeks burning. "What?"

She arches a brow, the corners of her mouth tugging in a knowing curve. "Don't 'what' me. I saw that."

"I—no, you didn't." The words trip over themselves, too quick, too defensive.

"Manu," she says, amused now, eyes flicking toward Connor and back to me. "You might want to work on your poker face."

I glare at her, which only earns me a smug smile. She smooths her hands down the front of her blue dress, like she's got nothing better to do than let me stew in my own fluster.

Connor heads in our direction, shoes steady on the planks. "Here," he says, voice low but certain. He reaches his hand out to me, palm up, waiting.

The world tilts around us, but all I can see is his hand, the steady weight of his gaze. My fingers slip into his before I can think better of it.

His grip is warm, strong, and when he guides me onto the boat, his eyes lock on mine like we're the only two people here. The look lingers, soft and startling, and I swear my breath stumbles in my throat.

"Got you," he murmurs, barely audible.

"Thank you," I whisper back, though my voice comes out shaky.

Behind us, Nicole's laugh cuts sharply, and I realize with a jolt that people noticed. A couple of heads tilt, curiosity flickering across their faces before turning away. Camila raises her brows but says nothing.

I slip my hand from his as soon as I'm steady, but the heat of it burns long after.

The boat sets off, gliding smoothly across the lake. Trays of champagne pass from guest to guest, the clink of glasses mixing with low music drifting from hidden speakers. The mountains grow darker as the sun dips, the sky painted in pink and orange.

Camila and I drift toward a group of women near the railing at the back of the boat—Nicole, Hannah, and a few of Elle's college friends, who I've seen once or twice in the past three years. Elle's family is somewhere around, her very pregnant sister, toddler niece, and mother wearing similar dresses in complementary hues, like an unofficial wedding party. Conversation swells around designer shoes and travel horror stories, laughter bubbling over the rim of champagne flutes.

"Connor seems different this trip," Hannah says suddenly, leaning against the rail with a sly smile. "More... relaxed."

Nicole snorts. "That's because Athena isn't here."

My stomach jolts.

Across the deck, Connor is deep in conversation with Cash and George, glass in hand, his profile sharp against the fading light. He doesn't look different to me. Connor looks exactly like himself—the version I know when no one's watching.

Camila hums, swirling her champagne. "Different how?" she asks casually, though I catch the flick of her eyes toward me and the slight curve of her lips. I want to glare, but I also want to know exactly what they are seeing.

Hannah shrugs, sipping. "Just... I don't know. Less uptight. Athena always kept him on edge, it seemed. Now it's like..." She waves vaguely toward him. "He's finally enjoying."

My throat goes tight. I press my glass to my lips, hiding behind the rim, hoping no one notices the flush crawling up my cheeks.

The ride is slow, deliberate, as if the boat itself doesn't want to disturb the moment. The lake stretches wide around us, mountains looming dark at the edges, fairy lights reflecting in broken ripples. Servers keep glasses full, and laughter rises, the entire evening shining with a gloss that feels very much like something Elle and Jack would do.

It's polished yet casual, and very intentional.

Elle and Jack circulate the deck, glowing, their hands never straying far from each other. She squeezes his arm when she thinks no one is watching, her smile too luminous to be just a welcome dinner.

"Something's up," Camila murmurs near my ear, eyes narrowed in observation.

I glance at her, confused. "What do you mean?"

She tilts her chin toward Elle, who's laughing too brightly, cheeks flushed. "I sense something."

Connor's eyes find mine again across the deck, a flicker of

something private threading through the noise and light, enough to make my pulse stumble. Camila's words echo in my ear, her knowing look still burning at the edges of my thoughts.

It feels like the night itself is holding a secret just out of reach—one we're all about to collide with.

37

CONNOR

"Thank you all for coming," Elle says, voice bright and clear, cutting through the chatter that's built steadily all evening. She stands now at the bow, champagne flute in hand, Jack firm and steady beside her. Fairy lights tremble overhead with the boat's slow movement, the water glinting darkly below.

Her laugh carries easily, a little nervous, a little tipsy. "Most of you just arrived today, and this weekend was meant to be a big celebration—all of us together, finally. But..." She pauses, turning to Jack, and the look they share is so charged that half the crowd goes quiet in response. "Waiting until the end felt impossible."

Confused murmurs ripple through the guests—the cousins craning their necks, Nicole whispering something sharp that earns a laugh. Georgie is whispering something to his wife, and she glares back at him, mouthing an aggravated *shut up.*

Jack leans toward the microphone someone has thrust into his hand, grinning so hard it looks like his face might split. "So we're not going to wait."

Elle beams, her eyes glowing with mischief and certainty. "We're getting married tonight."

The boat erupts. Gasps, shrieks, the clatter of silverware, champagne nearly sloshing out of glasses. Nicole yells, "Shut up!" and promptly drops into Amelia's arms, cackling. Sterling whistles sharp through his teeth, making half the deck cheer louder. Someone behind me shouts, "Are you serious?" while another guest is already fumbling for their phone, angling to record it all.

I can't help laughing, the sound torn straight from my chest. It's so Elle and Jack—impatient, bold, refusing to play by anyone's timeline but their own.

Servers appear from nowhere, clearing a space at the bow. Lanterns flare one by one, glowing warm against the rising dark. Guests shuffle closer, buzzing as though they've just been given an electric jolt.

I should be focused on Elle and Jack, but I can't stop watching Manuela—frozen midstep near the rail, champagne glass tilted, fairy lights scattered across her bare shoulders. She looks caught between awe and disbelief.

I'm about to move toward her when a familiar voice cuts through the din.

"Connor."

I turn. My parents are suddenly there, materializing from

the press of bodies like they've never been gone. My mother in silk and diamonds, my father crisp and immaculate even on a boat deck.

"Hi, darling." My mother leans in with practiced ease, air-kisses brushing both my cheeks, the scent of expensive perfume clinging. My father offers a brief, firm clasp on my shoulder—never more, never less.

"You didn't call us back," my mother adds lightly. Her smile doesn't falter. "We've been waiting to hear from you about the offer."

Now? Here? The officiant is being ushered forward, guests are buzzing, and still the email I haven't opened finds me anyway.

"I've been... busy," I say. "The itinerary was really packed this week, courtesy of cousin Jackie."

My father's jaw tightens, almost imperceptible. "Don't leave him waiting, Connor. This is the kind of chance people don't get twice."

Before I can answer, applause erupts. Elle and Jack have stepped into the light, hand in hand, glowing. The crowd surges forward. My mother pats my arm once, smile fixed, and they're swept away again, already absorbed by the spectacle.

But the knot in my chest pulls tighter. Everyone else is laughing, craning for photos, swept up in champagne and romantic love. I'm stuck replaying their voices: *Don't waste it. Your future doesn't wait forever.*

And then my gaze hooks back on Manuela. The dress

she's wearing is red, cut just above her knees, bare shoulders framed by draped fabric that falls loose around her arms. Her hair's down in soft waves, catching the candlelight glow, and it's not a look I've seen on her before. It knocks the air out of me.

Still by the rail, still glowing, lips parted in surprise as Elle and Jack kiss to cheers. She catches my eye across the deck and shakes her head, smiling into her glass.

The sound of the crowd fades, dim compared to the sound of her breath when I finally make my way to her side. We stand shoulder to shoulder, arms brushing.

"They're really doing this," she whispers.

"Of course they are." I tilt closer, enough to catch the citrus twist of her perfume. "It's very them. I'm surprised but also... not?"

The officiant starts speaking, but I barely hear it. Guests are laughing, crying, snapping photos, and all I can do is listen to her breathe beside me. Elle and Jack say their vows, Jack trips over a line, Elle laughs through hers, and everyone cheers when they finally kiss. Champagne glasses clink, sparklers appear out of nowhere, and the boat roars with applause that echoes across the water.

It should be about them. But the whole time, I'm aware of Manuela's hand just barely brushing mine against the rail and how it feels so natural for it to be there.

Servers sweep through with trays of champagne refills as the ceremony concludes, and Elle's mother raises her glass, her voice carrying easily over the noise. "Dinner and dancing will follow at the Edelweiss Ballroom once we dock. Please make your way there so we can keep the celebration going all night!"

Cheers rise again, glasses lifted, and I force a smile for anyone watching, but inside my chest, something dangerous stirs.

The music swells, shifting softer for Elle and Jack's first dance as the boat slows even more in its approach towards the dock. She glows in his arms, his cheek pressed to her temple, both of them radiant and sure. The crowd watches, half in tears, half still buzzing from the shock of it all.

Nicole swoops by, eyebrows arched. "You two look cozy," she teases, champagne lifted, before disappearing again. Manuela ducks her head, laughing into her glass, but her shoulder presses into mine, and neither of us move.

I should laugh it off. Deflect, the way I always do. But the words stick in my throat. Because Nicole isn't wrong. And because as far as she knows, I still belong to someone else.

Athena's name hovers like a ghost between the bubbles and the laughter, unspoken but present. No one here knows we ended it for good. Not my friends, not my parents, not Nicole. They're still waiting for her to walk in, perfect and sharp, with her hand tucked into mine.

Instead it's Manuela beside me, eyes bright in the fairy lights, her shoulder warm against mine. And for the first time in a long time, I don't feel restless or suffocated. I feel steady. Right next to a woman who makes me feel like I can breathe again.

The champagne burns down my throat, but it doesn't clear the knot in my chest.

"WOW," I murmur before I can stop myself. "Breathtaking."

She doesn't look at me. Her gaze stays fixed on the lake and the mountain range shadowing the horizon. It's dark now, but the faint glow of the scattered buildings across the hills paint a dreamy picture of the landscape in front of us. "Isn't it?" she replies, almost distracted. "Elle really has an eye for these things."

I step closer, bracing both hands on the glass railing that lines the deck of the main building at the resort, caging her in without really meaning to. "Why are you out here?" I ask, my voice softer than I intend. I dip low enough to press a quick kiss to the slope of her neck. She shivers, cheeks shifting into a ghost of a smile.

"I needed a minute," she says, turning toward me. Her makeup is subtle, just enough to catch the light, and it makes me focus on her mouth. Her lips shine faintly, full and soft, and all I want to do is taste her again. "It's a little loud."

"They'll call us in for dinner soon," I tell her, chin resting on her shoulder now.

She reaches for my hand, pulling it against her stomach, anchoring me to her. "Okay," she says, exhaling, but it sounds like surrender. Her fingers squeeze tighter, and suddenly the space between us hums with something I don't want to name. I know exactly what it is, though.

This is supposed to end. Five more days, and we go back to New York, back to our real lives. Pretend this was just vacation air, not something with this amount of weight.

"Okay," she says again, but this time her voice trembles.

"What's wrong?" I murmur, scanning her face.

She studies me, eyes flicking between mine and my mouth, searching. Finally: "I'm just tired."

I don't buy it. Her eyes tell me there's more, but I don't push. She leans forward instead, wrapping her arms around my neck, pressing the softest kiss to my lips. Chaste. Quick. A promise or a deflection, I can't tell which.

"Can we go to bed after dinner?" she whispers.

"Of course," I answer, smiling, though my chest feels tight.

Because I want to say more. I want to ask if she feels it too—this thing growing between us that doesn't fit the boundaries we set. I want to ask if maybe we could keep going in New York, if maybe this doesn't have to end. But if I'm wrong, if she doesn't want it, the crash will destroy me more than the end of this pact.

So I kiss her instead, soft and lingering, then tug her back toward the glass doors where the sounds of laughter and clinking glasses spill from the ballroom.

Inside, the crowd is already gathered—Elle and Jack flowing at the head table, servers weaving between guests with trays of champagne, music swelling warm and bright.

Manuela slips towards a table at the back and takes her seat next to someone I don't recognize, while I make my way to the bridal party's table.

I look across the room and find her already watching me, a small smile curving her mouth. When she realizes I've caught her, she blushes, lifts her glass, and tips it toward me in a silent toast.

38

MANUELA

THE STAFF MOVES in synchronized precision, placing plates in front of us, uncorking bottles of wine that glint ruby in the candlelight. The clatter of cutlery rises, laughter skipping across the tables, a hum of comfort that feels choreographed, like Elle willed this whole room into existence.

I stab at my appetizer, smiling faintly at something someone across the table says, but my eyes drift again—always, always—to him. Connor leans back, shoulder loose, his arm draped over the back of Cash's chair. He looks at ease. Radiant in a way that makes my chest ache so much.

It's ridiculous, really. He belongs here. Cousin of the groom, lifelong friend, part of the fabric of this group. But there's always been something in him that stands just at the edge, observing, calculating, never fully sinking in. Now? He looks woven into it. And maybe that's why my heart twists, because I recognize myself in that distance. Ninety percent of the time, I'm the outsider. Smiling, laughing, but still a spectator. And yet, this week, with Camila by my side, with Connor's eyes always finding mine, I've felt that shifting. I've felt the thread tug me closer. Which makes this twist sharper. Because just when I thought maybe I could fit into this world somehow, I see him, and he looks like he already does. Without me.

The chair beside me scrapes suddenly, and Camila slides into it, a little out of breath. Her ponytail is slightly skewed, a piece of hair slipping loose, and her lipstick looks freshly reapplied but imperfect.

"*Ey,*" she says, smoothing her dress down, trying to collect herself. It's a long-sleeved periwinkle thing that makes her eyes look impossibly bright. "What did I miss?"

"*Absolutamente nada,*" I reply, glancing around as the servers bustle through the side doors, balancing trays with military precision. "*¿Dónde estabas?*"

"Oh, umm..." Camila's gaze flicks across the room toward George, who's sitting across from Connor with his tie loosened and his shirt buttoned wrong, two holes mismatched like he dressed in a rush. "I needed to touch up my lips."

"Sure," I say with a chuckle, letting her excuse slide. Honestly, Camila's arrival has been one of the highlights of this trip. It feels like we've known each other our whole lives, and despite being roommates for more than a year now, the past few days have been a very welcome respite.

And the other highlight? Well, it's obvious.

So obvious that my eyes drift back to Connor. He thanks a server with a grin so wide it lights up his whole face, the sight making my pulse stumble.

"*¿Y vos?*" Camila asks, eyes searching my face as though she already knows the answer. "Ready to head home?"

"Yes," I say automatically. A small sigh slips out, and I pray she doesn't hear the crack in it. Because what I want to scream is, *No. I don't want to go.*

I don't want to leave this bubble, this impossible little world where he exists for me and I exist for him. Where my days aren't just commutes and deadlines and missing home so much it gnaws at me until I can't sleep. Tres Fuegos feels so far away in New York, like I left half of myself there.

Here, I feel... alive.

"Same," Camila says, eyes darting toward George, who is now standing off to the side, talking animatedly to a group of older guests. She's glowing just from looking at him, and the image makes a bubble of laughter rise in my chest before I can stop it. "But we don't leave until next Wednesday."

I groan, and she chuckles, swishing her ponytail like nothing in the world could bother her.

And then the air changes.

The door at the far end of the ballroom opens, a hush falling for just a beat before the chatter rushes back. I glance up absently, half expecting another service.

Instead, it's her.

Athena.

My stomach drops so violently I grip the edge of the table.

She's stunning. Of course she is. She always has been—the kind of beauty that makes people pause mid-sentence. Hair glossy, dress draped like liquid silk, smile polished to perfection. She walks like she owns the room, and maybe she does, because eyes follow her, people stopping conversations to say hi to her. Before I can blink, she's by his side.

"Connie." Her voice is syrup, warm and familiar, too loud in my ears. She places her hand on his arm, lingering, possessive. Athena's body angles toward his, like the two of them are magnets that naturally click back into place.

He startles, chair scraping faintly as he straightens. And before I can process his expression—shock, guilt, I can't really tell—two people are there flanking her. By the looks of it, they may be his parents. The resemblance to his dad is uncanny, and I'm too stunned to move. His mother is glowing, and his father claps him on the shoulder like the prodigal son has finally come home.

The table erupts around them. Hannah gasps, and Nicole grins wide. Someone else—Sterling, maybe—calls out something about it being too long since they've seen her. And everyone claps her back into the circle like she never left.

I can't breathe.

It's chaos—laughter, greetings, chairs shifting, silverware clattering against plates—but all I hear is the rushing in my ears. All I see is her hand on his arm, his parents leaning in, the circle closing tight around them.

And I realize, with a clarity that cuts like glass, that they didn't know. No one knew they broke up. Not his parents. Not his friends.

Which means that to them, she is still his. And he is still hers.

I press my palm flat to the tablecloth, trying to steady the shaking in my fingers. Camila says something in my ear, but it's drowned out by Athena's laugh, bright and familiar.

Connor glances across the room then, and for just a second, and our eyes catch.

There's something raw in his face, but it doesn't matter. Because the damage is already done. To everyone here, I am invisible. And she is Athena, the girl who fits.

Heat rushes up my throat, searing, burning. My vision blurs, and I have to look away before I shatter into a million pieces right here in front of them all.

I clear my throat and sip my wine just to keep my hands busy, but it does nothing to numb the ache. The glass is trembling when I set it back down.

Camila leans in then, her shoulder brushing mine, her voice pitched low enough for only me to hear. "Do you want to go outside for a minute?" The words take a moment to register. Her offer is soft and steady, an anchor against the chaos swirling around us. "Or we can leave now if you want. I'll walk you back to the house."

Laughter rises at Connor's table, Athena touching his sleeve again, his mother beaming like she's watching a dream come true.

And I sit there, smiling tightly, pretending I'm not unraveling. Pretending I don't feel like the floor just gave out beneath me.

Because of course. Of course this was never real.

It was always going to be her.

39

———

CONNOR

It's surreal, watching her slip back into the fold like she never left. I mean, she always had control over the group—more like it was her friends, and I was tagging along because we were together.

Hannah is hugging her while Nicole squeals loudly over her dress. Athena laughs easily, tilts her head just so, and every move is rehearsed perfection. My mother beams, and my father nods in approval like she's already the daughter-in-law he ordered. Everyone is enamored by her charm. She turns to me then, her smile landing like a weapon. "Connie. You didn't think I'd miss this, did you?"

And me? I sit there like a prop in my own life.

She leans closer, brushing my arm as if it's still hers. "It's been too long," she says warmly, eyes glinting. "I was just telling your mother I can't believe I stayed away this long."

"Yeah," I manage. My voice is flat by design, practiced.

Too many eyes on us for me to show how I really feel. "Time gets away."

One of my cousins steps in, greeting her, complimenting her shoes. More laughter. It's endless, this parade of welcome-backs, like the entire room has been waiting for Athena to walk through the door and make everything right again.

And I can't breathe.

When the tide of greetings finally ebbs, her attention snaps back to me, her hand slipping over my sleeve again. "Connie," she murmurs, low enough for only me. "Why don't you show me around? Catch me up?"

I force a tight smile that doesn't reach my eyes. "Sure."

I push back from the table, my chair scraping, and guide her away with a hand at the small of her back. She doesn't notice the stiffness in my touch, the way my jaw locks as we weave past tables, past the noise and champagne, until the double doors swing shut behind us.

The hallway is quieter, cooler.

I turn on her the second we're alone. "We need to talk."

She steps gracefully out of the doorway and turns to me with that perfect, polished smile.

"Connor," she says, voice low, amused. "Dragging me out like that? People are going to think we're sneaking away."

I don't smile. "Athena, what are you doing here?"

Her head tilts, glossy hair slipping over one shoulder. "I was invited. Your mother sent me the sweetest message—she said she hoped I'd surprise you." Her hand lifts to my arm again, familiar, practiced. "And I thought... why not?"

My stomach knots. "You shouldn't have."

She laughs softly, the kind of laugh that used to make me think she was untouchable. "You needed time, Connie. I gave it to you. I assumed that meant we'd pick up where we left off."

I exhale sharply, shaking my head. "There is no picking up. We broke up. "

Her smile falters but only for a beat. "You don't mean that."

"I do." My voice is harder now, echoing faintly against the marble. "We're done."

She folds her arms, eyebrows rising, coy again. "You've said that before, and yet here we are. You've always come back, Connor. Always."

She's not wrong. I ended things before—half a dozen times, maybe more. Each time she waited me out, certain I'd fold. And I always did. Until now.

I let out a humorless laugh, rough at the edges. "Not this time."

Her lips part, eyes narrowing, something sharp in them now. "So what, then? You throw everything away for some... fling? Nicole—"

Before I can answer, the doors creak open behind us. My mother steps out, concern tightening her face, and my father follows, his hand already raised in warning.

"Connor," my mother says quickly, scanning Athena, then me. "Please. Let's not make a scene, darling."

Athena straightens instantly, the perfect picture of composure. "We were just talking, Genevieve," she says lightly, as if my chest isn't on fire. "Catching up."

I can feel the rage climbing, pressing at my throat. And for once, I don't want to swallow it back down.

I laugh, sharp and ugly. "Catching up? Is that what we're calling this?"

"Connor," my mother hisses, her eyes darting toward the ballroom doors. "Keep your voice down. People will hear."

"Let them," I snap, my voice cracking with it. "I am so fucking tired of keeping my voice down."

My father stiffens. "Watch your tone, young man."

"No," I say, chest heaving. "You don't get it. Neither of you do. I ended this. *We* ended. Athena, I don't love you. I haven't for a long time."

She blinks, startled. The coy tilt of her head wavers for the first time. "You're just overwhelmed. You needed space. That's all."

I bark out a laugh that tastes bitter. "Do you know what nearly killed me? Pretending. Pretending to be the perfect son, the perfect boyfriend, the perfect future husband. Dying on the inside just to make everyone else comfortable. Space? Athena, I nearly collapsed from burnout six months ago. I thought I was dying. And do you know what went through my head in the emergency department? That I didn't even know who I was anymore. Not with my job. Not with you. Not with the life everyone else wanted for me."

"Connor," my father growls, "this isn't the time or the place—"

"It's always the same with you!" The words tear out of me, louder than I mean, but I don't stop. "Not the time, not the place. Don't say it here, don't rock the boat, don't embarrass the family. Do the job. Date the right girl. Get married, have kids, keep the image intact. Every box checked while I suffocate."

"Connor," my mother tries again, her voice sharp with the same warning she gave me during my teenage years.

I round on her. "I was drowning. And you didn't notice. Or maybe you did, and you just didn't care, because at least I was still performing."

Her face crumples, just for a second, but then it's gone, smoothed back into composure.

Athena steps forward, her chin high. "You're being dramatic. You'll regret this outburst. You always do."

My throat tightens, and something inside me snaps. "No. I won't regret finally telling the truth. I don't love you. I don't want you. And I will *never* marry you."

The words echo in the empty hall, final and brutal.

My mother gasps softly, and my father's jaw clenches. And Athena looks like I slapped her. But for the first time, none of them have a script ready.

And in the silence that follows, I realize I can breathe. My chest hurts, my hands are shaking, but I can breathe.

I drag a hand through my hair, the sound of muffled music and laughter seeping faintly through the ballroom doors. And suddenly, I know.

I know exactly who I need to find.

"I'm done," I say, voice raw but steady. "With this conversation. With all of it."

I don't wait for a reply. I shove the doors open, scanning the room, searching desperately.

But the table where she sat is empty.

"Where is she?" My voice catches on the question, too frantic.

Camila looks up from across the table, her face soft with something like pity. She shakes her head once. "She left."

The floor drops out beneath me.

Of course she did.

I push past the tables, past the music, out into the night air. My pulse is still pounding, my throat raw, my chest hollow with panic. Every path stretches dark ahead of me—back to the house, down to the lake, anywhere.

I don't care where she went. I just know I have to find her.

Because if I don't—if I let her slip away now—I'll lose the only thing that's ever made me feel like I wasn't drowning.

40

———

MANUELA

I DON'T EVEN REALIZE I'm moving until I'm already outside. The night air knifes down my throat, entirely too sharp to swallow. My hands are trembling, arms wrapped around myself like that can hold me together. Behind me, muffled laughter spills out as the doors to the ballroom swing shut, the sound of clinking glasses still reaching me, cruel in its normalcy.

My heels click against the stone path as I walk fast, faster, not caring where I end up, just as long as it's away. Away from her hand on his arm.

Away from the way his parents lit up like they'd been waiting for her.

I press a fist against my chest, trying to ease the ache. It does nothing.

The mountains loom dark around me, jagged teeth cutting into the night sky. The lake mirrors the resort's golden glow, so beautiful it feels cruel. I follow the gravel path upward until it bends into a small clearing. A wooden bench waits there, angled perfectly toward the calm water.

When I sink down, the silence presses in, so thick I can hear my own heartbeat. From here, the lake stretches wide, framed by ridges that feel impossibly familiar. It's not Tres Fuegos, but for a moment, I can almost trick myself into thinking it is—the same bite in the air, the same rough cut of the mountains against the sky. Home, except not.

The resemblance guts me.

I kick off my shoes, one after the other, and curl my legs under me on the bench. My chest aches, and before I can stop myself, the words slip out.

"No, *por favor.*"

The crunch of steps on gravel behind me makes me freeze. For a stupid, reckless second, I think it might be him.

But then I hear her voice.

"Manu."

Camila.

She slips into the clearing, softer than usual, her perfume curling faintly in the air. She doesn't sit right away, just stands there a beat, then lowers herself onto the far end of the bench. She's kicked her shoes off too, her dress bunched at the knees so the hem doesn't drag.

"You didn't have to follow me," I whisper, folding my arms tight across my chest.

"I know." She shrugs, leaning back against the bench slats. "But I didn't feel like staying there."

The lake glimmers below us, catching every light from the resort. The quiet presses too loud, and suddenly I'm unraveling.

"I don't belong here."

Saying those words out loud makes everything heavier, like I've given them a shape I can't take back. Camila tilts her head, not surprised. She doesn't argue, doesn't rush to say *of course you do*. She waits.

"I mean…" My voice shakes, my fingers digging into my arms. "I've never belonged. Not here, not in New York. I thought leaving Tres Fuegos would make me more—bigger, better. But all it's made me is homesick."

The tears come fast, stinging hot. I swipe at them with the back of my hand, frustrated, but they keep falling.

"Every single day, I wake up and I wonder if I made a mistake," I choke out. "In New York, I'm always the outsider. I don't get the rhythm and the references, the… everything. People are polite, but it's like I'm always five seconds behind."

I laugh bitterly, a sound that doesn't belong to me. "And it's worse with these people. At least in New York, I can separate from them. They've known each other forever. It's like I'm always the plus one that's invited after the first round of RSVPs comes in. Like an afterthought."

Camila leans forward, elbows braced on her knees, watching me with steady eyes. "You're not an *afterthought*, Manu."

"I am." My voice cracks. "You saw it. The second she

walked in—it was like I disappeared. Like I'd never existed at all. And the worst part? I let myself believe. For one second, I thought maybe... maybe this thing with him could mean something." My breath hitches. "But I was just the place-holder until Athena came back."

The image flashes again—Athena's hand sliding so easily onto his arm, his mother's delighted smile, the table erupting like they'd been waiting for her all along. My chest caves just thinking about it. I press my hands over my face, trying to keep the sob inside, but it breaks through anyway, rough and ugly.

Camila doesn't move at first. Then, slow and deliberate, she slides closer, her arm slipping around my shoulders. I collapse into her, forehead pressed to her collarbone, tears soaking into her dress. Her hand strokes circles on my back, grounding, unhurried.

"Manu," she murmurs. "*Vos estás lastimada.* That's all. You're allowed to hurt. You're allowed to miss home, even if you love your new life. You're allowed to be both. Just because you made this choice for yourself doesn't mean it hurts less."

My chest twists. I left Argentina with my chin high, telling myself I was brave, that chasing my career in New York meant I was finally becoming the person I always wanted to be. But tonight, watching them fold her back into his life like nothing had ever happened, I've never felt smaller.

"I'm tired." My voice is muffled against her shoulder.

"I'm so tired of not fitting anywhere. Too... invisible. I don't know where I'm supposed to go."

She tips her chin against my hair. "Maybe it's not about where but about who."

Her words pierce deeper than I want them to. I squeeze my eyes shut, more tears slipping free.

"And you're allowed to want more than being invisible," she whispers. "Don't you dare forget that."

We sit there a long time, my breaths shuddering, her dress damp beneath my cheek. The lake laps faintly at the shore, and it's barely audible from this high up. I can hear the bass of the music playing inside the ballroom a few hundred yards away, and it gives me pause.

Camila shifts, voice low. "You know he was looking for you, right? Right after you left the room."

Something flickers in my chest, dangerous and bright, but I smother it before it can take root. Hope has only ever made me look foolish. I stiffen, pulling back enough to see her face. "What?"

She nods. "He came back into the ballroom like a man on fire. He was scanning the room, desperate." Camila's eyes search mine. "Manu, maybe you need to talk to him instead of assuming the worst."

The words land heavy, tangled up with the ache still burning in my chest. I want to believe them. I want to believe he chose me, even if his world chose her.

My throat tightens as I whisper, "The thing is... with him, it's the first time in a long time I've felt like I belonged.

Like I wasn't just... watching life from the outside. And it happened immediately the night I met him, years ago." My voice breaks, and I press a trembling hand to my lips. "And now I don't know if I imagined it all."

Camila squeezes my shoulder, steady and sure. "You didn't imagine that. I saw it. Everyone saw it. I actually think Nicole tattled and told Athena to come to the wedding because she was definitely going to lose him. Whatever this is —it's real. And you owe it to yourself to find out where it goes. Not run before you even ask."

The silence that follows isn't empty. It hums with all the things I'm not ready to face, all the things I want too much.

Eventually, she shifts beside me, her hand squeezing once more at my shoulder. "We should head back," she says gently. "Elle will notice if you're gone too long."

I swipe at my face, throat raw. "Go ahead. I'll be there in a bit."

Her brows pinch, uncertain. "You sure?"

"Yeah." I manage a faint smile that feels brittle but true. "I just need a few more minutes. To... pull myself together. Elle deserves that much."

Camila studies me for a beat, then nods, brushing a strand of hair from her cheek. "Don't stay out here too long, okay?"

"I won't."

She squeezes my hand before rising and making her way back down the path, her figure swallowed by the soft glow spilling from the ballroom.

I stay put, the bench cool beneath me, the mountains towering like sentinels around the lake. The silence steadies me just enough.

For the first time since I left Argentina, I let myself whisper it out loud.

"I want to go home."

The words scrape raw against the dark, and no one answers.

41

CONNOR

THE BALLROOM IS TOO bright as I walk back in, even in the dimness of the candles placed on every table, and the music punches through my chest like it's mocking me. I don't see her.

I shove through a knot of cousins, scanning every corner. Empty chair inside, just like Camila said.

My eyes sweep the tables again. The panic claws higher. She wasn't outside on the terrace, either.

The hollow punch in my chest nearly knocks the air out of me. I move, fast, weaving through the crowd. Someone claps my shoulder, another cousin says my name, but it all slides past like static. I'm too aware of every second she's gone.

"Connie!"

Nicole's voice hooks me midstride. She's leaning back in her chair, one heel kicked off, champagne glass raised like she's already the star of some afterparty. Her smile is bright, careless, and her eyes glint sharply.

"I didn't think you'd mind," she says, and the words slice before I even understand them. "Athena kept asking if she should come. How you were doing, wondering if the trip finally knocked some sense into you." She takes a sip of her drink and places it on the table in front of her. "You were looking so relaxed, I told her of course she should join, that it was a great opportunity to rekindle things with you. And of course, the trip wouldn't be the same without her."

I stop dead. My pulse spikes hot in my temples. "You told her to come?"

Nicole shrugs, unconcerned, adjusting the strap of her dress. "She belongs here, Connie. You two were always the golden couple. People missed her. It just... made sense."

Her voice is breezy, like she's commenting on the weather and she hasn't just detonated my entire night. Possibly my entire future.

Rage roars up fast, white and blinding. I step closer, my voice low but shaking with it. "Stay the hell out of my life, Nicole."

Her smirk falters, just barely, but I don't stay long enough to savor it.

I push forward toward the doors, only to find another wall in my path.

"Connor," my father's voice cuts, cool as a blade. His hand clamps around my arm, steering me toward a tall man in a sharp tux, the tie already loose and undone. "This is David Lasker. He's Joe's partner."

Lasker extends a hand, teeth flashing. "Your father says you're as sharp as they come. Hopefully, you are seriously considering our offer. We know you'd be a perfect fit for us."

I don't take his hand. My chest is still heaving, the need to run clawing at my ribs. "Hi, David, nice to meet you. I'm not interested."

My father's fingers tighten around my arm like a vise. His smile is fixed, brittle. "Connor. This is an excellent opportunity for you. Don't be rude."

Something in me cracks. The part of me that used to flinch, used to fold under that tone, finally snaps in half.

"I said no." My voice is steady. "I don't want the job. I don't want your contacts. I don't want any of it."

A ripple of surprise flickers over David's face. My father's jaw tightens, his eyes promising the storm that will come later. I don't care. Not anymore.

I wrench my arm free and shoulder past them both. The room feels smaller by the second, walls pressing in, every laugh like a nail in my skull.

The doors swing shut behind me with a heavy thud, muting the ballroom into a muffled hum. The cold night air hits like a slap—sharp, clean, threaded with pine and lake water. For a second I just stand there, bent over with my hands on my knees, dragging in lungfuls like I've been drowning all night and finally broke the surface.

The gravel path crunches under my shoes as I move fast,

half-blind in the dark, every muscle wound tight. The mountains tower above, jagged silhouettes against the scatter of stars, and the lake spreads silver and restless at their base. It's too beautiful for a night like this. Too still, too vast, when all I can feel is panic clawing at my ribs.

My mind won't stop replaying the last twenty minutes. Athena's hand on my arm. My mother's satisfied smile. Nicole's smug little shrug when she admitted she invited her. My father trying to sell me like a stock. And through it all, the empty chair where Manuela should've been.

I change directions, heading for the house quickly, but when I get there, it's completely dark and every single room is empty.

I keep scanning, desperate. The dock juts out into the water, but she's not there, either. I curse under my breath, chest tightening. Then, farther up the path, I catch the faintest outline—someone sitting on the bench tucked into the clearing, shoulders hunched against the night.

Manuela.

Relief slams into me so hard my knees almost buckle.

I slow as I get closer, not wanting to spook her. She's staring out at the water, hands clasped tight in her lap, hair catching the moonlight like it's spun from something I'll never deserve.

For a moment I just watch because I can't seem to do anything else. Because she looks perfect, like she belongs here —like she was carved out of these mountains, rooted to this place in a way I'll never understand but want more than I've ever wanted anything.

Then she shifts just slightly, like she feels me coming before she hears me.

"Manu, baby." My voice cracks on her name, raw from too much silence and too much shouting.

Her head turns, slow. Her eyes find mine, wide and wet, and the sight nearly guts me.

I take another step, then another, until I'm standing in front of her. I don't reach for her—not yet. My hands are fists at my sides, shaking with everything I want to say and don't know how.

"I looked everywhere," I rasp. "Please don't run from me."

The lake laps gently at the shore, a sound so calm it feels cruel. She doesn't speak right away, and the silence is a blade at my throat. But I don't move. I won't.

Finally, after what feels like hours, she turns her body in my direction.

I'm standing at the edge of the clearing, breathless, jacket half off and hair probably a mess since I've been running around trying to find her. I'm sure she can see my panic because her eyes widen for a second and her hands twitch at her lap, almost like she's ready to jump off her seat and come to me.

Her eyes lock on mine, and she blinks a few times.

"Don't shut down," I gasp, the words echoing too loud against the stillness. "I love you."

Her head snaps up. The disbelief in her eyes cuts deeper than anything my father ever said to me.

"You don't have to say it back, and I don't care who hears it," I push, louder now, the words tearing free before fear can choke them down. "I don't care what my parents want, or my friends, or the whole fucking world. I'm done living their life. I want mine. And it's you."

For a beat, all I can hear is the water lapping against the dock below, steady where I'm not. My chest is heaving, but I've never felt clearer.

She shakes her head, voice cracking. "You don't mean that. This is just... vacation magic. It'll disappear the second we land in New York."

The ache twists hard in my ribs, but I don't look away. "I'm in love with you," I say, and my own voice nearly knocks me over with the force of it. I don't soften it, don't give her an out. "And if this is ever going to work, you have to start trusting me."

She tries to back away, panic flaring in her eyes, but I close the distance, steady and deliberate. "Trust the words I say. Trust the ways I show you. Because I have spent my entire life listening to people tell me what I should be. What I should want. Who I should love." My throat tightens around the word, but I force it out anyway. "And I'm done with it."

The lake throws silver light across her face, and it guts me how much she doesn't believe she deserves this. There are two swans making their way out of the water and onto the rocky shore, waddling like their shift on the lake is over and it's their turn to sleep.

"I won't let it happen here," I tell her, sharp now, steel behind the words. "Not with you. I won't let anyone—*including you*—turn this into a script I'm forced to follow. This is mine." I press a fist against my chest. "And if you can't believe in that yet, then at least believe that I will never stop proving it to you."

Her breath stutters, her hands trembling between us. She looks like she wants to bolt. I lift a hand, slow, careful, afraid she'll disappear if I move too fast. My thumb grazes her cheek, damp and soft. "I've never been more sure of anything. But you... I've never breathed easier than when I'm with you. Don't take that from me."

She whispers my name like it hurts her.

"I don't want perfect," I cut in, fierce because I need her to hear me. "I don't want polished and scripted. I want *you*. The way you make me laugh without trying. The way you see through me when no one else even looks. The way you make me feel like I'm not drowning anymore. Please." My forehead rests against hers, sweat and lake air between us. "Please don't walk away."

Her tears fall fast now, streaking down her cheeks. "I can't go back in there, Connor. Not after what just happened. Not with them looking at me like I don't exist, like I'm nothing compared to her. I can't survive that."

"Baby," I say, the pain making my voice unsteady. I cup her face, forcing her to see me even as her gaze skitters away.

"You've got to cut yourself some slack. You think you're invisible, but you're not. You've carved out space in this group whether you realize it or not."

Her brow furrows, wet lashes trembling.

"You don't see Amelia hanging on to every word you've said? Or the way Elle talks you up to anyone who listens? They notice you, Manu. Every single one of them. Maybe you don't believe it, but I've watched it happen all week." My chest tightens. "And I notice you. Ever since that night on the rooftop. Always."

She presses her lips together, like she's trying not to believe me.

"I know it feels easier to tell yourself you don't belong," I continue, softer now, thumb tracing her cheekbone. "But you're here. You're part of this. Just as much as Hannah or Amelia or anyone else. And even if you can't see it yet, I do. I always will."

"But Nicole—"

"Baby, Nicole' s just bitter because she's hoping to get engaged, but even Banks knows not to propose during someone's wedding trip. He's probably going to do it tomorrow."

The corner of her mouth twitches despite herself.

Finally, her shoulders sag, the fight bleeding out of her, replaced by something more fragile—hope, maybe.

"I'll go with you wherever you need to be," I whisper.

The words hang between us, heavy and certain, until finally she lets out a shaky breath and leans into my touch like she's been holding herself back for too long.

42

———————

MANUELA

FRIDAY

THE HOUSE IS quiet when I wake up.

Sunlight stretches across the floorboards in long strips, catching on the chaos left behind from last night—my shoes are toppled by the door, Connor's suit jacket is slung haphazardly on the bench at the foot of the bed, and there's a faint trail of glitter going into the bathroom like breadcrumbs. My heels are on their sides, straps tangled, and one of Connor's cufflinks gleams faintly on the rug, like it got displaced from its pair in the shuffle of us stumbling in and pulling each other apart.

Somewhere outside the room, someone's shower is running. Otherwise, it's just the soft creak of the wood floor as I move.

Connor is nowhere to be seen. His side of the bed is empty, sheets rumpled like he left reluctantly. My chest goes soft at the thought.

By the time I find him, he's in the kitchen with George, both of them looking devastatingly awake and suspiciously put together.

It feels impossible that just a few hours ago, we were still on the dance floor—sweaty, laughing, the music so loud it thumped through my ribs. Someone passed around champagne straight from the bottle, and by the time the staff started dimming lights and hinting that it was time to go, our group had discovered a stash of junk food in the catering kitchen. We ended the night barefoot in tuxedo jackets and gowns, eating pretzels and cold fries in small lounge areas in the lobby of the resort until the night auditors gently escorted our giggling selves out.

And the whole thing with Athena... no one told me what happened, but I guess she left as quickly as she came. I don't know if she slipped out quietly or if Connor asked her to, but either way, she's not here this morning.

George is on the phone, gesturing with a croissant, while Connor is leaning against the counter eating a slice of leftover cake straight from a to-go box. He's in gray sweatpants and a white T-shirt, his pair pushed back messily, and something about how unguarded he looks makes my heart thump faster.

He glances up when I step in wearing his clothes, and his mouth tilts in this small, private smile that's just for me.

"Morning, baby," he says, like it's the simplest thing in the world.

My stomach swoops. "Morning."

"*¿Café?*" he asks in perfect Spanish. It's a little accented, but it's enough to make warmth bloom in my chest anyway.

"*Por favor*," I say, and he grins like a child on Christmas morning.

He pours coffee into a mug and slides it toward me across the counter like he did that first morning, his knuckles brushing mine as I take it. My pulse stutters.

We take our warm drinks to the back deck and settle into the cushioned chairs that overlook the lake. The morning is still, the water a perfect mirror for the mountains. The air smells faintly of pine, lake water, and the unmistakable scent of recently cut grass.

For a while, we don't talk. I curl my legs under me, and Connor pulls me closer, wrapping his arm around my shoulders so I can rest my body on his. We sip slowly, watching the light climb higher over the peaks. Connor's hand plays with the ends of my hair, and a trail of goosebumps erupts all over my skin.

A few minutes later, Camila wanders out carrying a basket of pastries and a carafe of coffee. She's in sunglasses and a white dress, looking like she belongs on the cover of a yacht magazine despite the faint pillow crease still on her cheek. She drops into the chair next to me with a dramatic sigh, like sitting down is the hardest thing she's done all morning, and immediately tears into a chocolate croissant. Flakes scatter across her lap, sticking to her legs, but she doesn't seem to care.

George follows soon after, finally off the phone, his

sunglasses pushed up into his hair like he's pretending he's not exhausted. He kisses the top of Camila's head as he passes, swipes a pastry from the basket, and flops into the seat beside her.

"Did you just close a deal or end civilization as we know it?" Camila asks, mouth full.

"Little of both," George says around a bite of pain au chocolat.

Conversation drifts easily from there. We talk about who still needs to pack, who's flying out when, and whether the leftover wedding cake counts as breakfast (it does). George starts a debate about whether he should try skiing before they leave, which earns him a synchronized groan from everyone and a very pointed, "The ski resort is not open right now, sweetheart," from Camila.

"Details," George mutters, waving her off.

The sliding door creaks open, and Hannah appears, hair piled into a messy knot, wearing a giant sweatshirt that swallows her frame. She blinks at us in the sunlight like she's stumbled into a dream. Amelia trails behind her, looking refreshed and not a bit like we were out partying until the early morning hours.

"Oh thank god," she says, padding over to the table. "Human contact. Has anyone seen Nicole or Banks? Their room is empty, and their suitcases are gone."

"They left at dawn," George says. "Something about a day trip. Romantic boat rides. Possibly eloping, who knows."

"They're not eloping," Amelia says with a knowing smile

as she slides the door shut behind her. She drops into a chair, tucking her feet under her. "But honestly? I wouldn't be shocked if he proposes. She's been vibrating like a champagne cork all week."

"Huh." Sterling pours himself coffee, settling beside Hannah, his arm draped casually along the back of her chair.

The table goes quiet for a moment, only the hiss of the espresso machine from inside breaking it.

"Fondue for dinner," Hannah declares suddenly, like she's just solved world peace. "We should go out with a bang."

"Yes," Camila says immediately, lifting her mug like a toast. "Melted cheese and overpriced wine. I support this plan."

George groans, but it sounds suspiciously like agreement.

The door slides open again, and Elle appears at last—barefoot, hair a tangle, makeup smudged, looking wrecked but radiant. She blinks at us like we've materialized out of thin air, then grins.

"What are you doing here?" Hannah asks, head tilting. "Weren't you supposed to stay at the bridal suite last night?"

Elle waves her hand, beaming as she crosses to the table. "We did. We just... came back for snacks. And possibly my robe. And also because I missed you guys."

"Already?" George mutters, but he's smiling.

Elle ignores him, stealing a piece of pastry and dropping into the empty chair beside me. "So. Who's going to tell me why you're all sitting here like a Renaissance painting? It's giving... post-revolution brunch."

"Just planning dinner," Hannah says.

Elle squints at her, then at me, then at Connor, and her smile goes sly. "Right. Totally about dinner. Not at all about—"

"Elle," Connor warns lowly, but she's already gasping like she just cracked some ancient code.

"Oh my god." She slaps both palms on the table, making the cutlery rattle. "It happened. You two..." She points between us so aggressively her finger wobbles. "You actually happened. Do you have any idea how long I've been waiting for this? Since my engagement party, Manu. The rooftop."

Heat floods my face so fast I almost flinch. "Elle—"

"I *knew* it," she barrels on, ignoring me. "The tension. The smiles. The eye fucking! And don't even get me started on the waterfall detour, when you came back from that hike looking like..." She waves her hand vaguely at my face, then at Connor's, like that explains everything. "Like *that*."

Connor drags a hand down his face, groaning. "Earth, swallow me."

"Why?" Elle asks, beaming. "This is incredible, and everyone was wrong and I'm right." She twists toward the others, eyes wide. "Did you all know? Am I the last one to know? I've been *shipping* you for years."

"Pretty sure we've all known," Amelia says warmly, biting into a croissant.

George shrugs. "They weren't exactly subtle."

The air feels suddenly too bright around me. My heart is still racing. I'm waiting for the teasing to tip into something sharp, for someone to flinch or frown or ask what I'm thinking—what I'm risking. But no one does.

"God, this feels amazing. I'm so happy for you. Really." Elle whirls back to me, her grin softening, eyes shining. "I always thought there was something there. Gosh, it's the best day of my life."

"You just got married last night," Amelia says with a laugh, and the group erupts into loud laughter.

The scene feels so natural. Something in my chest unclenches, slow and tentative, like my ribs are loosening. I didn't realize how tightly I'd been bracing until now. My fingers brush Connor's under the table, testing, and when he doesn't move away—when his thumb curls softly around mine—I almost forget to breathe.

Elle claps her hands once, decisive. "Okay. Now that my heart is fully full, who's making dinner reservations? I refuse to leave Switzerland without drowning in a pot of molten cheese."

43

CONNOR

Three Weeks Later

THE KETTLE CLICKS OFF, and the apartment goes quiet again—just the hiss of the radiator and the low rumble of traffic six floors below. Morning light slants through the blinds in fat stripes, turning the air into glitter.

She's on the couch, hair shoved up in a clip, my socks slouching at her ankles, surrounded by the chaos we've ignored since we got back from our trip. Pizza menus, glossy catalogs for furniture we'll never buy, envelopes I probably should've opened already. And one thin, official-looking one with her name screaming in bold black letters that was delivered by Camila last night after we were already in bed. Alfred brought it up only minutes ago.

I watch her finger slip under the flap. I don't breathe until the card slides free.

I forget about the toothbrush in my mouth.

It's thicker than I expected, ugly in that government way, but her hands shake like she's holding a miracle.

She nods. A laugh bursts out of her, cracked and wet, and my chest squeezes so hard I nearly choke on mint foam.

"It's here," she says.

I spit and rinse in the kitchen, then cross the room in about three strides, hand wet from the sink when I cup the back of her neck and lean my forehead to hers. "*Hola, residente permanente,*" I murmur and can't stop smiling even if I wanted to.

"Ew." She shoves me, laughing through tears. "That's not what we're called."

"Legally, you are." I kiss the top of her head and pluck the card out of her grip like it's some sacred relic. "We're framing this."

"You can't!" she yelps and flies off the couch as I pluck the most important piece of documentation we'll ever own from her fingers. "I need it, Connie!"

"Fridge, then." I dodge her grabby hands and slap it under the NYC-taxi-shaped magnet on the fridge, crooked but proud. "We'll make a copy later and replace it."

Manuela stands there, hands clutched against her chest, staring at the fridge like it's a shrine. And I get it. To me it's just plastic, but to her—it's freedom. Proof. A key.

I hand her a cup of coffee and bump her hip. She takes it, but she's still looking at the card like it might vanish.

We've been home three weeks now. The suitcases are

finally unpacked and all the laundry is put away. The glow of Switzerland has worn off, but not the part of her that lets herself laugh like she belongs here, and not the part of me that stopped pretending I didn't want this.

I didn't take the job. The one my father kept dangling like a prize. I also walked into my manager's office and gave notice the day after we came back. My father called it career suicide. I call it breathing.

Now I'm interviewing for jobs that still count as corporate, technically, but sound like they might let me be human. Finance departments at companies where no one uses the word "bro" in casual conversation, where the people in the photos on the website are actually smiling. I've even been sleeping through the night again.

"Timer's about to go off," I murmur into Manuela's hair.

She sighs dramatically. "When did you even have time to start another loaf?"

"This morning."

"Connor—"

The oven beeps, and she sighs again but sits on the counter right next to me, waiting for me to unveil my latest attempt at edible food. It's been rough, but the starter is finally thriving, and I think this might be *the one*.

The smell hits the second I crack the door—warm and nutty and very much reminding me of the little vacation that started all of this.

"Okay," I say, pulling the loaf out and setting it gently on the rack. "Moment of truth."

"Oh wow," she says, a soft smile on her face like she has been preparing to let me down gently. "It has an actual shape."

"Don't sound so shocked."

"I'm just saying," she teases, tapping the crust with one perfectly painted nail, "this is very un-paperweight of you."

I grin. "I think that's the nicest thing anyone's ever said to me."

"Oh yeah?" she says, arching an eyebrow as she hops off the counter. She leans her hip against mine, mug cradled in both hands. "You must hang out with very mean people."

"Or," I say, brushing a lock of hair off her shoulder, "I just haven't been hanging out with the right ones."

We see people. Regularly. Camila drags us out for rooftop drinks at least once a week, and Elle insists on Sunday brunches that last five hours and include more drinks than food. Amelia comes over a lot, always with perfect hair and a huge smile on her face, and even Cash has grown on me —turns out I didn't dislike him, I just hated my job. He roped me into their fantasy football league finally, and last night I actually spent twenty minutes researching running backs. I can't decide if that's character growth or a cry for help, but I'm weirdly enjoying it.

She rolls her eyes, but her smile twitches like she's trying to hold it back. "That was smooth."

"I'm smooth," I say, deadpan.

"You're not," she counters immediately, laughing as she sets the mug on the counter.

I reach for her waist, tugging her in until she's pressed between me and the marble, the smell of bread still warm in the air. Her laughter softens, and for a moment, she just looks at me, eyes quiet in a way that makes my eyes sting with all the emotions.

"I love you," she says simply.

My heart stops.

Her eyes flick down to my mouth, then back up, like she's steadying herself. "I think I knew it that first night. The rooftop, remember? When Elle introduced us and you said something about standing by the olive tree. I don't even know what it was exactly, but..." She exhales, shaky. "I felt it. And I'm so glad you took me up on the no-pressure pact silliness. I don't think I would've let myself get here without it."

"Manu—" My voice cracks halfway through her name. I press my forehead to hers, the bread forgotten, the entire world forgotten. "I love you too."

"And I'm sorry I didn't say it sooner," she adds. She wraps her hands around my neck and gives me a soft kiss. "I just needed to be sure."

"Baby—"

"I like this version better," she cuts me off, eyes glinting like she remembers that night on the rooftop. When I said I hated small talk and she said, *Isn't this technically small talk*, and I told her, *I like this version better.*

"Of me," she adds softly. "The version I am with you."

She smiles then, this soft, disbelieving thing that wrecks

me completely, and kisses me slow, like we've got all the time in the world.

Fourteen months later

"Manu, babe," Connor calls the second he walks into the apartment. The door slams behind him, the sound echoing through the hallway, and I hear the dull thump of his shoes hitting the floor as he kicks them off. His steps move closer, unhurried but with purpose, like he's already tracking me by sound. "Babe."

"Nooooooo, go away," I call back, loud enough for him to hear over the hum of the bathroom fan.

"What are you doing in there?" His voice is curious, not suspicious, and I can feel the smile on his handsome face.

"Nothing! Go away!" I start laughing, because of course the boundaries don't exist in this relationship. It's like the moment we set foot in the same space, he wants to be right next to me, breathing my air. I don't blame him; the feeling is mutual. But can't a girl pluck her chin hairs in peace?

"Connie," I say, raising my voice so it carries through the closed door, "I say this with all the love in the world, but get the fuck away from this bathroom."

"Why? What's wrong?" His footsteps stop just outside. I can picture him leaning against the doorframe, head tilted, waiting for me to slip.

"Connor," I say, trying to keep my tone even as I angle the tweezers toward my reflection, "I'm just finishing up with something."

"You're just doing your makeup," he says, like it's an accusation. "I want to tell you what happened at work today."

"Connor!" I set the tweezers down with a soft clink and throw my hands up at the mirror. "Let me pluck my chin hairs in peace!"

There's a pause, then a surprised, almost offended, "What chin hairs? You don't have any chin hairs." I hear the shift in his voice—a thread of concern under the teasing.

"Well," I reply, meeting my own eyes in the mirror, "apparently, once you turn thirty-four, everything goes south."

"South where?" he shoots back instantly. "To Argentina?"

I laugh, shaking my head. "Oh my god, go away!"

"Okay, fine," he says, voice drifting like he's about to

retreat but not really. "But you are the prettiest girl ever. I don't care about your chin hairs."

I pivot toward the door, eyebrows up. "So you have seen my chin hairs then!"

"I still like you a lot," he says without hesitation. "Like, *a lot* a lot."

"Yes, I like you a lot," I admit, turning back to the mirror, "but not enough to let you witness this monstrosity."

The door creaks, and suddenly he's behind me, the mirror catching his reflection as he steps into the small space like he's been invited. His hands slide around my hips, pulling me back against his warm, solid frame. He's still chilly from his walk home, the damp edge of November clinging to his clothes.

"This winter seems to be dragging already," he murmurs, pressing a light kiss to my temple.

"It's barely November," I say, feeling his body heat seep into mine. "I do not care."

"But I do," he counters.

I meet his eyes in the mirror. "Connor. I'm getting old."

He frowns, but it's soft. "How can you get old at thirty-five? We're in our prime."

"Speak for yourself. I pulled a muscle the other day while getting out of bed." I reach for the tweezers again. "Really, there should be an unsubscribe button."

"Manuela."

"Connor," I echo, meeting his gaze in the glass.

"Why so serious?" he asks, his tone somewhere between

amused and genuinely curious. "Where is this coming from? I've never heard you talk about this before."

"Did you know that pregnancies after the age of thirty-five are considered geriatric?" I say, turning toward him now, leaning against the counter. "Literally, the classification is the same for a pregnant person in their seventies as someone in their mid-to-late thirties."

His eyebrows lift. "Okay. Do you know anyone who was pregnant in their seventies?"

"That's not the point." I wave him off. "The point is that I'm getting old, and I hate it."

"Babe." He takes a deep breath, then breaks away, stepping out of the bathroom without another word. I hear the faint sound of the closet door sliding open.

When he comes back, he's holding a white rectangular envelope, the kind that comes tucked into bills for mailing back checks. His expression is determined. "You leave me no choice."

"No choice for what?" I ask, glancing down as my phone buzzes on the counter—Camila, calling from somewhere in the Mediterranean. She's on her delayed honeymoon after the whole drama last year.

Before I can answer, Connor moves. In one smooth motion, he pushes the envelope into my hand and takes my phone from the counter, tossing it gently out into the carpeted closet hallway.

"Connor, what is going on?"

"Open it."

I hesitate, narrowing my eyes.

"Just open it and stop asking questions," he says, a lazy smile tugging at the corner of his mouth. "You are so impatient sometimes."

I glare, but I'm already sliding a finger under the flap.

"But I love you so much, baby. Just the way you are," he adds, his voice softer now. He leans in to give me a quick peck on the lips, then steps back, waiting.

Inside are photos—one per month, starting with January first and moving through the year. I shuffle through them slowly, my mind catching up to what I'm seeing.

The last one stops me cold. It's from Elle's new rooftop a few weeks ago, when the weather was still warm. She had a huge housewarming party for herself once they moved to a bigger house, and of course it was as extravagant as her wedding. We're lounging on her loveseat, the herb planters behind us overflowing. I'm looking at the camera, but he's looking at me with dreamy eyes—the same way he looked at me in Switzerland two summers ago, and last summer when we traveled through the United States in my attempt to at least visit a few of the national parks.

"What is this?" I ask, even as my stomach flips.

In every single picture, Connor is holding the same small, vintage pink box with decorative filigree on the edges.

"I've been trying to propose to you for months," he says, smiling wryly. "But for one reason or another, I haven't been able to. And since you're not getting old, I might as well do it—"

"In the bathroom of our home?" I cut in, staring at him.

"Yes, baby. In the bathroom. You leave me no choice." He slips into the most exaggerated Spanish accent I've ever heard. "Manuela Torres, *¿te querés casar conmigo?*"

The accent vanishes on the last word, replaced with perfect pronunciation. He even skips the *s* after *querés*, just like we do in Argentina.

"What the fuck?"

"What? What's wrong?" His brow creases, real worry flickering there. "Shit. Did I read this incorrectly?" He closes the box and sets it on the counter, where it immediately slides into the sink.

"Oh my god," I say, reaching for it. "Did you talk to my mother?"

"Who do you think's been teaching me Spanish?"

"You already speak Spanish."

"I mean, yes? I just... wasn't brave enough to speak it to you. We talked about my semester abroad in Chile already."

"Connor."

"So... no? You don't want to marry me?"

From outside, my mother's voice carries in: "*¿Qué dijo?*"

Every inch of my exposed skin flushes. "My mother is here? Connor, what have you done?"

"So, no? You haven't answered."

I flip the box open. My jaw drops. "Baby, what the fuck?"

"Manuela..." His voice dips into Spanish again, and I can feel the warmth in the way he says it, love threaded through every syllable. "*¿Te querés casar conmigo?*"

"Yes," I say on a breath, then laugh. "*Sí*. Do we speak Spanish now?"

"Manuela, *hija*—"

"Is my mother here?"

"Manu! Come out here!"

"Is that Amelia?" My head snaps toward the door. "Are my friends here too?"

Connor chuckles and pulls me into his body, and it's at that moment I realize I'm cry-laughing, tears streaming down my face and into my boyfrie—fiancé's shirt.

"I just wanted to pluck my chin hair. I didn't want to pressure you into proposing."

"What did you think tonight was? Elle was setting it all up in her new backyard."

"I thought we were going to have dinner with one of your clients."

"Baby, when have we ever gone to dinner with a client?"

"I don't know, Connor!"

"Manu." Camila's voice joins from behind the bathroom door. "Can I come in?"

"Aren't you supposed to be on your honeymoon? Why is everyone here?"

There's a pause, then—

"Oh my god, I'm engaged!"

THE END

ACKNOWLEDGMENTS

This book feels special. Different from my previous ones, though I can't quite put my finger on why. It lived rent free in my brain for a year before I could finally get the story out. Maybe it's because it touches on topics so close to me: being an adult immigrant, struggling to find where you belong, and navigating culturally nuanced relationships in a world that moves too fast... one that often feels like you're watching from the sidelines.

At its core, though, it's still a love story. Because even in the moments when life feels too big or too lonely, love has a way of grounding us. Writing this book reminded me that connection—messy, funny, tender, imperfect—is what makes everything else worthwhile. My hope is that somewhere in these pages, you see a little piece of yourself too.

Bekah, thank you for listening to me talk about this story for a full year and for reading every single version from its messy start to what it is now. Your encouragement kept me going, and I don't have enough words to say how grateful I am.

Hailey, I don't know who decided we should meet, but thank you to whoever did. Two years feels like a lifetime.

Thank you for your support, your honesty, and always being there.

Katie, you're the best editor a girl could have. This book is infinitely better because of you, and I can't imagine doing this author thing without you.

Menace Chat, you're probably the longest-standing group chat of my life and the only people who answer my ridiculous questions at any hour. Thanks times a hundred million. Bobbi, sorry we missed your birthday!

Amanda, gracias, gracias, gracias. Even though this book isn't set in NYC, the information you shared cemented so many details and made everything click.

Nela, you are a force and I'm so lucky to have you in my corner.

My family, thank you for giving me the time and space to write these stories and for always being in awe of what I'm doing. To my two young daughters: you don't need to figure out what you like at your age! Your passions will ebb and flow, and it's okay to find something you love at any point in your life. I know I did.

My friends, thank you for cheering me on, celebrating every milestone, and keeping me grounded when deadlines tried to swallow me whole.

And you, the reader—thank you for trusting my words and letting this book be your escape. I hope you loved reading it as much as I loved writing it.

Love in the Alps

The No-Pressure Pact

Tres Fuegos Series

After the Fire: An Enemies to Lovers Small Town Romance

Before the Storm: A Second Chance Small Town Romance

With the Wildflowers: A Fake Dating Small Town Romance

Love in Layovers

Misbooked for Love: A Valentine's Day Novella

Holiday Rules

The Twelve-Hour Rule: A Strangers to Lovers Christmas Novella

Maria Rigou is a US-based author hailing from Argentina. She writes love stories full of longing, tenderness, and the exact amount of ache right before the happily ever after.

She lives in South Florida with her husband and two daughters and loves to read.

The No-Pressure Pact is her fifth book.

———

CONNECT ONLINE

www.mariarigou.com

@mariarigouauthor